THE TRIALS

PROJECT PAPER DOLL

THE TRIALS

STACEY KADE

HYPERION
LOS ANGELES NEW YORK

For information address Hyperion, 125 West End Avenue,
New York, New York 10023.

First Edition, April 2015
1 3 5 7 9 10 8 6 4 2
G475-5664-5-15046

Printed in the United States of America

Library of Congress Cataloging-in-Publication Data
Kade, Stacey.
The trials/Stacey Kade.—First edition.
pages cm.—(Project Paper Doll; [3])
Summary: "After being on the run, Ariane Tucker finds herself back
where she started—under the cruel control of Dr. Jacobs, head of the
research facility that created her. Now she must participate in the
upcoming trials; a deadly competition pitting her against other alien
hybrids, each representing a rival corporation"—Provided by publisher.
ISBN 978-1-4231-8463-8 (hardback)
[1. Genetic engineering—Fiction. 2. Extraterrestrial beings—
Fiction. 3. Contests—Fiction. 4. Science fiction.] I. Title.
PZ7.K116463Tri 2015
[Fic]—dc23 2014037457

Visit www.hyperionteens.com

THIS LABEL APPLIES TO TEXT STOCK

This book is dedicated to you.
Yes, you, standing (or sitting) right there.
I love telling stories. Thank you for letting me.
Thank you for reading.

PROLOGUE

Ariane Tucker

PRIVATE JOSEPH "JOE" ZADOWSKI WAS YOUNG, MAYBE only four or five years older than me. His reddish blond hair was cut short, buzzed on the sides. He was about a foot taller and a hundred pounds heavier than me, though his green fatigues bagged loosely around him, like he was playing dress-up. Freckles stood out as dark splotches against the pale skin of his nose and cheeks.

He swallowed hard and shifted beneath my gaze. Extended eye contact made most full-blooded humans uncomfortable. Extended eye contact with an unknown quantity (me) while locked in a small cell in a secret lab made them downright jumpy, it seemed.

But if I was going to do this, I owed it to Joe to remember his face. It would haunt me for the rest of my life. Fortunately I didn't expect the rest of my life to be all that long. The trials were just weeks away. I'd survive long enough to see my personal mission through, but that was it.

"They told me you're dangerous," Joe blurted, surprising me.

Interesting. The techs or Dr. Jacobs? Likely the former. I had a hard time imagining Jacobs deigning to meet and greet the human being he'd brought in to serve as a guinea pig.

"What else did they tell you?" I asked Joe.

He shifted his weight from foot to foot, his fingers tapping against his leg. I didn't see a weapon on him, but I suspected that nervous twitch was him wishing he had one. He hadn't come in farther than was necessary for the door to close behind him. "That, uh, I'm supposed to subdue you by any means necessary." He produced a pair of clear zip ties from his pocket, a prop provided by Jacobs or the techs. There was no way he'd actually get close enough to use them, even if he didn't know that.

"And?" I prompted.

"107." Dr. Jacobs's voice sounded over the intercom in warning.

Joe jumped. I ignored it. Dr. Jacobs was, I was sure, watching on the monitors in the observation room. The glass wall was opaque at the moment, preventing me from seeing him. But his impatience and eagerness crawled over my skin like a thousand biting ants.

"And?" I said again to Joe, drawing his attention back to me.

His expression flashed irritation mixed with fear. "You'll fight me the whole time, supposedly." Already he was making assumptions about me, based on my size and gender. Not smart, but inevitable.

I had just a couple more questions. "You're a volunteer?" I asked, confirming what I'd been told.

"Yesss," he said, drawing out the word, not understanding at all why this was relevant.

"And they told you you'd be risking your life?" I pressed. More than "risking," actually, but that wording was the only compromise Dr. Jacobs and I had been able to reach.

Joe lifted a shoulder in a shrug. Even with the strangeness of the situation and all the unknowns I could hear circulating through his head (*What is this place? There's definitely something wrong with her. Why is she so calm?*), he wasn't nearly as concerned as he should have been.

"I like my odds," he said, staring back at me for the first time, his ego rising up against that quiet voice of doubt, the niggling sense that something was "off." After all, I was just a girl, and a small one at that.

Oh, Joe.

"107, time is wasting," Jacobs snapped over the intercom.

He must have been running a timer along with the camera that would record what was to transpire. Yes, heaven forbid I did not break world records in speed *and* manner of killing.

"You know the consequences if you don't do as you're told," Jacobs continued.

Without warning, Joe took two large steps toward me, zip ties in hand. Evidently he'd decided enough was enough.

I let him come at me, feeling a bit of grim enjoyment for the momentary panic that caused on the other side of the observation window, and then slid out of his reach, my back to the opposite wall.

"Don't make this difficult," Joe said, shaking his head with exasperation. The fact that he'd charged at me and nothing had happened—not that he was sure what to expect, exactly—had boosted his confidence.

Guilt sprang to life in me, throbbing like an infected cut. Delaying wouldn't change anything, and by doing so I was toying with him, giving him hope where there should be none.

So, when he came at me again, I stopped him, lifting my hand and directing my power to wrap around him, freezing him mid-lunge. It involved little more than a thought from me, no longer the struggle it had once been.

"I won't make it difficult," I promised him as his eyes bugged out in panic. His muscles tensed, fighting against me as he struggled to free himself. It was pointless, I could have told him. We were both trapped.

Finding his heart, thumping madly in his chest, wasn't hard. Neither was the process of stopping it. Just a squeeze of directed power around that muscle, which, though powerful and necessary for life, was no different than any other.

It's a necessary evil to save others.

This is the least of all the atrocities that will be committed if I don't *do this.*

I don't want *to do this.*

But none of those thoughts helped as I watched Joseph "Joe" Zadowski, he of the freckles and the nervous fingers, recognize that something was very, very wrong. His face turned from a flushed red to a disturbing purplish blue as his heart slowed and he stopped trying to escape and worked instead to keep breathing, to keep living. His last thoughts were of his family, a flash of his mother—a woman with graying hair, round cheeks, and a perpetual but tired smile—and a younger brother sticking his hand up to block Joe on the basketball court, a triumphant grin when he succeeded.

"I'm sorry," I whispered, my throat tight as Joe's body sagged in my grip and his eyes closed.

But I didn't stop.

I couldn't. Not now.

CHAPTER 1

Ariane Tucker

TWO MORE DAYS. TWO MORE DAYS. TWO MORE DAYS.

I repeated that refrain in my head, over and over again, blocking the errant thoughts and memories that threatened to interrupt my concentration as I pushed myself through another round of sit-ups on the shiny white floor of my cell.

I'd kept a running countdown of days, based on the cycle of the lights in my room and the dates I'd overheard from the staff. It had been almost a month since my return to GTX.

Almost a month since the parking lot. Almost a month since Zane's blood on my hands, so red and wet . . .

I squeezed my eyes shut, focusing harder on the burn in my stomach muscles and the dull ache in my head from the strain of pushing my abilities too far, too fast. I could no longer see my metal-framed cot swaying above me, held there by the force of my mind, but I could feel it pulling at that part of my brain, like a weight attached to a limb not quite accustomed to bearing the burden.

In the far corner behind me, a stack of books, a much lighter target, was also levitating near the ceiling, theoretically. I'd turned my attention away once I'd lifted them off the ground, relying on my ability to keep them up without my gaze on them, a stretch for me. A second stack waited in front of me for similar treatment, though I hadn't managed two at once (plus the cot) yet.

I was improving but not fast enough. Time was almost up. I needed to be ready; I needed to be *better*. The trials would start the day after tomorrow somewhere in the Chicago area.

I was pretty sure.

One of the disadvantages of being a mouse in a GenTex cage is that people don't exactly bother to keep you in the loop. They probably thought it didn't matter. After all, I was just "the product." It wasn't as if I could do anything to change my situation.

Sometimes I thought the uncertainty would kill me before anyone else had the chance.

Until recently, I'd never thought much about dying. That sounded great, enlightened even, like a lack of concern about my own mortality was a gift of higher spiritual knowledge via my alien half. But to be honest, that had nothing to do with it.

The truth was there were things worse than death. I'd been far more worried about ending up back in the small white room where I'd lived the first six years of my life, longing to see the world outside.

Here's the funny thing, though: once the worst has actually happened—well, what you thought was the worst, anyway—you learn that that line was only a low watermark, an indicator of your own naiveté. The idea that there is a cap to the horribleness that can happen to you is ridiculous.

It can always get worse. A lot worse. I know that now. Back in that parking lot by the Illinois border, when I was caught between Dr. Jacobs and Dr. Laughlin with Zane looking on, I'd have leaped into the black unmarked van with the retrieval team to come here—hell, I'd have driven myself—if I'd known what was going to happen instead. There is no maximum threshold for the worst that can happen to you. To believe otherwise is just daring someone to prove you wrong.

Those who would want to show you the opposite, that life can be better than you'd ever imagined, were few and far between.

One fewer now.

At the thought of Zane, a horrible pang of longing and sadness struck my heart with unerring accuracy. But I pushed it away, trying to refocus on the cool, emotion-deadened spot inside me, the one that had opened up shortly after I'd awakened in Laughlin's facility with an IV in my arm and Zane's blood all over my hands.

Ford, my counterpart at Laughlin's company (and probably my clone, if such a thing were possible), made it look so easy—just stop caring. Do what needs doing. Shut off the consequences and the fear and the guilt.

I'd managed to do exactly that for a while, but the relief of that emptiness wasn't to be found today, not with anxiety and anticipation warring within me, my body tired and my concentration stretched too thin.

Not to mention the all-too-familiar high-pitched nattering filling my ears.

"—and then Cami told me what Trey said. Too high maintenance to be worth it? Seriously? What does that even mean?"

My eyes snapped open against my will on the down motion of a sit-up, showing me Rachel Jacobs perched, as usual, on a swivel chair just outside the glass door to my room. With her ankle wrapped around one of the casters to control her movement, she spun a few inches back and forth, like a child.

She'd been here every day after school for hours, for almost two weeks now. Dr. Jacobs's master plan. Forget waterboarding, spikes under my fingernails, or strategic electrocution; Rachel's presence was worse punishment than any of those. She was a constant reminder of my old life, what I'd had and lost, what I'd deluded myself into thinking could be mine forever. It was a finger poking into a still bloody wound, making it impossible to ignore.

I hated it. I hated her.

Which was exactly what I suspected Dr. Jacobs wanted. I just wasn't sure why.

"Someone to keep you company," he'd announced cheerily before her first visit, and damn him and my stupid broken heart that wouldn't stop hoping for miracles, I'd thought for a second that maybe it was my father or somehow . . . Zane. Even though I'd left him bleeding out on the pavement in a Wisconsin park.

But then Rachel had entered the hallway beyond my cell in a swirl of her trademark red. Dr. Jacobs set her up in the chair outside my door and left before I could pin down his thoughts beyond the noise of Rachel's. My telepathy was spotty at best, even worse around a broadcaster like her. She was so loud; she drowned out everyone else.

Rachel had glared after him, still pissed, but she sat down, anyway. He was, after all, paying her to be there, according to her thoughts. All she had to do was talk. And she hadn't shut up since.

"Just because I know what I want," Rachel continued huffily. "What's wrong with that?"

Rachel shook her head as though I'd responded, her shiny dark hair tumbling forward over her shoulder as she tapped away at her phone. I didn't know what she was doing; it wasn't as if she could get any kind of signal down here.

I imagined the flood of waiting texts that would soar from her phone, like evil flying monkeys released from the holding pen of her outbox, the second she ascended to a point where phone service kicked back in.

"And then Trey wouldn't even apologize! He acted like I was the one with the problem. He's never done that before." She sounded almost hurt, if she were capable of such emotion.

In the beginning, Rachel had done exactly as I'd expected, taunted me, said every mean thing she could think of, even repeated a few that she was particularly proud of. All trying to provoke a reaction, just because she could. She thought she was safe on the other side of the door. She wasn't, but I had zero interest in diverting my focus just to scare her. (Okay, the thought did cross my mind, but only for a moment. I didn't want to give Dr. Jacobs the satisfaction.)

After a few days of insults and taunts, though, something changed. It was as if Rachel had forgotten I was there or she didn't care. She'd turned the threshold of my cell into a confessional, treating these afternoons like one long series of free therapy sessions. Either way, for some reason, her monologues were harder for me to ignore.

Maybe because they showed she was human, much to my dismay. (I was half human, after all, and frankly that was already too much in common with her.) Or maybe because, as usual, Rachel had no idea that what she bitterly complained about were things others would be overjoyed to have.

Like the guy who loved her still being alive but shunning her (rightly so) for being too demanding.

"I mean, whatever. It's not like I care or anything," she continued in that tone that screamed anything but. She was a child who wanted sympathy over a toy she'd broken herself.

Rage welled in me, breaking past the barriers I'd erected so carefully over the last few weeks, and spilling into the empty, emotion-free zone.

Zane was *dead*. He'd been in the wrong place at the wrong time. He was there because he'd cared about me. And Rachel was bitching because she couldn't manipulate Trey into playing one of her popularity games? The injustice of it made me want to scream until I was hoarse.

"His loss, you know?" she continued, blithely unaware. "I can do better."

As if love was disposable, easily discarded and forgotten, just as easily replaced.

Maybe for *her*. My one chance was gone.

My control splintered. Overhead, one end of the cot dipped alarmingly. I yanked my legs out of the way a bare second before the cot clattered to the floor in front of me. In the corner, books thumped to the floor, pages making a ruffling noise. Then I whipped around to face Rachel.

"Trey's worshipped you for years and you treat him like

crap, like he's yours to do with you as you please," I snapped, frustrated with myself for responding and yet unable to stop it. "What did you expect?"

Rachel froze, her fingers still poised over her phone. Then she raised her eyebrows. "It speaks," she said, with a sniff of disdain. "Guess you're not brain damaged, just a freak still."

I flopped back on the floor, cursing myself for breaking. "Go away."

She gave a harsh laugh. "Believe me, I'd love to. You don't think I have better things to do with my time?"

"No," I said flatly. Rachel, for all her willingness to express her opinion and dictate to others what theirs should be, seemed to be lacking a sympathetic (or unresponsive) ear to listen to her discuss all the endless trouble in her life. She gave me a hostile look. "I'm not getting paid enough for this," she announced to no one in particular and everyone within hearing range before returning her attention to her phone.

But once I'd opened up the barrier—burst through the waxen layers of resistance and determination that had distanced me from Rachel—I couldn't reseal it.

I sat up. "Does of any of this even register with you?" I asked, sweeping my hand in a gesture that encompassed my cell, the observation window above, and pretty much the entirety of the corporation, levels above me. "People are going to die because your grandfather and Dr. Laughlin are determined to one-up each other."

The trials, in theory, were a competition to determine who had the best product, a term they used to describe genetically engineered alien/human hybrids like me. The prize:

a lucrative government contract to create a whole line of soldier/assassins of the not-quite-human variety, according to Dr. Jacobs. The losing products would not survive. They would either die in the competition or be destroyed afterward. No reason to keep them around.

There were three companies competing. I didn't know who Dr. St. John would send, if anyone. (Jacobs didn't seem concerned about him.) But I knew it was me from GTX and likely Ford from Laughlin Integrated. Laughlin and Jacobs had a history, hating each other for past sins and slights and using us to act in their stead in this grudge match.

It was more than a contract at stake here; it was pride and ego. And those were far worse.

Ford and I, sisters of a sort, would end up at each other's throats, perhaps literally, vying to win. Ford, because she would fight until the end to save the only other hybrid we knew of, Carter. And I would kill to end this program, to destroy us all and the ones who'd made us. In fact, I'd *already* killed for that cause, as much as my mind tried to shy away from that memory.

The only question was which of us—Ford or me—would succeed. And it had to be me. If I was going to die—and that was a certainty, only the timing was in doubt—then it needed to count for something.

I pictured Ford on the ground, her face, identical to mine, turning red and then shades of purple, veins bulging as she struggled to breathe while I held her heart still in my mental grasp. Now that I'd actually done it—stopped a beating human heart—it was all too easy for me to picture.

A wave of sadness washed over me. Even in trying to do

the right thing, Ford and I would both end up hurting each other instead of the people who deserved it.

I definitely didn't wish Ford dead. She and Carter were the closest thing I had to family. I didn't like Ford, exactly—she was difficult and strange—but I admired her. She hadn't had it any easier than me, living in Laughlin's facility and forced to attend school as part of a humanizing effort, all the while trying to protect her "siblings." She'd never had a chance at true freedom, either. But the photo of a gorgeous lake surrounded by mountains—somewhere in Utah, maybe?—that she'd hidden away in the cubby where she slept told me that she'd dreamed about it, at least.

"Not *real* people," Rachel muttered defiantly, meeting my gaze with a challenge in her eyes.

It took me a second, lost in my thoughts as I was, to put Rachel's words in context.

I stiffened. People were going to die, but they weren't real people to Rachel. I wasn't a real person.

It wasn't exactly a surprise she held that opinion. A lot of people involved in Project Paper Doll, including Zane's mother, Mara, shared it. And yet hearing those words from Rachel sliced at me. I'd been in classes with her. She'd known me as Ariane Tucker before she knew I was GTX-F-107.

I pushed myself up off the floor, ignoring my overworked muscles, and approached the door.

"You think this is about aliens and hybrids and creepy crawlies made in a lab?" I demanded.

Rachel pushed her chair back until it slammed into the bottom step leading from the hallway above, and then she jumped up, as if she might run. As if that would save her. "Stay away," she said, her hands clutched tight around her phone, her life preserver of normal in the ocean of alien strangeness around her.

I leaned against the glass door, pressing my palms flat on it, the lines on them the same as hers, as human as hers. "They're going to use us as assassins, spies, and mercenaries," I said, staring her down, knowing the fear and discomfort my too-dark and almost irisless eyes provoked in people. "Who exactly do you think we're going to be killing and spying on, Rachel? Not other 'freaks' like us."

She stumbled up the first step and glared at me, hating me for making her afraid. "God, Ariane, okay. What do you expect me to do about it?"

"I don't know. Care about someone other than yourself. Or pretend, at least." I turned away from the door and her beyond it, returning to my place on the shiny white floor, near my now-overturned cot.

I waved my hand at the cot, flipping it upright easily and then lifting it up toward the ceiling again, and prepared to resume my physical training.

Push-ups, maybe. My upper body strength was definitely lacking, my bones too fragile to support much of the muscle development. But every bit would help, especially against Ford, someone who was, in all likelihood, my exact match in strength and abilities. It would come down to some less definable element—surprise or willpower or cunning.

I couldn't let it be Ford. This had to end. Jacobs and Laughlin, they couldn't be allowed to keep using us, taking from us.

An image of Zane's face, a smile pulling at his mouth as he leaned over me, flashed across my mind.

"Did you know they're having a memorial service at school

on Monday?" Rachel asked, startling me. She'd been so quiet I'd assumed she'd stormed off in a huff to report me to her grandfather. Instead, a quick glance in her direction showed her back in her chair, albeit still pushed away from the door. "For Zane, I mean," she added.

My heart stuttered. I'd been expecting this or something like it for weeks now, ever since Dr. Jacobs, in one of his many attempts to elicit a reaction from me, had broken the news that no one could find Zane. But somehow the expectation hadn't prepared me for the reality of hearing those words.

I sat back on my knees and lowered the cot to the ground quickly before it could crash again. "What?" My voice sounded rough even to my ears.

"Well, I guess it's not really a memorial service," she said in a considering tone. "Since they didn't . . . they haven't found his body." She winced visibly.

I stared at Rachel, making an effort this time to hear her emotions and thoughts as well as her words. Grief mixed with anger, cloudy and pervasive, pulsed through her. "Why are you telling me this?" I asked.

She ignored my question, staring holes through me instead. "His mom, she's back in town now. I met her. She seems nice. She wants to have a funeral—Quinn, too—but they can't do that, can they? I mean, what are they going to do, bury an empty casket? Maybe some of the blood the police scraped up from that parking lot?" She raised an eyebrow at me.

My hands clenched into fists.

"The hospital still says his body never got there. I mean,

they have the record of the ambulance call and everything, but that's it. Nobody seems to know what happened to him after that," she said, lifting her shoulders in an exaggerated shrug. Then her eyes narrowed. "But you do, don't you?"

I looked away. "No."

I didn't, truly. But I had my suspicions, given the people involved. There was no way that Jacobs or Laughlin would risk police involvement, as there inevitably would be with a shooting death. No, it was better that Zane Bradshaw, an inconvenient victim/speed bump on the road to progress, just mysteriously disappear as a bureaucratic error, lost in the system. Perhaps even delivered to an accommodating funeral home and cremated "by mistake," a discovery that would be made months or years from now. Or never.

Or maybe Laughlin or Jacobs's lackeys, whomever they'd charged with cover-up duties, had gone old school and simply buried him in a grave that some early-morning hunter or jogger would stumble over one day.

My stomach lurched, and I rocked forward to my hands and knees, the imagined scene pictured too clearly in my head, the white of his shirt, now dull and dirtied, wrapped in tatters around bones.

Bile rose up my throat. I coughed and choked it out, bright yellow on the pristine white floor.

"So, see?" Rachel asked, watching me, satisfaction heavy in her expression. "I'm not the only one who's selfish. You got Zane killed, and you won't even help his family and those of us who really cared about him say good-bye."

Her words struck deeply, where I was most vulnerable. Because she was, after all, absolutely correct. I might not know where Zane's body was, but I was definitely the reason he was dead.

"Screw you, Rachel," I said, wiping my chin and glaring at her through my tears. "I hope you get everything a real person like you deserves."

"Girls, girls," Dr. Jacobs said in a scolding tone, catching both of us by surprise.

He stood at the top of the steps behind Rachel, having emerged from the private elevator or perhaps even the observation room behind my cell. I wasn't sure. I didn't care.

Rachel stood up immediately, scooping her bag up from the floor and slinging it over her shoulder. Then her hand shot out toward him, palm up. "Cash," she said flatly.

His smile was tight with irritation. "Good afternoon to you, my dear," he said. "Manners do still count for something, you know." But he reached into the pocket of his white lab coat to remove a silver, or more likely platinum, money clip.

"Yeah? How about you save your lectures for the grandchild you didn't try to have murdered?" She paused for a moment, pretending to think, tapping her finger against her mouth. "Oh, wait . . . there's just me."

Rachel was holding tight to her grudge. Not surprising. Dr. Jacobs had once thrown her into my cell, hoping she'd annoy me enough that I'd kill her and therefore meet the entrance requirement for the trials. When a family member, the only one who seems to really care about you, is willing to have you killed to prove the worthiness and ability of his science experiment—namely, me—that's probably not something you get over quickly or easily. Unfortunately, that didn't change the fact that he was still pretty much all she had.

Dr. Jacobs paused counting out hundred dollar bills to give Rachel a sharp look.

"You know, if you'd just give me access to my trust fund, we wouldn't have to go through this," she said. "You bribing me to talk to your toy, me pretending not to hate you." She waved her hand in an airy gesture.

"Not until you're eighteen," he said with a weary air that suggested this was a conversation that had taken place multiple times in various iterations.

I pushed myself to my feet to snag the roll of toilet paper from my bathroom—a toilet, sink, and shower set up in the corner of the room behind a privacy curtain that was more of a suggestion of such than the real thing.

I wanted, if at all possible, to get the floor cleaned up before Jacobs noticed. But I forced myself not to rush; that would surely draw his attention faster than anything.

"I could hire a lawyer," Rachel continued, snatching up the money he held out and shoving it into her bag.

"Not one that's better than all of mine," he shot back. "It's untouchable for the next fourteen months, Rachel. Get used to it, please."

"Whatever. I'm late to meet Cami," she said, spinning off in a huff.

I mopped up the floor as Rachel stomped up the stairs, her heels cracking loudly on the tile.

"I've already made your excuses for your absence on Friday, as you requested." Jacobs's voice was muffled as he turned away from the intercom outside my cell to call after his granddaughter. "I explained your trip to Chicago has an academic aspect, and Mr. Kohler has agreed that a five-page paper on the architecture of the city should be more than enough to—"

"Five pages?" Rachel shrieked.

"Chicago? She's coming with us?" I blurted, the wad of toilet paper forgotten in my hands. He was bringing Rachel to the trials? Since when had this top secret competition become a spectator sport? The thought of her smug face watching from the bleachers made me feel ill. I still didn't know exactly what the trials would involve. Dr. Jacobs claimed not to know. The event was supposedly shrouded in secrecy, to prevent one competitor from having an advantage over another.

Dr. Jacobs turned to me, startled. "Don't be ridiculous. Rachel is accompanying her friends on a shopping outing." He glared at me, as though I was the one revealing secrets.

"Wait, you're letting her out?" Rachel asked her grandfather, a beat too slow on the uptake. Was it just me, or had her face gone a shade paler?

"It's nothing for you to be concerned with," Dr. Jacobs said, lifting his hands reassuringly.

Rachel shuddered. "Just keep her away from Michigan Avenue. I don't want her spoiling anything for us. Cassi's always filling out those stupid giveaway cards. It's about time she actually won something nonpathetic. They're sending a car for us on Friday." She paused with a frown. "I hope the driver knows to bring spring water—the carbonated kind, not that cheap regular stuff."

Then she turned and stalked off toward the elevator. I felt Dr. Jacobs's attention return to me.

I chucked the toilet paper into the tiny plastic trash can (white, just like everything else in here) and resumed my place on the floor, forgetting until I was in position that I'd already done sit-ups and my stomach was not in a forgiving mood.

"That was more emotive than you've been in a while," Jacobs said conversationally as I forced myself through another set of five.

I didn't know whether he meant my shouting at Rachel earlier or the vomiting on the floor, but I wasn't going to ask.

What he said sounded like a statement, but I knew better. It was bait with a bright, shiny hook buried inside. He'd been trying to get me to talk for weeks now, to open up, as he said.

A horrible idea that brought to mind the image of my skull being cracked open with everything spilling out for further examination, speculation, and admiration of his handiwork.

I gave a shake of my head, more to myself than him. No, damn it. My feelings and thoughts were mine, at least. The only things that were, in this place. And I was going to keep them.

Instead, I lay on the floor, giving my abused muscles a break, and retrained my efforts on the other side of my new exercise regime. With barely any exertion, I had my cot suspended above me again, along with my initial stack of books, gathered and reassembled in midair. Once, something like this would have been difficult for me and the results unpredictable. The lightbulbs overhead would have blown and anything not bolted down would have been shaking and shifting.

Not anymore. Amazing what grim, uncompromising determination would do for you.

"Your improvement is quite impressive, particularly for such a short amount of time," Jacobs said, after a moment. "Then again, I suppose that might be due to your newly acquired motivation."

I went still, and the books wobbled slightly. Was that an oblique reference to Zane's death? If Jacobs had guessed my intention to raze Project Paper Doll to the ground, personnel included, I wasn't sure what he would do. He needed me to compete in the trials but certainly not at the risk of loss, humiliation, and death.

I let out my breath slowly, straining to maintain an impassive expression. *Steady, stay steady.* I wasn't sure if I was talking to my cot and the books or myself.

"Your desire to seek vengeance against Ford is understandable," he continued. "And I certainly can't argue with the results."

I relaxed. That was a logical assumption on his part. Of course I would blame the person who pulled the trigger on the bullet that had killed Zane. In Dr. Jacobs's arrogant mind, that was the only reasonable response. No way would I hold him responsible. *He* hadn't hurt anyone.

Except me. Over and over again, in almost every way possible. He had vastly underestimated the depths of my anger and desire for retaliation.

A grim smile pulled at the corners of my mouth. His loss. Or, it would soon be.

Yes, Ford had shot Zane, but it had been unintentional, a by-product of her attempt at self-defense against Laughlin's guards. Zane's death was her fault only because she, like me, was a pawn in this game Jacobs and Laughlin were playing with us.

"But *we*," Dr. Jacobs said with a wink at me, as if we were somehow collaborating, "need you to be *you*. Everything that makes you special, not some flesh-and-blood robot." He made a disgusted noise at the idea and then smiled at me as if I understood what he was talking about.

Which I didn't. Not at first. Robot? What?

Then, suddenly, his meaning clicked. Oh. If I were too much like Ford, too obviously different, inhuman and nonemotional, his methodology wouldn't shine through, demonstrating the obvious advantages of his technique (i.e., she walks, talks, even smiles just like a real human, but she's not!) over that of his competitor, Dr. Laughlin.

And that, in turn, explained Rachel's persistent presence. Rachel had the ability to crawl beneath my skin and set up camp, like a rash that would not go away. She irritated me, to the extreme. He'd been counting on her for that, to force me to react and dissolve the walls I'd put up around my feelings.

He wanted to make sure that if he pricked me, I'd still bleed. Especially in front of the audience we would have waiting for us at the trials.

And I'd fallen right in line with his plan.

A fresh cascade of self-hatred washed over me, and I let my cot and books fall to the floor.

I stood on shaking legs to turn my back on Dr. Jacobs's gloating face. He'd won, yet again.

"You'll be pleased to hear that Private Zadowski is being released from the hospital today," he said smugly.

My breath caught in my throat at the name; a vision of that soldier's face, young and unlined, growing purple from the effort to stay alive, was so bright in my mind.

"Minimal permanent damage to the heart, despite clinical death, thanks to your resuscitation efforts. He's going to be fine." He paused. "You really are quite capable of amazing things, 107." He sounded impressed, pleased, but there was a layer of smugness beneath it all, as if to say, "Of course you are. Because I made you."

Then he walked up the stairs and away from my cell, whistling, his shoes clacking happily on the tile floor.

My fingernails dug into the vulnerable skin of my upper arms, the pain sharpening my focus and reminding me of my true purpose.

Oh, Dr. Jacobs, you have no *idea what I'm capable of.*

I lowered myself into push-up position on the floor and sent that second stack of books into the air, where they held steadily for the first time.

Two more days.

CHAPTER 2

Ariane

"107," Dr. Jacobs snapped.

His voice over the sudden pop of the intercom jolted me awake. I sat bolt upright, my heart pounding in triple time.

I blinked rapidly, trying to reorient myself, the rush of adrenaline making me shaky. I was in a cell at GTX, just like usual. Well, the usual for the last three weeks, anyway. My eyes were gritty, and my neck had a painful kink.

I tugged at the collar of my tunic, which was damp with nightmare-induced sweat. In the dream, I was being chased by an unseen enemy, while Zane, a pale spectral vision with a blood-soaked shirt, watched in the distance. And no matter how hard or fast I ran, I couldn't seem to get any closer to him, nor could I shake my pursuer.

Nothing like your subconscious to be as subtle as an anvil to the skull.

"I said, how soon can you be ready to go?" Dr. Jacobs sounded brusque, annoyed even, at having to repeat himself.

I looked for him at the door first but found him instead at the observation window above me, his forehead pinched with irritation. I wondered how long he'd been trying to wake me.

"Go?" I repeated dumbly. "Now?" The trials weren't until tomorrow. I hadn't been asleep for *that* long.

"How soon?" he asked again, through clenched teeth.

"I don't know . . . fifteen minutes?" I shook my head, trying to clear it. What was going on? This was odd.

"Excellent," Jacobs said. "I'll make the arrangements. In the meantime, please be clean, dressed, and ready to go as soon as possible." Strangely, his words were clipped, completely devoid of the arrogant, anticipatory triumph I'd expected from him on the day before his "great victory."

I frowned up at him.

He avoided my gaze. Like that would help him. The trouble with creating an alien/human hybrid that can sometimes read minds is that sometimes that mind is *yours*.

"You're upset about something." More than just my unwillingness to be conscious at his command.

. . . Laughlin behind this. I'm sure of it. Why else would they . . . Security will be almost impossible and 107 has run before . . . He must have told them . . . otherwise, why select such a location . . .

"They changed the venue. No," I amended, listening more intently to his thoughts. "The venue isn't what you thought it would be." Interesting.

"Enough, 107," he said sharply. "I have clothes for you." He nodded at someone to his left, and a tech appeared at the door, watching me with open trepidation written on his face and shrieking at me from his brain.

I remained still as he opened the door and hurled a pile

of clothing—bra, underwear, socks, jeans, and a shirt—and a pair of shoes in my general direction before pulling the door shut again.

"There's a meeting this afternoon for all the participants and their companies to make sure everyone has an equal understanding of what is expected of them and what will constitute a fair win," Dr. Jacobs said, his mouth puckered as though the words tasted sour.

How complicated could it possibly be, I wanted to ask. Wasn't pretty much the only rule, "Kill or be killed"? But those words lurched to a stop on the tip of my tongue as the ramifications of this meeting's existence sank in. My plan had been to win the competition while looking for the opportunity to end everyone involved in it, one by one and over weeks or months if necessary. But if I understood Dr. Jacobs correctly, all the major players would be in the same room today.

My heartbeat increased until I could feel my pulse in my fingertips. Was that even possible? Could I finish this before it even began? Taking on multiple opponents at once made it riskier, but if I got it started, maybe Ford and Carter would join in.

I fought the urge to grin.

"—both know, it's a dog and pony show, a chance to look at you and the others up close while you all run through your 'tricks,'" Dr. Jacobs said with distaste, drawing my attention back to him. "But we can use that against them."

Oh yes. Yes, *we* can. Well, *I* could. I wasn't sure what Dr. Jacobs had in mind.

"I've had to make some adjustments to my original plan."

He sounded miffed. "So we'll discuss additional strategy details . . . later. Just be ready." He paused. "I need you on my side for this one, 107." He glared down at me as if that would help impress the words upon me.

I nodded quickly, obediently. I'd come this far and done so much with everything working against me, I needed this opportunity. Whatever he needed to see/hear/feel to take me to that meeting, I was willing to do.

Jacobs gave me a curt nod before snapping off the intercom and stalking away from the observation window.

Legs shaking with repressed relief and giddiness—I might really have a shot at ending this all today!—I moved to the other side of my narrow room and gathered up the clothing the tech had tossed in to me.

It was only after I touched the jeans that I realized they were mine. From my old life. Jacobs must have sent someone to my former house, the one I'd shared with my father for ten years.

A house that GTX probably owned, now that I thought about it. But even knowing that, it was still home to me. The first place I'd ever felt safe.

I couldn't stop myself from picturing it as it probably looked right now.

The grass in the front yard had to be overgrown, likely prompting comments from the neighbors. Our breakfast dishes from that last morning, still in the drying rack, probably had a fine layer of dust. My backpack with all my books still on the floor of my bedroom, weeks of homework collecting at the school office, never to be retrieved. The bathtub with its slow-drip faucet, still dripping. The stacked packages of blue contacts beneath the sink, no prescription, just color.

I wondered if my father had been able to retrieve the photo albums of his daughter, the original Ariane, before leaving town. I hoped so. I wanted to think of him having those with him, wherever he was.

Would GTX send movers? Someone to go through our stuff and pack it up so they could destroy it or sell it? Maybe they already had.

A powerful ache started inside me. I wanted to be home, sitting across the breakfast table from my father, talking to him about my day.

But that home, that life, was gone. And so was my father. I'd hated him for what he'd done, for lying to me for all those years, secretly reporting on me to GTX. But now . . . now I could see it another way. He'd saved me the only way he could. Teaching me what it meant to be human even as he'd encouraged me to own my distinctly nonhuman abilities.

He would have hated my plan, hated who I'd become to accomplish the goal in front of me. He'd warned me, told me to cut ties and run, but I hadn't listened. At least, not well enough to save myself or Zane. So this was all that was left.

I stroked one finger down the velvety softness of the denim in my hands. By complete chance they'd brought my favorites, my Luckys.

I'd worn these on my first "date" with Zane to the activities fair. The beginning of a sequence of events that led me to this time and place.

It seemed appropriate that they were also part of the end.

Whenever I'd thought about the trials, I'd always been far more preoccupied by *what* they would be instead of where.

In my head, the setting was always dark, vague, anonymous.

An old abandoned warehouse or an empty hangar on a military base of some kind, perhaps. I'd never paid much attention during my imaginings. The spotlight, sometimes literally, was always focused on us, dueling or punching or levitating stuff in front of an unknown audience, hidden in the shadows.

But if I had considered it, I would have said that an isolated location, in a low-res area with a perimeter that could be easily secured, seemed only logical. No witnesses, plenty of time to clean up, and room for lots of plausible deniability.

In short, absolutely nothing like downtown Chicago.

But from my seat in the very back of a GTX van—the security team accompanying me was not taking any chances—it looked like that's where we were headed.

We'd left the interstate behind to enter a grid of congested one-way streets. Madison, Monroe, more president names flashed by my window, reminding me of Ford and Carter. And Nixon.

Nixon. The memory of his hand on mine, seeking reassurance, as we headed into Laughlin's facility, made me flinch inwardly. The recollection was paired, as always, with the image of Nixon on the ground, his eyes staring up at the sky unseeing and the pool of blood spreading beneath his head.

I squeezed my eyes shut, trying to blot out that horrible picture.

A horn blared, and my eyes snapped open. The van jerked to the right suddenly, nearly toppling me over.

The security guy at the wheel cursed under his breath. I watched as a cab shot over a few lanes, still honking at everyone in his way.

We were most definitely heading deeper in the city. Why?

I sat forward in my seat. "Where are we going?" I asked, speaking for the first time since I'd been escorted from my room up to Jacobs's office and then down through a service elevator to the waiting van in the GTX parking garage.

All four security guys ignored me, except for a slight tensing of shoulders in the one nearest me. Two rows of seats away. Clearly my reputation preceded me. Their thoughts were buzzing with anxiety and anger, making them difficult to read.

I tried again. "Where is Dr. Jacobs?"

Again, silence.

The driver was torn between watching me in the rearview mirror and trying to pay attention to the cars around him. "I'm just going to keep asking," I said, using that flat tone that so many humans—well, the ones who knew the truth about me—interpreted as threatening.

"He's already on location," the driver said curtly. "Because of the delay."

Ah yes, the delay again. The fifteen minutes I'd suggested as the time I required had stretched into an hour and then two and then more before anyone had shown up to retrieve me.

It was already late afternoon. The sun was a bright orange blaze in the west, reflecting off mirrored high-rise windows in bright flashes as we passed.

Had we missed the meeting? Was that Jacobs's brilliant plan? Just not show up?

I forced myself to inhale and then exhale to a count of ten. Staying calm and alert was my best bet.

Watching out the window, I counted off blocks and turns, memorizing our route. It kept my brain occupied.

When we drove past the sweeping entrance for the Manderlay Hotel, I didn't think much about it, except to note that it looked like something out of a movie. The bustling valets and bellmen in red coats, the flags flapping on poles overhead, and the limousines idling in the drive.

But then the van slowed and pulled into the attached parking garage. The Manderlay? Seriously?

I moved to the edge of my seat. Maybe we were going somewhere else, another building that used the same garage.

But no, the driver was following the signs inside for hotel parking.

What the hell? The Manderlay looked expensive. Luxury, even. I would have felt better pulling up to a former meatpacking plant full of rats and tetanus or something.

This just didn't make sense: a fight to the death in a place that turned down your covers and didn't bolt the remote to the bedside table. I could understand why Jacobs would pick a nice place for the duration of the trials. Laughlin, too. And the as-yet-unknown military contacts who would be judging the trials. (Jacobs called them the Committee.)

But why bring me here? I was missing something, some important detail or fact that would make it all click. It made me uneasy. If one of my assumptions was wrong, then my read of the entire situation—and my plans, accordingly—might be wrong.

The driver parked and cut the engine.

I stood up, my head bent to avoid the roof, but before I could start for the van door, the guard closest to me, the nervous one, held up his hand to stop me. "No," he said loudly, as if speaking to a stupid but large puppy. One with sharp teeth.

I raised my eyebrows. "I am fully fluent in English and four other languages. There's no need to shout. I am more than capable of understanding basic human speech."

He twitched at the word *human* but otherwise ignored me. I couldn't resist tweaking him, though. "For example, *no*, *bù*, *nein*, *nyet*, *la*."

No longer fearing for my life made me bold in ways that were probably not so good for my survival.

He glared at me as he climbed out of the van with his buddies.

I made him uncomfortable, which meant I'd need to keep an eye on him, if he was sticking around for the duration. Someone that edgy might be more likely to shoot first and never ask questions. Maybe I could use that to my advantage.

I watched as the four of them did a visual sweep of the area.

Apparently, someone was worried I'd die on the way to my death match. Interesting.

The guard nearest me gave a nod toward me through the van's tinted windows.

As soon as I stepped out, the four of them positioned themselves around me, two in front and two in back, and led the way through the garage to a set of doors marked LOBBY.

Really? This should be fun.

Beyond the doors, the smell of new carpeting and fresh paint in a recently redecorated walkway filled my nose, making it hard to breathe until I adjusted.

The walkway had a few other people in it—families, a few couples, some of them heading toward the garage, others ahead of us in the trek to the lobby.

We earned curious glances, but nothing more. My hands weren't bound, and I was dressed in my regular clothes. If anything, I probably looked more like the privileged child of someone important—progeny worth protecting, coddling even. Oh, hello, irony.

As soon as we reached the polished black-and-white floor of the lobby, my escorts took a sharp left at the koi pond in the center of the room, heading for a narrow hallway tucked to the side of the massive mahogany registration desk.

At the end of the hallway, we went through a set of swinging wooden doors and ended up in a significantly less posh section of the hall. Linoleum floors, thick yellow paint on the walls, the faint smell of old food, and rolling carts full of folding chairs stacked on either side. A service corridor, most likely.

One short trip up in a battered and small elevator to the third floor, and we'd arrived. To where, exactly, I wasn't sure. But Dr. Jacobs was there waiting, as the doors rolled back.

He reached in, past my guards, and hauled me out, his hand tight enough to bruise my forearm. "What took you so long?" he hissed at me, flecks of spit landing on my cheek.

"We stopped to sightsee," I snapped, pulling my arm back. As if I'd been even remotely in control of our arrival time.

He released me, shaking his hand as if touching me had in some way contaminated his skin. I'd never seen him this agitated. Normally, the angrier he was, the more pleasant he got. When the man smiled, it was absolutely terrifying.

But this . . . this reaction was something else.

As the guards exited the elevator and fanned out in what proved to be another service corridor, I studied Jacobs, rubbing my forearm. He wore an outdated suit (that still screamed money) beneath his pristine, white lab coat, his cheeks were flushed, and his forehead was damp with perspiration.

Either he was coming down with a deadly disease (fingers crossed!) or this was Dr. Jacobs being nervous. I wanted to enjoy his misery, but if he was worried, I wasn't sure what that meant for me. His thoughts were too jumbled and buzzy with adrenaline for me to read.

He reached into a white plastic bag resting on an abandoned room service cart behind him, pulled out a bundle of bright red fabric, and thrust it at me.

I took it reluctantly. Unfolded, it proved to be a sweatshirt with UW–MADISON in big white letters across the front. The letters were soft around the edges from wear, and the cuffs were ragged. This was definitely not new.

I glanced at him in question, and he held up an equally battered backpack. Not mine. This one was dark blue with a tiny, yellow Minion figure dangling from a keychain attached to the hook strap at the top. From the shape of the bag, it appeared to be full of books or something equally weighty. That was . . . strange.

"It's not ideal, I realize," Dr. Jacobs said. "But it will have to do. We had a fully detailed and tailored navy uniform all ready for you, but the location was not—" He cut himself off.

Ah, the venue change from this morning. Evidently Jacobs had assumed we'd be at a military base of some kind. That, or he'd gotten bad intel. Either way, that explained his foul mood and the delay while he scrambled for a Plan B.

"Just put it all on." Jacobs dropped the bag at my feet,

where it landed with a solid thud. "These, too." He fished a small, familiar-looking package from his lab coat pocket: tinted contact lenses, the same brand I'd worn every day for years.

He tossed them at me, and I caught them automatically.

But when I hesitated, still trying to piece together what was going on here, Jacobs waved a hand at me, as if that would cause some kind of magical transformation, instant wardrobe shift, and I felt a flash of anger.

I'd crossed a lot of lines in pursuit of my goal, and I'd given up a lot of things; rather, I'd had them taken from me. Freedom, individuality, basic human rights (assuming I was entitled to them). Changing my appearance on command was a relatively small straw by comparison, but it felt like the last one. I was not a toy, not a lab monkey to be dressed up and paraded around for the mockery and pleasure of others.

But I was so close to the end, just minutes away from the meeting that would change everything. What was one more violation if it got me closer to my objective?

Gritting my teeth, I turned my back on Jacobs and the guards. I pulled the sweatshirt over my head first. It smelled faintly of bonfire smoke and spicy deodorant, but not unpleasantly so. And it was about three sizes too big; my arms swam in the armholes, and the hem dropped halfway down to my knees.

I ignored the backpack at my feet for the moment and concentrated next on carefully tearing open the packaging on the contact lenses. I was used to doing this at the bathroom counter with a mirror in front of me, so it took me an extra few seconds to figure out how to juggle the packages and then get the lenses in my eyes without a guide.

Eyes watering fiercely, I bent down and scooped the backpack off the floor and jammed the empty lens packaging in a front pocket that was empty but for what appeared to be a half-eaten granola bar. Lovely.

I turned and faced my audience.

Dr. Jacobs looked me up and down in evaluation. His lips pursed in displeasure.

"Pull your hair up." He fished around in his pocket and pulled out a dirty green rubber band that looked as though it had recently been wrapped around mail or something.

"What exactly is the point of this?" I asked, hoisting the backpack onto my shoulder and then gathering my heavy hair into a rough ponytail. Were we going to be judged by our ability to assemble a ridiculous ensemble from items from the lost and found?

"No," he snapped. "Braid it."

"I don't know how," I said through clenched teeth. I hated him so much, sometimes it felt as if it were burning a hole outward through my chest.

He paused, seemingly mystified by this gap in my education.

"Not a lot of slumber parties in my recent past, remember?" I asked.

He heaved an impatient sigh. "I don't care what you do with it. Just make it look normal."

I laughed. I couldn't help it. As if I hadn't been trying to do that for most of my life, with little success. "Is this a costume party?" I asked, wrenching my hair up into the barely contained ponytail I'd worn to school every day back in my "real" life. "I'm going to look like a little kid playing dress-up."

He pursed his lips. "It doesn't matter, 107. The point is simply for them not to recognize you for what you are."

I raised my eyebrows. Wasn't the whole point of this to show us off?

With some impatience and more than a little pride, he explained, "We're emphasizing our strengths."

"By dressing me in someone else's clothes?" I asked slowly.

When that wasn't enough, he elaborated impatiently. "We want to give them a chance to see what they're getting, 107. First impressions are everything, and we want to win them over as close to the start as possible by demonstrating our advantage."

And Jacobs's big advantage in me? That I already knew: I played human far better than Ford.

I stared at Dr. Jacobs. That was his magical plan? I was going to walk in and . . . out-human her? By what? Looking normal and harmless, I suppose. It was either the most brilliant or ridiculously stupid scheme in the history of such things. And in other circumstances, where I didn't intend to strike first, it might well have gotten me killed by giving off "easy target" vibes.

"Sounds great," I said in response to his questioning look. Whatever. I wasn't here to see him succeed in selling me.

I managed to get my hair somewhat under control, though the individual strands would continue to frizz and wave without the addition of product.

"Good enough," Jacobs said in a tone that suggested

anything but. He took my elbow, pulling me along down the hall, toward a door I hadn't noticed until now.

"Just remember," he said to me as the guards fell in behind us. "You're a regular human." A vein in his forehead, throbbing and blue, pulsed with intensity behind his words, as if it might burst at any second.

This from the man who'd done everything he could to take that "regular" humanity away from me, to remind me that I had no right to it?

The urge to help that vein on its way to an embolism *right now* seized me, but I resisted. Barely. The idea, though, made me smile, twisting my mouth into something ugly. And I found I didn't care anymore.

I wanted to defeat Dr. Jacobs, to stand over him in triumph.

Or, okay, at the very least, see him howling in immense pain and possibly—no, definitely, bleeding.

See? Compromise. That really is the key to success.

CHAPTER 3

Ariane

THE DOOR DR. JACOBS PULLED ME THROUGH LED TO, what else, another hallway. This one, though, was in the hotel proper. Music played faintly in the distance, and my feet, which were still in my old Chucks, sank into plush carpet. Dim, soothing lighting, a harsh contrast to the brightly lit service corridor, made it difficult for me to see more than a few feet ahead.

Fortunately, we weren't going far. Dr. Jacobs headed toward the first door on the left, marked THE MEADOWLANDS. It was a glossy wooden door, not the banged-up, overpainted versions I'd seen in the service portions of the hotel, and it was closed, with another pair of black-clad guards in front of it.

But as we approached, they didn't move away or defer to Dr. Jacobs as I would have expected.

"Let us pass," Jacobs said through clenched teeth.

It was only then that I noticed the bright blue logo of

Laughlin Integrated on their sleeves. Oh, now it was a party. BYOST. Bring Your Own Security Team.

They backed up a step reluctantly, so much so that I wondered if Laughlin had given them specific instructions to give Jacobs a hard time.

"Wait out here," he said to the four GTX sentinels behind us. Then he barged between Laughlin's men, pulling me after him by the arm.

The handle turned easily, not locked, and I held my breath, not sure what to expect, as Jacobs yanked the door back and crossed the threshold, letting go of me as soon as I was in the room.

I resisted the urge to rub my arm as my eyes adjusted to the much brighter fluorescent light inside. Whatever I'd been anticipating, it wasn't this.

Three long tables covered in white tablecloths were arranged in a U-shape, with a fourth table at the front of the room. The tablecloth on the fourth table was black, though, which made it seem more important.

Each table held a pyramid of shining drinking glasses and a sweating pitcher of water. A whiteboard, housed in a large wooden cabinet with the doors partially open, dominated the far wall, behind the head table. Glass decanters of juice, a tray of muffins, and a bowl of fruit held prominent position on a built-in counter to my right.

All absurdly normal. Almost insultingly so, considering why we were there.

That is, until you lingered long enough to pick up on the massive waves of tension rolling through the space.

The man closest to us was at the bottom table in the U

by himself. He looked over his shoulder at us briefly and then resumed studying the phone in front of him, as if urgently awaiting a call or text or the summons to raid in *Book of Heroes*. He was younger than both Dr. Jacobs and Dr. Laughlin, who was what my friend Jenna's mother would have called "well preserved." This guy was probably in his late thirties. His dark hair was rumpled, and his leg was jouncing with anxiety, making the glasses on his table wobble and clink in their formation.

I frowned. This must be Emerson St. John. Something about him seemed familiar, but I couldn't figure out why or how I would know him. Dr. Jacobs would certainly never have let him in the GTX lab. But where was his "product"? Was St. John already disqualified in some way?

On the right side of the U, several faces I knew stared back at me. One I knew *very* well. Ford, my clone for lack of a better term, stood on the inside of the semicircle created by the furniture arrangement, next to Carter. They were wearing their school uniforms: white shirts beneath blue blazers with a plaid skirt for Ford and khakis for Carter. Laughlin's attempt, no doubt, to make them seem relatable and human. If anything, it emphasized how human they were not. The dark blue of the coats only made their hair look whiter and their skin more gray. The preternatural stillness they . . . we have was so much more noticeable in isolation.

Full-blooded humans twitch, sigh, bite their nails, expressing their anxiety in motion. We are the opposite. It had taken many years for me to adapt to that particular quirk, to create one of my own. Now I bite my lip out of habit, rather than imitation, but it hadn't started that way.

Ford glanced over her shoulder at me, her expression flat. She looked harder or sharper somehow, as if the last weeks had compressed her from raw material into something more deadly. Grayish blue circles marred the skin beneath her eyes, and a new hash mark decorated her cheek.

It hurt to see those marks on her face, a reminder of what had been lost. One for Johnson, the hybrid who'd been eliminated when she couldn't blend in at school, and the other for Nixon.

Nixon. He'd never had a chance. To survive or actually live. I wondered if they'd preserved his body in the gallery with all the others, leaving him permanently staring out at the quarters where he'd once lived.

Ford gave no acknowledgement of our previous acquaintance. Angry at me, perhaps, for our failed attempt at rebellion, the one that had cost her Nixon. Carter, though, greeted me with the corner of his mouth lifting in the tiniest of smiles.

He, too, looked weary and paler than usual. Whatever he and Ford had been through since I'd seen them last had taken its toll. The fact that he was still capable of smiling made me hate everyone else in the room just that much more. He deserved better than this. We all did.

At the table, Dr. Laughlin cleared his throat, glaring at Ford and Carter and jerking his head in an indication that they should both face forward. His two assistants, dark haired, beautiful, and strikingly similar, sat up straighter, their tablets at the ready for any words of wisdom he might drop.

It wouldn't be a hardship to kill Dr. Laughlin when the time came. I eyed him carefully, a greasy feeling of anticipation slipping through me. Perhaps that glass water pitcher to the head. The base of it looked heavy, and it only takes fifteen pounds of pressure per square inch to fracture a human skull. *Your bones may be stronger than mine, but that does not make you indestructible.*

The left side of the U was empty. I trailed after Dr. Jacobs, avoiding Dr. St. John's chair as we walked to our seats.

At the head table, two men and a woman were seated. None of them were wearing anything to identify them as military, but it seeped through in the details. The old white guy on the far end had a buzz cut that screamed armed services. The blond woman in the middle, her hair in a blunt cut that stayed out of her face as if it was too afraid to stray, had her back so straight that she didn't even appear to need the chair. The younger man was African American and wore a serious "don't mess with me" expression on his acne-scarred face.

In short, though they weren't wearing uniforms, you'd have to be blind to miss what they were.

This was the Committee—our judges, our jury, our executioners.

I watched them watching Ford and Carter. Then those evaluating gazes shifted to me, cold, unemotional, and yet still eager. The open avariciousness in the woman's expression made my stomach churn and my palms sweaty. Under those eyes, I felt small and stripped of not just my human "disguise" but everything that made me me. They did not see us as people. We were something to be acquired.

"Dr. Jacobs, I assume this is your submission . . . finally?" the one I was calling Morpheus, after the character in *The Matrix*, asked suddenly, his voice ringing loud in the otherwise quiet space.

The back of Dr. Jacobs's neck flushed with color as the attention in the room shifted from me to him. "It is. My apologies again. There were final preparations to make," Dr. Jacobs said.

As one, the three Committee members looked to me again with critical eyes, as if to determine what last-minute enhancements might have been performed. I doubted any of them would have honed in on the sweatshirt, contact lenses, and freaking backpack.

I didn't care if Jacobs's ridiculous "out-humaning" gambit actually worked, but given my plans for ending all of this as quickly as possible once everyone was in place, I'd have preferred *not* to have stares pinned on me.

Fortunately, Dr. St. John, who'd been staring at me as well, chose that moment to pipe up. "We have a prototype and a special model arriving shortly." He tapped a message into his phone and sat back in his chair, looking all too pleased with himself suddenly.

"Might I point out that our prototypes are functional *and* capable of telling time?" Dr. Laughlin asked with a smarmy smile.

Blech.

"We're not waiting any longer," the woman warned, pointing a pen at St. John. "It'll be up to you to make sure your product is informed of the boundaries and restrictions." She paused with a tight smile that wreathed her face in wrinkles, revealing her true age. "Disqualification would be . . . unfortunate."

"Not a problem," Dr. St. John assured her.

Dropping my prop backpack on the floor, I sat down next

to Dr. Jacobs, my heart tripping over itself suddenly. I could feel the irregular beat shaking me from head to toe. How had I ended up here?

A little over a month ago, I'd been getting ready to start my junior year, and my biggest worry was about blending in. Zane Bradshaw had been a stranger, a pretty boy lacking a spine, at the periphery of Rachel Jacobs's circle of piranhas. I'd had no idea that my life Outside was a complete sham, a scheme to teach me more about being human and help me regain the abilities I'd blocked.

Now Zane was dead and I was here, in a surreal version of the world that had me facing down not only my creator but also the people who were even more responsible for my existence. After all, there's no point in supply if there is no demand. And the three at the head table—or someone within their organization—had provided the alien genetic material and asked for the impossible: alien-enhanced soldier/assassins. Which GTX, Laughlin Integrated, and presumably Emerson had happily leaped to provide.

My palms were damp, and I wiped them unobtrusively down the legs of my jeans, out of sight beneath the table.

Focus. Be calm. Evaluate the situation. Prioritize your objectives.

The old guy cleared his throat. "Thank you, gentlemen, for coming today. And for your work in support of the security of this great country."

Because the best defense is a good offense. The line from an old movie, a comedy and one of the few my father had actually watched and enjoyed, ran through my head.

"Melody has additional information for you regarding the specifics of what will be required," he said, gesturing carelessly at the woman next to him. "Melody?"

Her mouth pinched in clear displeasure—pissed that he'd used her name, perhaps, or that the doling out of details had been delegated to her—but she nodded. "You have an assigned target for this mission," the woman said, speaking to Jacobs, Laughlin, and St. John, as if they were the ones doing the work. Now that the novelty had worn off, Ford, Carter, and I had ceased to exist, no more a party to this discussion than the furniture. "In the packet, which you'll receive at the meeting's conclusion, you'll find the target's photo, some basic information about the target, and a phone for designated check-ins. Find the target, confirm identity by taking and transmitting a photo, and then await further instructions."

Well, that explained why we were here in the middle of the city. Dumping us all into an echoingly empty warehouse wouldn't be much test of our tracking skills.

If that was, in fact, what they were testing. The "await further instructions" bit gave me a weird vibe. I couldn't read Melody's thoughts—she was military trained and, obviously, they'd all been briefed on what we were capable of—but excitement glittered in her eyes.

I shifted slightly in the chair, taking a slow, deep breath. If I was going to do this here and now, the three of them—Old Guy, Melody, and Morpheus—had to be first priority. They were soldiers, past or present; they had, most likely, faced some form of attack in the past.

People like them never let their guard down completely.

"From the itinerary our sources have assembled, the target should be within the city limits for the next forty-eight hours," Morpheus added.

I ignored him. The trick would be taking out as many as

I could at once. The moment one of them went down, the room would dissolve into chaos. And I'd have to devote my effort to holding the doors against the guards and addressing any additional threats inside the room.

"Discretion is a mission requirement. No exceptions. But you may eliminate the competition as you see fit, provided it doesn't violate that order," he said. "This is a test of strategy as well as skill."

I reached out with my abilities and tugged gently at the wooden cabinet housing the whiteboard, testing. It wobbled, spilling out a blue marker that landed on the floor behind the three with a quiet *thwap* on the carpet.

Ford stiffened. She'd noticed.

Crap. I released the cabinet immediately, letting it settle gently against the wall again.

But no one shouted or pointed as Morpheus continued outlining mission standards. Dr. Laughlin was too busy rocking on the two back legs of his chair and smirking at Jacobs, who was glaring death at him. St. John had resumed the study of his phone.

Ford risked a sharp glance over her shoulder in my direction. Warning or questioning me? It was impossible to tell.

I returned my attention to the cabinet. It was loose, definitely. If I could pull the entire structure free of the wall and send it at their heads with enough force—

"Is the target aware of his status as such?" Ford asked abruptly.

The ensuing silence was breathtakingly loud.

I froze. What was she doing? They hadn't, as far as I knew, been instructed to keep quiet, but these military types likely weren't used to being questioned, particularly by beings they equated to weapons, nonsentient tools.

Laughlin set his chair down with a resounding thump, his angled face a dozen shades of furious. "Ford," he barked. Carter cringed, inching closer to Ford, whether for protection or to protect her, I wasn't sure.

But the one I'd dubbed Morpheus nodded approvingly. "No. It . . . she is correct. That would change the parameters." To Ford, he said, "The target has no reason to feel hiding is necessary."

Jacobs reached over and pinched my arm, signaling in a flurry of confusing motions that I should stand and *do something*. Evidently, he didn't want Ford getting too much positive attention from the Committee.

But as I stood reluctantly, the door to the hall flew open, startling everyone except Dr. St. John, who turned with an expectant smile.

"Oh, good, you're here," he said to someone just out of sight. Then he stood and swung his arm out in a welcoming gesture. "Everyone, may I present Adam."

I made a face. Adam? Really? Naming with numbers (107) wasn't particularly inventive, either, but Adam was such a tired cliché.

Adam himself, though, was anything but, especially when it came to what I knew of alien/human hybrids. At a quick glance, I wouldn't have thought him more than a normal human. In his early twenties probably, he was dressed in khakis and a bright yellow T-shirt stretched to its limits. He was broad and muscular, almost absurdly so. He actually had to turn slightly sidewise to fit through the door. He could probably have ripped the wooden cabinet off the wall without any additional abilities beyond his strength.

Which made sense. As I understood it, Emerson St. John's approach involved introducing alien DNA through a virus and rewriting portions of the human genetic code. Picking a fit human specimen was not only logical but probably necessary to ensure survival.

Upon closer look, though, there was something . . . off about Adam. It wasn't the same kind of "differentness" that people saw in me. His brown eyes were dilated, making the pupils strangely large. And he seemed paler than he should have been, but his cheeks were flushed pink with color.

I couldn't quite put my finger on what it was.

Adam walked in and took a position behind St. John's table, standing instead of sitting, as if waiting for instructions. I studied him, trying to get a read on what it was about him that screamed "wrong" to me. Other than the fact that if it came down to hand-to-hand, he would crush Ford and me. If he had even remotely the kind of psi abilities we had, we were severely outclassed.

"And, of course, the primary advantage to our method is demonstrated in our special model," St. John said proudly.

I was too busy squinting at Adam to pay attention to St. John's sales pitch, which was a mistake.

Ford sucked in a sharp breath. I automatically glanced back and found her staring at the door. I followed her gaze. My body went cold as soon as I saw what she was looking at.

Who.

The person in the doorway, the "special model." Like Adam, he was dressed in khaki and yellow. But he was taller, well over six feet with dark hair that was mussed and eyes that, when not so dilated, would have been a perfect shade of gray-blue.

Zane.

I stumbled backward, blinking rapidly, as if a trick of the fluorescent light was responsible for the mirage of the dead boy I loved.

But, no, he was still there. He wasn't looking at me, staring fixedly ahead. But it was unquestionably Zane.

I couldn't breathe.

Laughlin laughed. "Impressive, I must admit."

Next to me, Jacobs shot to his feet. "What is the meaning of this?"

"Our method can be applied to anyone," St. John said, continuing his speech. "No need for the time-consuming process of growing personnel with special skills. With our formula, you can enhance anyone you want. Key contacts within an organization, informants, those with a personal connection to the target." And with that he looked straight at me.

St. John had done this intentionally. Why? What did it even mean to "enhance" someone? How deep did St. John's process go? My thoughts were consumed by this shift in reality. I was afraid to move, to inhale or exhale with any degree of force, as if that might cause the sight of Zane to dry up and crumble away.

"Assuming they survive," Laughlin said dryly with a sniff. But he didn't seem upset, more amused than anything.

"This is unacceptable!" Jacobs shouted, his fists clenched.

"Oh, don't be a poor sport just because he outmaneuvered

you," Laughlin said gleefully. "Picked the boy up off the pavement, did you?" he asked St. John. "Smart."

"What is going on?" Melody demanded.

I ignored all of them, the din around me fading into a faint hum, as I watched Zane. His chest was moving in and out steadily, and there was no sign of the bullet wound that had seemingly killed him.

He was here. He was alive.

The urge to see him close up, to touch him, swept over me, squeezing my chest. I lurched in Zane's direction.

Jacobs made a grab for my elbow, but I pushed him away before he made contact, sending him stumbling and crashing into his chair under the invisible force of my mind, the very ability he'd gifted me with.

Then I shoved at our table, swinging it neatly out of my way. The fastest route to Zane was through the U, not around it.

Chaos erupted then, with someone shouting for the guards, who piled into the room, moving around Zane like water flowing around a rock as they searched for the threat.

And still Zane didn't react. What had they done to him?

"Stop her!" Jacobs's shriek pierced the fog in my head.

But I didn't need to be stopped. I halted all on my own in front of St. John's table, two feet from Zane.

His face was pale, but his cheeks were flushed, just like Adam's.

"Zane?" I asked, my voice hoarse and scared sounding.

He didn't move, but his gaze flicked to mine for the barest of seconds. Any farther from him and I probably wouldn't have seen it.

He knew his name, at least. But that appeared to be it. The look he'd given me had held no recognition or significance.

Knock, knock, knock, but nobody's home.

My knees wobbled, weak suddenly, as a huge, wrenching sob rolled out of me, catching me by surprise before I could stop it.

Not that it mattered. The GTX guards were on me seconds later, pulling at my arms and shoulders, tugging me away.

No. I fought out of instinct, breathing hard and fast through my mouth, like an animal in attack mode. I pushed back against every hand on me, throwing them off me.

One of the men flew into Laughlin's table, colliding with it hard and setting off a chain reaction. The glass pitcher and glasses hit the floor, and Laughlin scrambled out of the way, his assistants following with a shriek as the table collapsed.

Then, without moving from where he stood, Zane reached out and righted the man without touching him, pulling him away from the table and the glass shards with telekinesis as naturally and easily as if he'd been born to do it.

I froze, adrenaline thundering in my veins and air trapped in my chest.

Oh. Oh no. What had they done to him?

The GTX guards grabbed me again, but I didn't fight this time, my mind reeling from the possible implications. Zane shouldn't have been able to do that. What did it mean that he could? Was the Zane I knew still in there somewhere? Or was this some new version? Someone molded and fashioned to be like me, just to prove St. John's point?

"I think perhaps it's best if we postpone the remainder

of this meeting until it can be held without disruption," Morpheus said with obvious disapproval.

"Wait! That's not necessary," Dr. Jacobs protested immediately, with desperation and fury in his voice. "My product is perfectly stable. She was reacting only to this ridiculous stunt." He threw Dr. St. John a glare that would have melted glass. St. John didn't seem to care; if anything, he was amused.

But when Morpheus nodded at the GTX guards holding me, they dragged me toward the door.

Somewhere inside me, I was dimly aware that I was losing my chance, my opportunity to end Project Paper Doll in one fell swoop, but I didn't care in that moment. How could I when I didn't know if Zane was okay, if that person standing there wearing his face could even still be considered—

TOMORROW MORNING. WEST ENTRANCE.

The words boomed and echoed in my head as my guard entourage and I reached the doors. I flinched at the volume, costing me the extra second I needed to realize that I knew that voice.

Zane. He wanted to meet.

Except as the guards opened the door and pulled me over the threshold, Zane gave no sign of attempting to communicate with me. No look in my direction, no wink or smile, no further attempt to think words at me loudly enough for me to hear them. Actually, I could get nothing from his mind, which had never been the case before. And certainly shouldn't have been the case now, if he really wanted to "talk" to me.

That's when I realized that the message I'd received could just as easily be interpreted as a challenge: St. John's special model calling out Dr. Jacobs's product for a one-on-one elimination.

My heart collapsed in on itself, extinguishing the tiny flicker of hope.

A challenge was logical, far more so than any other explanation that I would have preferred. And recognizing that was like living through Zane's death all over again. Only so much worse.

Because, this time, as the conference room doors closed after us, he was standing right there, just a few feet away and completely unreachable all at the same time.

CHAPTER 4

Zane Bradshaw

THE SCAR ON MY STOMACH STILL BURNED AND ITCHED sometimes. But the fact that it was a scar and not a gaping wound with the accompanying destroyed muscles and organs—or worse, a stitched-up hole on my very uncaring corpse—was enough to keep my mouth shut with gratitude. Most of the time.

But it always got worse when I was stressed. Like now.

"He should have been back already," I said, resisting the urge to dig at the raised edge of the scar as I paced the plush hotel room that had been assigned to me, twenty stories above the conference room where my fate as a trials competitor was being decided. I swore I could detect the tingling of little foreign cells zooming around beneath my skin, dodging my slower human ones. Emerson said it was my imagination, or possibly nerve damage that was still healing. I wasn't so sure about either of those explanations.

I *felt* different. And it wasn't just the itchy/tingling scar or even the occasional unintelligible buzz of other people's thoughts in my head. For the first time in my life, I wasn't struggling to keep up, to be better. I just was. The abilities, the powers I'd gained, made me see the world from a new perspective, one in which I had more control than I'd ever dreamed.

I could do things no other human on the planet—except Adam—could do.

But that only made helpless moments like these, where I had zero control, that much harder to bear.

Lifting my hand to direct my power, I took my frustration out on the room drapes, using my newly acquired abilities to jerk them back along the track set in the ceiling and let in the last of the daylight. But the tiny burst of satisfaction that came along with every demonstration of skill vanished almost immediately.

"It's only been fifteen minutes, bro," Adam said from where he leaned against the opposite wall. He sounded, even looked, bored, but it was an act. He had almost as much at stake as me, and if you knew him well enough—as I now unfortunately did from living in close quarters with him at St. John's lab in Rochester, New York—the forced nature of his relaxed position was screamingly obvious. Mainly in the way he kept flexing his fists and cracking his knuckles.

"Dude has to justify *you* to everyone," Adam continued with a smirk. "That's going to take some time."

"Shut up," I snapped, even though he was exactly right. Adam was the more obvious candidate to represent Emerson Technology, Incorporated in the trials in just about every way possible. He'd been recruited from the army. He'd had years to train and practice for these trials, not to mention the deliberate and gradual introduction of RSTS47—Emerson St. John's DNA-altering virus—to his body over the course of many months.

As opposed to dumping a whole bunch of it in at once and hoping for the best.

That was what had happened to me, and Emerson's impulsive actions had saved me. The bullet wound and the resulting internal injuries had been healed within days.

The virus hadn't been created for healing purposes, though; rather, transformative ones. So there were consequences. The least of which was simply that I hadn't had a chance to master the new skills I'd acquired. (My show downstairs, pulling the guard to his feet, had been to demonstrate that I possessed the abilities, that I had the right to be present. That was it, which was good, because that was about all I was capable of. For the moment.)

But Justine, Emerson, and I were hoping that the Committee—as Emerson called them—would be intrigued enough to allow my candidacy, even with the creative answer Emerson had come up with for my entrance qualifier.

If not, Adam would be sent instead, and while I had no doubt about his ability to win the trials—or at least make a good show of it—I was significantly less sure of his capacity to accomplish our true mission here. Ariane didn't trust easily. Or at all, really.

And evidently, Emerson and Justine agreed with me. For now.

"No news is good news at this point," Justine said without looking up from her phone. "Jacobs is bound to strenuously object to your presence for the effect it will have on Ariane."

Her tone was flat, factual without a hint of empathy. But that was just Justine.

Hers was the first voice I'd heard upon waking up three weeks ago. "I don't care. You weren't authorized for this." She, whoever she was, had been pissed about something.

A doctor? I had wondered vaguely. I hadn't been awake, not entirely, my thoughts slipping away from me like those tiny fish in the lake up north, the ones Quinn and I had tried to catch in our hands when we were little.

Quinn. Something about my brother. What was it? I couldn't think. My head hurt, as if my skull had swollen to three times the normal size. More disturbingly, there was a low-level hum and buzz inside my mind.

Then an image clicked into place behind my closed eyes. Quinn, his face pale, his arm in a makeshift sling. He'd been in the hospital? No, I'd been in the hospital. I remembered that, sort of. The smell of antiseptic; the cool, unfamiliar sheets rough against my skin; and the pain, an unrelenting throb in my left side.

"You wanted a way to get to one of them, Justine. I'm giving it to you," another voice, male and a little petulant, argued.

"We had people working on it. Now you've just compounded the problem. This boy will have people searching for him." A weird tug at my left arm suggested that by "this boy" the woman meant me.

"The hospital records have been modified. They'll think he's dead," the man, who'd turned out to be Emerson St. John, had protested.

"Not without a body," Justine had said, sounding like maybe she intended to make that happen.

I'd opened my eyes right then.

Justine looked like someone's mom—a little soft through the middle, a rounded face, with dark red hair pulled back into a tight ponytail—and today, at the hotel, she was dressed like it. A sweatshirt that shouted GO LIONS in black and gold lettering, jeans that were too short at the ankles, and bright white Keds, their brilliance suggesting they were fresh out of the box.

But that outfit, like her appearance, was pure camouflage. Justine "You Don't Need to Know My Last Name" was a hard-ass connected to DHS. Department of Homeland Security. She had a badge and everything. Whether it was hers or legit, I had no idea. But motherly looks aside, she was about as comforting as a steel beam, and equally communicative.

"And?" I prompted her. "Or . . . so?"

She looked up from her phone, her mouth pursed at my willingness to question her. "*So*," she said, emphasizing my word with clear displeasure, "if St. John isn't back yet, that means they're hearing him out, at least. The argument is still going on. *And* that works to our advantage."

The Committee had cleared the conference room of all candidates after the GTX guards had hauled Ariane away. Dr. Jacobs had been shouting about my presence being a stunt and insisting that I could *not* be considered a qualified competitor, all while Laughlin sat back and laughed.

And now Adam and I were stuck waiting to hear the verdict. And not just us. Somewhere in this hotel, Ariane, Ford, and Carter waited too.

Ariane had looked small and tired, like she hadn't slept since I'd seen her last. She'd been trapped at GTX, forced to do God knows what. . . .

Pushing that thought away, I stepped up my pacing.

"Hey, if this is all too much for you, I'm ready," Adam said with a shrug.

I glared at him.

"I'm just saying, any time you want to trade places, assuming you actually end up getting a place, that is . . ." He trailed off.

"Gentlemen," Justine said with mild annoyance, barely even looking up from her phone. Of course, she could afford to be calm about this. Regardless of which of us was sent in to the trials, she still had a chance of getting what she wanted: Ariane.

The funding and the contract behind Project Paper Doll came from the Department of Defense, but the good people at Homeland Security, a separate department entirely, had other plans.

Justine had made promises about Ariane's future, talked of using her as an expert resource rather than a test subject. She'd hinted that Ariane was needed to help them with some equipment or documents recovered from the New Mexico desert.

This was my chance to prove myself and make a difference. I wasn't going to let it go without a fight.

"I still say I can be pretty convincing when I need to be," Adam said with a leer.

He was trying to get under my skin, provoke a reaction. I knew that, and I still couldn't stop myself. The buzz of power was like static electricity dancing over my skin. The room lights flickered in response. That was me, losing control.

But then blood gushed down from my nose to my mouth, and the gathering power dissipated.

Damn it. I fumbled in my pocket for a tissue. The process had been designed as a gradual one, intended to be administered over weeks instead of hours, as I'd experienced it. So my head ached now, almost constantly, with frequent nosebleeds when I accessed new parts of my brain that the DNA embedded in the virus had opened pathways to. (I'd spent a decent chunk of each week staring up at the inside of various diagnostic devices—CT scanners, MRI machines, and others I didn't even recognize.)

"You are so not ready for this," Adam said in disgust.

The lock disengaged on the door suddenly, loudly, in the relative quiet of the room. Even though we'd been expecting it, waiting for it, the sound froze us.

Emerson came in, appearing more rumpled than usual, his hair standing up in tufts and his glasses pushed up on his forehead. His mouth was a thin grim line.

Crap. This could not be good news.

Even Justine slipped her phone into her pocket to pay attention for once.

But before Emerson could say anything, he noticed me with the tissue stuffed against my nose. Again.

"What happened here?" Emerson asked with a frown. He approached me, tossing the envelope toward the bed, but Adam, with a simple gesture, diverted it to land gently in his hand.

"It's nothing," I said quickly. "It's getting better. What did they say?"

Emerson shook his head, ignoring the question to focus on me, checking the dilation of my eyes. "Have you been experiencing the headaches again?"

How about all the time? Not that I was going to mention that.

Behind Emerson, Adam ripped open the envelope without waiting for permission and pulled out a sheet of paper. "You're kidding, right?" he asked with a laugh. "*He's* my target?"

"No," Emerson said. "He's Zane's. Technically."

It took a moment for his words to sink in. I was in the trials. I felt a rush of relief, followed immediately by the falling sensation of panic. I'd fought hard for exactly this, but I hadn't thought beyond this moment to the next obstacle or series of obstacles, which were looking pretty monumental at this point.

But I would do it. I could do it. I wasn't the same helpless human I'd been before.

Adam looked up sharply. "No way. No way they're letting him in." He shoved the page back in the envelope. "I can win this for you," he said to Emerson. Then he switched his attention to Justine. "I can get that girl to do whatever you want. I'm the better candidate," Adam said with the supreme confidence of one who believes himself to be incontrovertibly right.

"Not for what we want anymore," Justine said calmly.

"We still need you," Emerson, always the peacemaker, said. "They're going to be monitoring Zane very closely." He gave me a worried look. "You're going to have to—"

"I didn't sign up for this to be the fucking B-Team," Adam snarled, his face distorted and red with anger. He was in love with the idea of being a supersoldier. I'd heard him talk about it night after night. And I kind of didn't blame him. He'd fought for his country and then he'd given up two years and a chunk of his humanity to be the first in the line of new and improved. He didn't deserve this outcome for all that work. Even if he was a total douche.

Justine raised her eyebrows. "You signed up for whatever we tell you, soldier."

He stiffened. "Yes, ma'am," he said. Then he dropped the envelope on the bed, like it was covered in filth, and stalked out of the room, the door banging shut after him.

Emerson sighed after him and then sat down heavily in the desk chair.

"I wasn't kidding," he said to me, scrubbing his face with his hands, as though he'd been downstairs for hours instead of minutes. "You're going to have to be really careful. It's not going to be as straightforward as we thought. Getting her alone long enough is going to be tricky." He looked to Justine as if for confirmation or help.

She waved away his concern. "That's why we have Zane, isn't it?" she asked, the threat implicit in her tone. *If he can't do this, then why are we sending him?*

I nodded quickly. "Yeah. I can do it." As if there were even room for another answer now.

Justine's phone chirped, and she pulled it from her pocket, examining the screen with a frown. "I have to go. Keep me apprised."

She left hurriedly, not bothering with anything resembling good-bye or an explanation.

St. John twisted back and forth in the chair, the base of it squeaking shrilly in the now otherwise silent room, before leaning forward to balance his elbows on his knees.

"Is that any better?" he asked, tipping his head toward my nose.

I shrugged, lowering the tissue. "Think so." I didn't want to commit either way. Needing another injection too soon would mean that my body was continuing to reject the changes rather than stabilizing.

NuStasis was nothing to mess with. Emerson had shown me a video of a test animal, a rabbit, that had "destabilized." I'd had nightmares. So much blood everywhere. It was nothing but a limp pile of fur and bone in the end.

But that was not going to be me. My body would eventually adjust and accept the changes, as Adam's had, and I'd be Zane 2.0 permanently, new and improved. Okay, yes, it was taking me far longer to stabilize than it had taken Adam, but that was probably just because of the way I'd started treatment.

This *had* to work. I was determined to ignore any other possibility.

Like reaching the point where my body would make the choice for me, rejecting all of my virus-altered DNA, and no amount of NuStasis injections would save me. Then, instead of the bloody rabbit stew, it would be me in the middle of that mess. Whatever was left of me, that is. Which wouldn't be much.

Running a hand through his rumpled hair, Emerson got up with a sigh and moved to crouch down in front of me. Then he pulled a pen light out from the inside of his coat. "Follow my finger." He held up his index finger and waved it from right to left, with the light shining on me with blinding intensity.

My eyes watering, I did my best. The new sensitivity was brutal. I wasn't sure if this was something Ariane had had to deal with, or if she'd simply grown accustomed to it after years of practice.

"What number am I thinking of?" he asked, pulling a small pad of hotel stationery he'd swiped out of his shirt pocket and jotting something down. Emerson was unorganized and kind of . . . all over the place. Not exactly the mastermind Dr. Jacobs was, but dude was obviously smart. Like one of those kid geniuses who'd never grown up. He was prone to impulse and not always thinking things through. A trait I was exceedingly grateful for, since it had resulted in me being alive still.

"Seventy-two," I said immediately.

"Yes," he said, startled.

"You need to think of a new number." I couldn't really hear thoughts. Not reliably, anyway. Just bursts of random noise, like a bunch of people shouting all at once. It was usually strongest right after an injection. I could occasionally get a few words here and there, along with a blinding headache. It was mostly useless, more of an annoyance than anything.

Emerson blinked at me, as if he'd been the one staring at the bright light. "What?"

"You always pick that one. The year you were born." Emerson was a good twenty-five years younger than Dr. Jacobs and at least a decade younger than Dr. Laughlin. He'd been the last to join this circus of experimentation and blood sport. And he seemed to actually care about Adam and me, possibly because we represented his life's work, but it didn't feel like that. I didn't mind him. Other than the fact that he'd signed up to play in this field, but at least his method let people choose to participate rather than forcing it on unwilling subjects.

Then again, maybe I was just more willing to cut him slack. Kind of a side effect of someone saving your life, I suppose.

"Oh, sorry." He tucked his pen light away, only to pull out a temporal thermometer, running it across my forehead. "Ninety-nine," he said absently, writing that down as well.

I waited, not moving, holding my breath for the verdict.

"You know," he said to me, "people like Justine don't do anything without a dozen reasons."

I stared at him, surprised by the shift in conversation. "What?"

He shrugged. "Just letting you know."

In effect, warning me. Of something I already knew but I couldn't acknowledge, not even to him.

"And you're different?" I asked. I thought he was all right, but that didn't mean I was about to trust him.

He grinned, unashamed. "At least I'm up-front about it."

That was true. If Ariane, the top competitor, disappeared, and there were serious concerns about Ford's emotional and psychological problems—common knowledge among the Committee, according to Justine—then that left Emerson as the last man standing, so to speak. He'd have to overcome the mark against him for choosing me as his candidate. But the big point had already been made with me today (you can enhance anyone, including someone with an emotional connection to the target). It would then be driven home with a separate demonstration, post-trials, from Adam (and look what happens when you choose someone who's already strong and trained).

At least, that was the plan.

But I also knew that, thanks to Justine, Emerson had plans beyond the trials for his creation with the pharma companies. He'd thoroughly documented my recovery from the brink of death, and the healthcare market was eager for the next miracle drug, no matter what it happened to be, including pieces of alien genetic material.

There were these pesky side effects: DNA alterations, new powers, the increased possibility of strokes and/or brain damage, blinding headaches, the occasional test subject hemorrhaging to death, etc. But he seemed to think all of that could be worked out in development, while he was sitting on his pile of millions.

"I'm just saying, there's frying pan into the fire and then there's frying pan into the volcano." His tone was casual as he tucked his thermometer back into his lab coat. I could take or leave his advice; he didn't care beyond whatever had motivated him to say something in the first place.

I nodded. I got what he was saying. A bigger cage was still a cage, and that was what Justine's promised future would likely be. But I was kind of hoping this one, whatever it turned out to be, would have bars easier to slip through.

He studied the page in front of him. "As soon as you're done tomorrow, mission accomplished and all, we could start reducing the injections, wean you off before trouble really starts," he said, avoiding my gaze. "The earlier we start, the better your chance of survival."

I stiffened. This wasn't the first time he'd made the

suggestion, and I should have known he'd feel compelled to bring it up again.

Weaning myself off the injections might mean a better chance of survival, yes, but it would also mean saying goodbye to all my newly acquired abilities. And that feeling, finally, of being *enough*.

A wave of possessiveness swept through me. No, I needed to be this new, better version of myself.

I shook my head. "No. I'm good," I said firmly.

He gave me an exasperated look. "Why did I know you were going to say that? Zane—"

I cut him off. "So, my numbers are okay still?" I tipped my head toward the pad of paper, refusing to continue the previous conversation.

Emerson's shoulders slumped in response, but he didn't pursue the topic any further. "Yeah. For now," he said, tearing the top page off and stuffing it into his pants pocket, and then the pad of paper after it. "But you should rest. Tomorrow's going to take a toll." He hesitated. "You'll need to come back after it's all over, right away."

I nodded. Going too long without an injection was just as dangerous as too many at once. So was giving myself an injection without someone to monitor my possible reaction.

Emerson grabbed the envelope off the bed, clearing it out of the way so I could lie down.

I didn't argue with him. The virus in NuStasis was still hard at work in me. And ironically, the super, juiced-up immune system that was the first side effect was now working against me, fighting off the "invaders," the bits of alien cells, as an infection.

I flopped back on the bed, thinking too late that I probably should have taken the tissue box off the desk. The white covers would show blood like none other.

But I wasn't about to get up again. The weariness that had become an all-too-familiar facet of my life the last three weeks was pulling me down, pinning me against the thick mattress. And thinking about tomorrow, the pinch of eagerness and sharp stabs of anxiety, only exhausted me further.

I would convince Ariane. I had to.

"Call me right away if your symptoms get worse," Emerson said on his way out the door.

"With what phone?" I asked, summoning enough energy to make myself heard. The hotel phone had been removed before I'd even walked in. Justine didn't want me making contact with anyone without her knowledge and supervision, afraid I might give something away even unintentionally.

He paused, tucking the envelope under his arm. "Right. I'll come and check on you."

"Fine," I mumbled.

I shouldn't have reminded him of my lack of a phone. The more freedom I had, the more room I had to maneuver, assuming there was somewhere to maneuver to. But whatever. I was tired of thinking twelve steps ahead. Unlike Ariane, I hadn't had the years of training for it, nor did it come naturally. I had to work at it. And I could only hope, for her sake and mine, I was getting better at it.

CHAPTER 5

Ariane

AMAZING WHAT A GUN BEING POINTED AT YOU WILL DO for clearing the fog of shock and emotion from your mind. Add three more and my thoughts were practically crystalline, transcendent even.

"If she tries anything, shoot her." That had been Dr. Jacobs's final order. He'd stepped out into the hallway outside the conference room just long enough to give the instruction, not shouted but uttered with teeth-gritting contempt for me.

So now the four guards who'd removed me from the conference room—the same ones who'd accompanied me to the hotel in the first place—were all jammed in a shockingly nice hotel room with me.

My shoulders ached from my hunched position in the desk chair—my knees drawn up to my chest—but I didn't dare make an adjustment.

Dr. Jacobs wouldn't be pleased to return from protesting St. John's trickery to find me riddled with bullet holes. But

I'd decided to take him at his word. The urge to not die had suddenly rekindled itself in me with such ferocity, I was surprised I wasn't hot to the touch from it.

Zane was alive. And here. Neither of which I would have classified as possible prior to today. Just thinking about him and his sudden reappearance made fear and longing surge inside me, loosening my grip on my power.

The desk lamp beside me, a strange wooden block with an equally square lamp shade that probably made sense in the designer's mind, wobbled. The bulb sizzled and popped inside.

My guards eyed the lamp and then me. "Stop," said the nervous one from the van, his finger hovering above his trigger.

Anger sparked to life inside me, catching on the resentment like dusty curtains in the flame of a forgotten candle. They were keeping me here, away from the answers I needed, holding me prisoner. But they were not nearly as effective a barrier as the glass cage at GTX had been. And the fear in his voice tempted me, whispered at me to push further, to really show him something to be afraid of. Four of them? I could manage that easily, especially now that I'd been practicing.

The blend of human emotion and the cool, practical knowledge that I could do more, be more, and beat them was a volatile mix. My human side was screaming, dying to punish them for their role in all of this, and my alien half was more than willing to show them exactly how outmatched they were.

I let out a slow breath, concentrating on my control. Letting my emotions rule would not serve me in this circumstance.

If I proved capable of dispatching four guards, Jacobs would only call for eight. And I wasn't leaving here without understanding what was going on. Period.

So I forced myself to do what I'd been taught: evaluate what you know, consider each fact individually and as part of a larger whole, determine the potential ramifications, and devise next steps.

First, unless Emerson St. John had perfected not only cloning but also some kind of advanced growth process—so unlikely—it was Zane I'd seen downstairs. The same person I'd known in Wingate.

In terms of his outward appearance, at least. But my Zane—was it wrong that I still thought of him that way? I wasn't sure—had been completely human. Definitely not capable of picking that guard up with just his mind.

The most logical answer was simply what St. John had implied: he'd selected Zane as a candidate for "enhancement" through his formula, the virus he'd engineered to deliver and insert alien DNA into an existing human.

That also fit, I realized, with another detail: Zane's body missing from the parking lot and/or hospital, and staff being unable to confirm what exactly had happened to him.

Somehow, St. John had found Zane in time to save him, likely by introducing the alien DNA into his system. Our ability to heal rapidly would be an enormous advantage in saving someone on the brink of death, if such a thing were possible.

But that wasn't the big question. The real question—with those changes—was Zane still . . . Zane?

He'd looked right at me. Just for a second, but that was

long enough. No meaningful glance, no expressive pleading with his eyes, just . . . nothing.

Zane was alive, yes, but possibly so damaged that he was no longer himself. And while I should have been relieved to find him breathing, the knowledge that he was no longer the same was almost worse.

And then, beyond that—in yet another level of horribleness that must be considered—there was a second question that I couldn't shake, one I desperately needed an answer for: why? Why save Zane and bring him here as a potential competitor?

It was deliberate, not a happy coincidence; I had no doubt of that. St. John had been looking right at me when he talked about the advantages of his approach. In fact, thinking about it now, I had to wonder if St. John had held Zane out of the room until he was sure I was there.

So it wasn't just saving a mortally wounded sixteen-year-old male. It was saving *this* one.

Why? Why? Why? The question beat in my head in time with the throbbing of my accelerated pulse.

The obvious answer was that introducing Zane as a candidate in the trials was designed to throw me. If St. John had somehow gotten wind of our . . . closeness, then Zane might be an excellent tool for distracting and disorienting me, keeping me from winning the trials.

But following that idea to its logical conclusion, St. John would also be forced to assume that I would want to save Zane, get him back. Which presumably might interfere with *his* winning of the trials.

Unless St. John was just hoping that I'd go all Victorian

fainting female and have to be removed, too overcome by all my untidy human emotions?

Sorry, wrong girl, wrong species. Yes, I'd been shocked to see Zane alive, but that had lasted less than a minute before my training and instincts kicked in. I wasn't as frail as I looked, an assumption St. John wouldn't likely live long enough to regret.

But even that logic was flawed. It assumed that I was the leading contender, when even I, under normal circumstances, would have put my money on Ford.

Ford would not be swayed by Zane's presence. If anything, it would give her a clearer path to victory. Kill Zane—an easier target because, no matter what St. John's formula had done, it couldn't make up for the instincts and skills honed over years—which would then compromise me emotionally, far more than discovering him alive. A two-for-one special. Witnessing Zane's death (again) would, at the very least, make me sloppy, slow to react, and Ford knew that. It would create the opening she needed.

After that, hunting down the provided target would be no problem; Ford would have all the time in the world and no distractions. It's not hard to win when there's literally no competition.

And that was the problem. Since St. John presumably wasn't (a) an idiot or (b) in league with Dr. Laughlin to give him the easy win, none of this made sense.

I was missing something.

I bit my lip. Like . . . perhaps the answers to my two questions—Was Zane still Zane? And why was he here?—were related.

Maybe Zane was here because *he* wanted to be. Not the old Zane I'd known, but the new one. The idea settled in my stomach like a rock with razor-sharp edges.

I didn't know how St. John's formula had changed Zane. But considering what I'd observed—Zane's nonreaction to my presence, his obvious willingness to participate (there'd been no guards pushing him in the door, as far as I'd seen), and his driving belief that he'd never be good/fast/strong enough as he was, thanks to his father—a very different Zane seemed like a distinct possibility.

I pulled my knees closer to my chest, against the chasm I could feel opening beneath my ribs. There was only one way to know for sure: talk to Zane.

And possibly be killed in the process, thereby answering all my questions.

TOMORROW MORNING. WEST ENTRANCE.

Was it worth giving up my last opportunity to do what I'd come here for just for answers I wasn't sure I wanted?

Before I came to a conclusion, the hotel room door banged open.

The guards jumped, and I moved my hand up automatically in defense against their guns. Never startle edgy people with weapons. That had not been one of my father's Rules, but, considering it now, it seemed to be a worthy addition.

The guards parted when Jacobs charged toward them, a battered file folder and a large envelope in one hand.

"Wait outside," he said to them over his shoulder with a dismissive and impatient wave. Which was good, because this space was not meant to hold four large men, one medium-sized scientist, and a smaller-than-average alien/human hybrid. (As if there were enough of us for there to be an average.) It was starting to feel claustrophobic.

"They're allowing him to continue," Jacobs spat at me as soon as the door closed behind the guards.

I sat up straighter, finally feeling safe enough to put my feet on the floor. I wasn't sure whether the "him" Jacobs was referring to was Zane or St. John, but either way, it amounted to the same thing.

"St. John lobbied that his death, and his subsequent recovery and alteration, should qualify him for entry. And they agreed," he said, his voice trembling with outrage. "It's a mockery of the entire process." He paced in front of the dresser, as if making his case before an invisible jury. "Completely unacceptable!"

"Right. Because the purity of the sport is your top priority," I said, unable to help myself.

Jacobs spun around and glared at me. "You think this is funny?"

I didn't care for the method or how St. John had chosen to execute it, but it was kind of amusing—in a really dark, depressing way—to see Jacobs being out-Jacobs-ed and how much it rattled him.

"Welcome to the other side of manipulation, Dr. J." I gave him an icy smile.

"Careful, 107," he said, flecks of spit flying outward in a spray. "Don't enjoy this moment too much. You're valuable to me only as a competitor. You're lucky they didn't disqualify you based on your behavior. What was that display?"

I stiffened. He was not going to pin this mess on me. "If

you don't want me to react poorly to the sudden resurrection of loved ones, perhaps you should try to avoid killing them."

He made a sound of disgust. "Do better, 107. Laughlin's products are the only ones that made a decent impression today. Between St. John's ridiculous showboating"—yep, he was definitely jealous of what St. John had accomplished—"and your emotional outburst, we are at a disadvantage."

He paused long enough to chuck the bulky manila envelope at me. Acting on instinct, I stopped it before it hit my face, forcing it to float down into my hand instead.

It was a testament to the level of his distraction that he didn't even notice or pause to admire his own work, as he perceived it.

I pulled the envelope open and tilted it so the contents would spill out onto the desk. Five crisp twenty-dollar bills clipped together. A smartphone, fully charged. An unidentifiable triangle of black plastic about the size of my fist, with a removable paper backing. A sheaf of pages, all surveillance photos of a girl. Not much older than me, if the pictures of her wandering what appeared to be a college campus were accurate.

"What is this?" I asked.

His eyes bulged such that I thought one of them might pop out and roll on the floor. "Were you not listening at all to the—"

"Yes," I snapped. "The target. Follow, confirm identity, await further instructions." I held up the sheet of photos. "You're telling me this is the target?" She was distinctly younger, and less . . . grizzled than I'd expected. In all the training scenarios I'd been given over the years, the targets had been hardened and elusive criminals. Warlords, fellow spies, drug kingpins, dictators, anyone who threatened the safety of the country.

Not a girl who looked like she should be rushing a sorority or protesting the use of Styrofoam in the cafeteria.

Jacobs glared at me. "You waste time questioning the facts while your competitors are no doubt using them to develop a plan of attack."

Please. Unless this girl was something more than her photos revealed, Ford would eat her for breakfast and still have time to grab a latte. Assuming Ford knew what a latte was.

"You want to obsess over something, how about this? It makes no sense for St. John to allow Zane to compete as his candidate," I said, lobbing the words out there like a grenade, one I would not be able to escape if it blew up in my face.

Jacobs threw his hands in the air. "Of course it does. You're distracted, which keeps you from performing at your optimum—"

"And allows Ford to take the lead," I added.

The good doctor stopped, his mouth open in anticipatory protest. Then he snapped it closed and looked at me with a grudging glimmer of respect.

"The other one, Adam, would give St. John a far better chance," he said slowly, thinking it through for the first time.

"Yeah," I said.

He grunted, but the outrage in his voice had died down into something that sounded like reluctant curiosity.

"There were rumors a while ago that Emerson St. John was a ringer," he said, more to himself than to me.

I raised my eyebrows in question.

"Someone with connections to another government or organization," he explained. He was pacing again, the file folder tucked under his arm, but in a contemplative manner. He looked more professorial than ever. "It's the only explanation for how he was able to advance his formula in less than ten years and at half the cost, according to financials submitted to the Committee."

That, or maybe St. John's method was just more viable than, I don't know, growing and raising your own alien/human hybrids in a secret and expensive lab.

"Be on your guard and stay away from the boy. Kill him if he opposes you; otherwise, avoid him. It's possible that St. John sent him in simply for recruitment or sabotage." He frowned. "Until we know what his objective is, it's better to prevent a confrontation."

I nodded. Not great, but better than being ordered to kill Zane on first sight.

"We'll be monitoring your positions through the GPS in your phones," Jacobs warned.

I swallowed a sigh. That would make the Zane encounter more difficult to pull off, though not impossible. "What, no tracking chips?" I muttered.

"And give the Committee the idea that there's cause to doubt your obedience?" Jacobs asked sharply. "No. A well-trained dog requires no leash, electronic or otherwise. But they will have monitors on you for your vitals."

Ah, that explained the little black plastic triangle in the envelope. They wanted to know when to cross off names of the dead. Lovely.

"But should you require additional motivation . . ." He

dropped the folder he'd been carrying on the desk, and it landed with a loud slap.

I flinched at the noise, and then felt a flash of my anger returning. Honestly, who was left for him to hold out as a potential punching bag? My father was gone, and Zane might as well be.

I set my jaw and made no move to open the folder. I wouldn't give him the satisfaction.

But Jacobs, as always, wasn't particularly keen on what I wanted to give.

He flipped open the folder and held it up in front of my face. Short of closing my eyes, which would have only proved to him that he was on the right track, I had to look.

On the right side, several sheets of paper covered in charts, numbers, and medical information. On the left was a photo, the old-fashioned kind, a Polaroid, with the thick white border at the bottom. I'd seen similar ones in the photo albums Mark had had of his daughter, the original Ariane Tucker, the one for whom I'd been named in the elaborate scheme that had first introduced me into the world outside of GTX. The developing fluid had left strange streaks across the surface of this photo, but the figure in the center was still plainly visible.

The woman was blond and thin, sickly thin if the stick-like arms emerging from her sleeves were any indication. The voluminous dress she wore—dark blue with white polka dots—only made her look smaller, lost within the fabric. Her delicate features—a long, thin nose; high brows and cheekbones—seemed even finer with the strain of weariness obvious on her face, though she was smiling.

That smile . . . it set off a twinge of recognition, a feeling of familiarity even though I couldn't place it.

"Do you know her?" Jacobs prompted, watching me carefully.

My mouth was dry, and it took me a second to unstick my tongue from the roof of my mouth and make it work. I could think of only one woman who'd have relevance in this conversation, not to mention features I might recognize. "No."

He shook the folder in front of my face, moving it even closer. "Are you sure?" he asked with a hint of ugly eagerness. He was enjoying himself.

The desire to reach up and break his neck swelled in me. A simple solution to a complicated problem. Except it wouldn't really solve anything.

"She looks familiar," I said through gritted teeth.

"She should," he said with satisfaction.

"Who is she?" I asked, hating myself for giving him that advantage but needing the confirmation.

"This? This is the surrogate who carried you. Six months, from implantation to full term. Or, one of your DNA contributors, if you prefer," he said with a shrug, as if that were irrelevant.

My mother. Dizziness swirled in my head.

I sat forward in my chair. "Is she still alive?" It hadn't escaped my notice that the photo was old. *What's her name?* That question I managed to keep to myself. He'd never share that information; it would give away his bargaining position. If I had her name, I could find her and ask her all the questions that were suddenly bubbling up in my brain. I wasn't musical in the slightest—was that a deficit from my human side, or something I'd inherited from alien ancestors? Were my long, thin fingers hers? How about the annoying tendency to get the hiccups after a meal with too much sugar?

When you're created in a lab, it's like existing in a void, no sense of connection to a larger world or family. I liked the color green because . . . I liked green. There was no one to tell me that perhaps that my affection for that hue had come from an early incident in childhood or even a genetic predisposition.

I wanted to snatch the folder from Dr. Jacobs's hand and examine every detail of the photo, but I restrained myself. It would only give him more leverage if he knew how badly I wanted information.

"107, I generally don't make it my business to keep track of former employees who behave themselves and obey their nondisclosure agreements," he said with exaggerated patience.

I relaxed slightly, even though the ramifications of his words were still sinking in, leaving behind a dull hurt. My mother, then, had been a willing participant. And she had walked away from me. Why? Had she been sorry? Or was she more concerned about how quickly GTX's check would clear?

I hated how much I wanted, no, needed to know.

"But making an exception this time seemed prudent," Jacobs added with a glint in his eye that I recognized too well.

So she was alive and he knew where she was. "You're threatening her," I said flatly.

"You think so little of me," he said, and *tsk*ed at me. "I could certainly find and threaten her, but I prefer to think of it as an inducement. The carrot instead of the stick. Behave yourself and perhaps I will tell you more about her. Maybe even set up a meeting, a chance encounter, of course. She could never know who you are," he added with a casual dismissive wave.

The corollary, then, would be what would happen if I *didn't* "behave."

I felt sick, my head swimming from the picture, the threats, and the roller coaster of my own emotions from the last few hours.

"I just want to make sure you're very clear on what's at stake, 107," he said almost gently, the blustering furor of a few minutes ago gone. "Not just for me or for the company. If you follow my instructions and do your best tomorrow, it'll be beneficial for others besides yourself."

If one could consider "beneficial" to be defined as surviving, unharassed and untortured, I suppose that were true. I knew nothing of this woman. Maybe she deserved everything Jacobs could rain down on her. She'd left her child to a laboratory and a lifetime of experimentation. But . . . how much had she actually known about what she was doing? Jacobs lied as easily as he breathed. And even if she'd been aware of the truth, who was I to argue with her actions when I knew exactly how manipulative this man could be when it came to getting what he wanted?

Either way, I owed her the benefit of the doubt. All I knew for certain was that this woman had participated in an experiment almost two decades ago. She'd probably moved on long ago. Maybe she had other children of her own. A garden. A job. A life. And I'd be the one who, indirectly, would destroy all of that.

Dr. Jacobs was such an asshole. Unfortunately, in the way of this world, that did not also make him wrong.

"I understand," I said, my voice thick.

And I did. My choices were as ugly as ever. To win the trials, I'd have to kill the target, a girl who might very well be as innocent as she looked. It was, after all, a test, not just of my capabilities but also of my obedience. And if I didn't do as I was ordered, I'd lose the slim chance to stop the Project Paper Doll program, and the woman who was my mother, for better or worse, would feel the repercussions of my rebellion.

"I knew you would," Dr. Jacobs said with a smug smile as he closed the folder and stepped back, and my fury, long held in restraint, slipped its leash.

I lifted my hand and stopped him dead. My power wrapped around him from the knees down, holding him in place.

Even with his knowledge of my capabilities, Jacobs reacted as most humans did: looking down at his legs as if they'd suddenly been removed from his ownership, which they had, in effect.

Then he glared at me, his jaw clenched tight. "I could call for the guards." But his face was pale. He didn't like me holding him. Too damn bad.

I cocked my head, letting him get the full effect of my stare, which most humans found unnerving. "You could," I agreed. "But remember, I'm valuable only as a competitor."

I stood and inched closer to him, watching with gritty pleasure as sweat beaded on his forehead. "It would be unfortunate if something happened to me the night before the big event, right? Or, if word got out that your 'product' wasn't as compliant as you claimed?" I smiled, feeling it stretch my face into something harsh.

"What do you want?" he asked, anger bubbling in his voice, but he couldn't quite meet my gaze.

"Just for you to remember *what* you made," I said, deliberately choosing the word he would use for me, "what" not "who."

His upper body jerked as if I'd slapped him. "And you'd do well to remember that if I made you, I can destroy you," he snapped.

Except he couldn't, not yet. And we both knew it.

I held him for a moment longer, just long enough for him to truly feel the start of panic and for one of those beads of sweat to trickle down the side of his face.

Then I released him. There was no point in pushing him further anyway, not now; I wanted to shake him a little, not scare him into pulling me from the competition.

Jacobs stumbled backward, catching himself on the dresser. He straightened up, squaring his shoulders and tugging his lab coat into place. "Be careful, 107," he said in that smooth tone that never failed to raise goose bumps on my skin. "You don't want to test my resolve, I promise you. Push hard enough and my choice might surprise you."

Then he turned and stalked out. Just a little bit faster, and he might have been running away from me.

My harsh smile returned.

Even better.

CHAPTER 6

Zane

THE TRIALS STARTED WITHOUT FANFARE. NO HORNS blaring, no voice shouting over an intercom, "On your marks, get set, go!"

Just a tiny chirp at nine A.M. sharp from a timer app on the Committee-provided cell phone, as the numbers started rolling backward from twenty-four hours, and the growing sense of dread and anxiety in my stomach. Somehow, the subtlety of the start made it feel all the more real and dangerous.

This was it. My last chance to make things right. And somehow, while wishing for it and anxiously awaiting it, the moment had still managed to sneak up on me.

I resisted the urge to pick at the edges of the vitals monitor that Emerson had attached to my chest before I left my room this morning. It felt conspicuous, the black plastic forming a dark leachlike bump beneath the stupid yellow shirt that had been designated as the uniform for Adam and me during this whole mess. It matched the yellow in the Emerson Tech logo, I guess. The phone the Committee had provided, now in the pocket of the khakis—seriously, who picked these clothes? Who goes on a secret mission in freaking lame-ass Dockers?—felt less invasive and obvious. But maybe that was because I was used to carrying a phone, even if it normally wasn't one being used to track my location. At least as far as I knew.

I shifted my weight from foot to foot and wiped my sweaty palms across the bottom of my shirt. "Come on, Ariane," I muttered. This particular side corridor of the hotel, which included double glass doors labeled as the west entrance, was empty, for the moment. The restaurant, O'Malley's, was closed for renovations, according to a sign on a stand blocking the entrance just behind me. But I couldn't stand here for much longer without risking that someone, whoever was monitoring our locations through the phones, would notice that I wasn't actually leaving the hotel and trying to find the designated target.

If Ariane didn't show up now, if she'd somehow mistaken my message or just not received it, I'd have to leave and try to find her out in the city. That would be a nightmare.

Assuming that she'd even want to be found by me.

She might have heard me just fine yesterday but want nothing further to do with me. She could easily still blame me for screwing up her plans with Ford. I bet Ford did. And if Ariane had something in mind for getting out of all this, she might not want to take the risk of involving me again.

That was a mistake I could not make again. If I was given the chance.

I studied the metal push bar on the doors to the sidewalk,

focusing on the way it gleamed in the early morning sunlight, how it was probably warm to the touch. Holding those sensory details in my head, I reached out and gave the doors a push, using that newly accessible part of my brain.

They opened, just as if I'd given them a shove with my hands, and a thrill shot through me, as always. I would never get used to this. And I was getting better, the more I practiced.

The only comparison I could make was that it was kind of like flexing your knee after you've hit the ground, bruised the hell out of yourself, and taken off a few layers of skin. You don't have a full range of motion while it's healing, and it takes extra effort to move, but it'll still work and eventually you won't even notice the hurt.

In the same way, it took a great deal of concentration to make my new abilities work as they were supposed to right now. But it was getting easier, and Emerson promised that once I'd stabilized and my body adjusted, it would become second nature. I wouldn't have to think so hard about using these powers any more than I thought about using my individual fingers.

Strangely enough, smaller objects were tougher. They weren't as difficult to move, but just touching them required more concentration and focus. Less surface area, or something. Pushing at the door release alone was trickier than shoving at the whole door. But if I wasn't careful and directive, I'd end up breaking the entire thing. At Emerson's, I'd destroyed several desks trying to get a pencil to roll. Adam had apparently gone through that stage as well. It was the difference between using tweezers and a bulldozer.

I wasn't sure whether or not Ariane had the same issues. If not, I wasn't sure why she didn't move/touch/pick up everything this way. It was amazing. I'd never have to leave bed to turn the lights off again. No more getting up to retrieve the remote from halfway across the room. No more flinching when my dad chucked a newspaper at me or hit the wall in frustration or anger. He would know better than to mess with me.

Not that I'd be going home again, ever, anyway.

The idea sent a weird, uneasy twinge through me. I didn't want to go home. Didn't want the life I'd had before. And yet, the thought of never being there again made me feel . . . off-kilter somehow. As if some part of my identity had centered on being the younger Bradshaw boy, the screwup, and now I didn't know how to be me without that. Or, maybe, more like I'd cheated by cutting off that part of my past instead of dealing with it.

Stupid. I shook my head in disgust at myself. I was much better now. What difference did it make how I got here?

I returned my attention to the door, but before I could test my control further and try flipping the lock mechanism, an eerie feeling of being watched settled between my shoulder blades.

I turned swiftly, checking the corridor behind me.

Empty. Just a set of vending machines farther down the hall, buzzing and clanking as the cooling units inside kicked on.

There wasn't really any place to hide, either. The restaurant windows were on the right side, dark and papered over from the inside. On the left, large floor-to-ceiling windows looked out onto the sidewalk and the flow of blissfully ignorant pedestrians, busily going to work or shopping or wherever normal people were going on a regular Friday morning.

Someone approaching me from behind would have to cover fifty yards in the open hall without me seeing or hearing them. It wouldn't be an impossible feat but definitely not easy, which was another reason why it was a good place to wait for Ariane.

Still, I couldn't shake the feeling of being observed. Maybe I was just being jumpy.

Or maybe not. Ford was here somewhere. And maybe even more eager to meet with me than Ariane (i.e., kill me horribly for what I'd done).

A warm trickle of blood slipped free of my nose and rolled down over my mouth. I pressed my lips tighter together to keep it from seeping in. Blood in your mouth is just not something you ever get used to.

I turned, putting the closed restaurant's doors at my back so I could watch both ways, and fumbled for tissues in my pocket. Emerson had reluctantly given me another injection this morning. So the nosebleed thing was, theoretically, supposed to be getting better, but not so far.

Ariane rounded the corner then, from the portion of hallway that led from the main lobby, her feet moving silently on the carpet. Her hair was pulled up in a messy ponytail, and she had on a T-shirt and jeans, similar to what she'd always worn to school.

If I ignored the fact that she wasn't carrying her tattered green canvas bag and that we were alone in the hallway instead of being jostled this way and that, we could have been at Ashe High. Maybe even on that day we first talked and struck a deal to get back at Rachel.

Ariane met my gaze warily, her eyes that beautiful, uninterrupted darkness that had once seemed strange to me. The buzz of thoughts in my head grew louder, adding hers to the noise. I couldn't pick anything out, though.

"Hey," I said, my voice cracking. I'd been imagining this moment for weeks now, but the reality of it fell painfully short.

Ariane wasn't smiling, didn't seem pleased to see me. If anything, she looked alert, cautious, her breathing short and fast as if she were preparing for fight or flight.

It reminded me so much of that first day, the first time we'd talked. I took two long steps toward her, intent on closing the distance between us. But then she jerked to a stop, holding her hand up, palm out. "No," she said sharply, and I could feel the light but insistent pressure of power against my skin from the neck down, holding me in place.

She'd never done that before, ever.

She didn't trust me.

I froze, making no effort to move against her containment. Had she come here just to say that to me? To tell me in her cool, unemotional way that I should leave her alone, that "it would be better if we didn't do this"? That was another possibility I'd imagined.

"Ariane," I began.

She shook her head, a curt movement that screamed rejection. Her gaze searched my face, as if an answer might be written there. Or like she was trying to memorize it before leaving forever.

"Don't," I said. "Please." I *needed* her to give me this chance. Everything would be totally fucked if she just walked away.

She tilted her head to the side and frowned. "Are you . . . still you?" she asked finally.

Her question took me aback. "Who else would I be?" I asked.

"That's not an answer," she said.

I stared at her. "I'm still me," I said slowly, feeling faintly ridiculous. "I'm still Zane."

"You would say that no matter what," she murmured. Then, raising her voice, she asked, "Why can't I hear you anymore? Yesterday I caught that one thought at the end, one you intended for me to receive, but that was all."

"I can barely hear myself sometimes," I said. "It's static and noise. I have to concentrate to push through it. It's a side effect of my treatment."

She nodded, but not like she believed me, more as if she was simply giving herself time to think and/or me time to incriminate myself on some matter that I didn't even understand.

"St. John found me and saved my life," I said. "His virus—he calls it NuStasis—it amped up my healing and—"

"I know what it does," she said. "I just don't know how far it goes."

"It doesn't work like that," I said quickly. "I'm not brainwashed or anything. I just have access to new areas in my brain." For now. Some of the time.

"Then why are you here?" she asked.

I hesitated. "At the trials or in this hallway?" I asked, stalling. Justine had been very explicit in what I could and could not reveal. In short, nothing.

Ariane narrowed her eyes at me.

"I can't tell you," I admitted. "Not yet. Please, just trust me." I paused, trying to find the right words. "I know I don't deserve it. But, please."

For a second, my words seemed to reassure her; she released her hold on me, and her shoulders relaxed, the harsh blankness in her expression easing fractionally. But as quickly as that moment started, it ended. "Competitor elimination is supposed to be discreet. A public hallway hardly qualifies," she said, glaring at me.

I stared at her, her words not clicking at first. Then I got it. "What are you . . . Do you think I wanted to meet here to hurt you?" I shook my head. "Ariane, I would never—"

A soft sigh came from behind me, close enough that I could feel it on the back of my neck. Or maybe that was the chill that immediately skittered across every inch of my skin, making the hair stand up.

I spun around to find Ford leaning against the alcove that housed the restaurant entrance.

Unlike Ariane, Ford was wearing what she'd had on the day before, her school uniform. Maybe it was another attempt to make her look "normal," or maybe that was all she had to wear.

"You continue to be tiresome," Ford said to Ariane, her voice almost identical to Ariane's, just with a flatter inflection. "It's only against the mission specifications if I'm *caught* killing him here."

That was, as ever, reassuring. I took a step or two back, raising my hand in her direction.

Ford glanced at me with a mirthless smile, amused by the gesture.

The urge to prove myself—and wipe that smirk off her face—thundered through me, until I trembled with it. Heightened aggression and competitiveness seemed to be part of my new deal, along with the physiological changes from NuStasis. Or maybe that was just me, a chip permanently affixed to my shoulder and finally able to do something about it.

"What do you want?" Ariane asked Ford, giving a tiny warning shake of her head at me.

"No thanks for saving you yesterday?" Ford asked.

Ariane raised her eyebrows.

"They would have killed you, with that pathetic attempt at destruction," Ford said.

"Not if you had helped," Ariane snapped.

I had no idea what they were talking about. It must have been something that transpired before I came in.

"There were too many of them in one room," Ford said dismissively.

"It wasn't like I had a lot of options," Ariane said through her teeth. "And at least I'm doing something."

Ford narrowed her eyes. "As am I. Family comes first. I would have thought even you would recognize that by now." Her disdainful gaze slid to me and then back to Ariane.

That was a jab at me and what I'd done, calling in Jacobs. "If you have something to say—" I began.

Ford ignored me. "I've run the scenarios," she said to Ariane as she emerged from the alcove into the hall. Strangely, she seemed unsteady on her feet, wobbling as she approached. "We are fairly well matched." She folded her arms across her chest, but not before I saw her hands shaking, like she was in withdrawal.

Maybe she was. I knew from our last encounter that it was not easy for her to be separated from the others. Well, now just Carter, I guess. I didn't know what that looked like, but this might be it.

"Killing him," Ford inclined her head at me, "which I'd very much enjoy, would even the competition, making it a true test of our skills and ingenuity."

"You can try," I snapped, my blood heating for battle once again.

"But I suspect that would only fire your desire for retribution," Ford said.

Ariane nodded slowly. "That would be accurate."

"Or maybe Ford's just afraid we'll team up against her," I pointed out. In her weakened state, Ariane and I probably had more than a decent chance of putting Ford out of commission.

Ariane frowned at me. *Don't stir up more trouble.* It came through as a barely intelligible whisper in my head, beneath the noise, but clear enough, particularly with her expression.

"In exchange for his life, I want you to stay away," Ford said to Ariane flatly.

That was . . . not what I'd expected. Ariane either, given the look of surprise on her face.

"Carter is gone, removed from the premises," Ford said, after a long moment, as if it pained her to speak the words. "But Laughlin has promised to return him, unharmed, and let him continue with school and live out the remainder of his life as he chooses at the facility, if I win."

"And you believe that?" I asked.

Ford looked at me directly for the first time. "I believe it's better than what he'll do to us if I lose. And Carter is family, mine to protect." The fierceness in her words spoke to how far she was willing to go to see him safe.

She returned her attention to Ariane. "The two of you will likely seal your own fates with disobedience. All I ask is that you do so far from me and the target." Her shoulders were tense, her mouth tight as though she were being forced to chew gravel and trying to keep from spitting it out.

Ah, this was Ford asking for a favor.

Ariane's gaze dropped to the floor. "I don't know if I can do that," she said.

I felt a stab of fear. She didn't know about Justine. She didn't know about the other possibilities. But her defeated manner spoke to something more; a vital part of her had changed. She'd always been lit by this inner fire and determination. I'd seen that at every turn, even when she was locked in GTX with Rachel and me staring at her through that observation window.

But now . . . had she given up?

Ford nodded, a curt jerk of her head that looked more like an involuntary muscles spasm than actual communication. "Understand that you cannot split your priorities, sister."

Ariane jolted at the word. It was, I was sure, the first time anyone had ever referred to her as a sibling. Powerful, even if it was only a blatant attempt at manipulation.

"It will be either his life or your success," Ford continued. "You cannot have both."

She turned on her heel and disappeared into the closed restaurant. Maybe they should try locking those doors. Not that it would have stopped her. Or any of us, I guess.

"Are you all right?" Ariane asked me, her voice guarded. She hadn't moved from her spot at the other end of the hall, her posture stiff as if she was holding herself back, and the gap between us felt uncrossable suddenly.

I swallowed hard over the lump in my throat. "Yeah, I'm fine."

"I'm glad you're alive," she said, but her words held awkwardness and distance, like she was speaking to someone she used to know.

"So you believe me?" I had to ask.

She tilted her head, considering her answer before speaking. "I was giving you the opportunity to hurt me. You didn't take it."

I winced. "Ariane." I started toward her.

"No." She held up her hand, stopping me. She pulled out her Committee-issued phone from her pocket, checked the screen, and then let her breath out slowly, collecting herself. "Listen to me. I have about thirty seconds more before Jacobs sees the two of us here alone and assumes we're collaborating and decides to start hurting people."

"Who?" I asked, holding my breath with dread. Had he dragged my mom or Quinn into this mess again?

"My mother."

I blinked. "Who?" As far as I knew, Ariane's only family had been her adoptive father, Mark Tucker.

She shook her head. "I don't have time to explain. You need to get out of here. Forfeit, run away, have them send in that other . . . Adam. Whatever you need to do to leave the competition, do it. Go home and hope they all forget they ever saw you."

I stared at her. "I can't leave without you."

She gave me a sad smile. "There is no way out for me. Things have changed. I don't belong out there. I've . . . done things." Her gaze skittered away from mine, something like regret washing over her features, and I strained to hear her thoughts, but anything coming from her was lost in the noise.

Then her expression turned fierce. "But you need to leave. Ford is right. If I'm caught between two competing priorities, she'll find a way in, and she'll hurt you." She checked her phone again, her posture determined, unyielding.

"I have a solution," I said recklessly. Justine would kill me if she found out I'd been this direct.

Ariane froze.

"But not here." I jerked my head up toward the ceiling and the security cameras overhead.

MEET ME AT HOLE IN ONE. BAGEL PLACE. TWO BLOCKS OVER AND THREE DOWN. TRACKER WON'T BE A PROBLEM. I focused on the words, picturing them flowing out from me to her, stock ticker style.

Ariane frowned, tipping her head to one side, as if hearing something just out of range.

Damn it.

Ariane. Did you hear me? Trust me. PLEASE.

Keeping her hand at her side, she flashed two fingers and then three rapidly.

Then she shook her head. "I'm done, Zane. I'm sorry, but I can't. I hope you'll take my advice. Go home, be safe, have a good life," she said, louder than before and with the almost robotic inflection I'd come to associate more with Ford than with this girl.

Then she spun around, her hair flying out behind her, and headed back the way she'd come, moving without hesitation. At the last second, before she vanished around the corner, she signaled me with two fingers and then three.

That had to mean she was coming, right?

My heart crashing against the wall of my chest, I waited ten seconds, just to make it look good, like I was stunned by what she'd said. Some of it might not have been acting.

Then I pushed out through the west doors onto the sidewalk.

"Took you long enough." Adam greeted me at the opening of the designated alleyway. The narrow gap between a bank high-rise and a rundown-looking restaurant offered a fairly invisible meet point. No security cameras, according to Justine, who'd done the recon. It also reeked of rotting grease and old food; nobody would be lingering any longer than necessary.

"Shut up," I muttered. I slapped the phone into his hand, slowing down only enough to make sure he didn't fumble it. I still had to cover a couple more blocks, and I didn't want to risk Ariane arriving too much ahead of me and deciding not to stick around.

But Adam grabbed my shoulder with his free hand as I passed, his fingers digging in.

I shook him off. "What the hell, dude?" The leftover adrenaline and aggressiveness from my encounter with Ford rose to the surface in a heartbeat, and I clenched my fist.

"You want to go? Ready to take me on?" Adam sounded amused. "Thought you had better things to do today." He was in a much better mood, for some reason.

"What do you want?" I asked through gritted teeth. I didn't like Adam, never had. He enjoyed all of this too much. He and Ford were perfect for each other. God, there was a terrifying thought.

"The vitals monitor." He nodded at my chest.

Reflexively, I clapped my hand over the black plastic triangle that clung tightly to my skin, thanks to about four pounds of adhesive on its reverse side. "They're using the phones to track us, not these." Supposedly. It was hard to know what information to trust. But Emerson had said nothing to me this morning about giving the vitals monitor to Adam.

Adam snorted. "Right."

Okay, maybe he had a point. No matter what they'd told Emerson, it was better not to take chances.

I tugged down the collar of my shirt and flicked at the edge of the monitor experimentally. It was, as I'd suspected, pretty solidly attached. "We have to be careful. It might send off an alert if we mess—"

Before I could stop him, Adam reached over and ripped the leach free, along with a good chunk of skin, or so it felt like.

I shoved him, my eyes watering. "Asshole." My chest was red and raw where the monitor had been, but it wasn't openly bleeding, at least.

"Don't be such a princess," he said with a smirk as he tugged down his shirt and slapped it into place.

I held my breath, waiting for lights to flash or a beeping to emerge from beneath the fabric. How many seconds had been lost in the transition? Two, maybe three?

But nothing happened. On our end, anyway. Who knew

what the Committee saw. Emerson wouldn't be expecting to have to cover for that. Hopefully, if it was noticed at all, it would be written off as a random blip and nothing more.

If not, there wasn't anything I could do about it now.

Well, there was one thing.

I hit Adam, my fist connecting hard with the side of his face.

Caught off guard, he stumbled a step back, his hand flying up to his mouth and coming away red.

He looked from the blood on his hand to me. "You are so dead, kid," he said with a disconcertingly wide smile.

I flexed my hand; the skin had split over the knuckles, but nothing was broken, as far as I could tell. "Not today," I said, shifting forward, my weight on my toes.

He pushed up on me, getting in my face, and I braced myself for impact, to roll and turn his momentum against him. I'd had years of practice, between lacrosse, my dad, and my older brother, Quinn. My dad and Quinn were built like Adam but on a smaller scale. Everything was on a smaller scale compared to Adam.

But the anticipation surging in my veins, that was new. I'd always gone into any fight or clash on the field with jaw-clenching determination, but that was different than enjoying it.

I *wanted* him to take a swing at me. I *wanted* to feel the impact of his fist. It would fuel the fire burning in me to stand over him and howl in triumph.

But then, as if he could read my mind and sense my eagerness, Adam grinned at me, his teeth bloody from the cut on his mouth. "Even better. It'll be a surprise."

He turned and jogged out of the alley, heading away from the bagel place, as was the plan. Which was probably better because, as he'd pointed out, we were already running late, and Justine would not put up with that.

"TBD, bro!" he called over his shoulder to me.

I exhaled slowly, trying to quiet the thundering drum of my pulse in my head.

Fucking Adam. I wasn't sure how Justine or Emerson were compensating or rewarding him for his reduced role in all of this. More steroids or whatever he was already doing, maybe?

I hoped whatever it was involved permanent ball shrinkage.

My hand starting to throb in time with the raw patch of skin on my chest, I hurried out of the alley and the remaining blocks to the restaurant.

It didn't take me long, under five minutes. Hole in One was a small place, taking up a corner in the lobby of another skyscraper. Through the windows, I could see that the half-dozen booths appeared occupied, and the line of caffeine and carbohydrate-deprived businesspeople snaked out through the door and onto the sidewalk, where damp metal tables sat under closed café umbrellas, waiting for the lunch crowd.

The popularity of the eatery was, I had to guess, part of Justine's plan to make Ariane feel less exposed.

But there was no sign of Ariane in the window-facing booths as far as I could tell without going inside, and I had a hard time imagining her joining the line of coffee seekers.

I turned and checked the sidewalk in both directions, hoping to see her approaching, her white-blond head tucked down against a nonexistent wind, just as I had seen it innumerable times at school.

But no, she wasn't in sight. And she should have beaten me here.

The worry I'd felt at the hotel, that maybe she'd been saying good-bye for real, returned with a vengeance, until the pain in my hand was nothing more than a vague memory. I crossed the sidewalk and pushed my way in through the door, earning more than a few glares for stepped-on toes and a few mumbles about "the back of line is that way."

Inside, it smelled of coffee and fresh bread and a not-unpleasant mix of colognes and perfumes from the impatiently waiting patrons. On any other day, I might have appreciated it more, my stomach rumbling for food.

But today I barely noticed, my focus pulled elsewhere.

A quick look around didn't reveal anything that I hadn't seen from the outside, except that the line of waiting people was even longer than I'd realized. It zigged and zagged through a series of a poles and ropes, like the ones they use at amusement parks to keep the line under control, with a set of bakery racks on the right side to box everyone in.

Ariane wasn't here.

Then, with a sinking feeling, I realized, neither was Justine.

I looked for her dark red hair in that tight ponytail—when you're tall, that's how you recognize people, by the tops of their heads—but no luck.

What did *that* mean? Had I missed them both entirely? Had Justine been able to convince Ariane that quickly and without me present? That didn't seem likely.

Or was this meeting an elaborate trap I hadn't seen coming, Justine in league with the other government people and hiding it for some reason?

Maybe they'd already hauled her away, drugging her so she wouldn't protest. I'd seen it happen before, the night I first learned who she really was and what she could do. GTX security had shot her with sedative darts outside a party at Rachel Jacobs's house and then carried her off to a van.

Crap, crap, crap.

I forced myself to slow down, take a breath, and pay attention to the room. No one here had the ruffled, excited air of someone witnessing a possible abduction or a girl fainting for unknown reasons and someone carrying her off. All I could see was boredom, irritation, and possibly the need for the bathroom from a couple people unwilling to give up their place in line, even as they shifted from foot to foot.

So probably I'd missed something. That was all.

With that in mind, I started looking again. And this time, on a second, more thorough search, weaving in and out of people, I caught a glimpse of pale hair, that unique shade that belonged exclusively to her and, well, Ford and Carter, through the shelves of muffins and bagels on the bakery rack marked "to go" in the ordering area.

My heart leaped with relief. *Thank God.*

I squeezed through the line, ducking carefully around the rack, and found a small seating area. Three tables were pushed against the rear wall, well out of the traffic pattern and visible only to those entering from the skyscraper lobby rather than the street. In other words, it was as private as you could get in a situation like this.

Which was probably why Justine had picked it. She sat facing me at the second table, wearing another of her soccer mom outfits, a Mustangs sweatshirt. Her expression was strangely strained, her cheeks flushed and her eyes wide with surprise . . . or alarm. A paper cup lay tipped over on its side, coffee slowly leaking out of the plastic top, forming a steaming puddle on the table while she made no move to address the issue.

Ariane stood at the edge of the table, partially turned away. I could see only her profile, but that was enough for me to recognize the forbidding set of her features. Oh boy, I'd seen that look before. She was *not* happy about something. I couldn't read her thoughts or Justine's at the moment, but I didn't need to. Waves of tension emanated from both of them.

Then I noticed Justine's hand locked on Ariane's arm, her fingers in claw mode around Ariane's wrist.

Oh, shit.

CHAPTER 7

Ariane

THIS IS A MISTAKE. THIS IS A MISTAKE.

The words ran over and over in my head, my logical side lecturing me again. *You know this is a mistake.*

Yeah, I did know that, and yet my feet kept moving, following the directions Zane had given me. They were taking orders from the emotional part of me that was still, insanely, harboring hope.

Hope for what, I had no idea. The smartest, safest thing I could have done for Zane was to stay away. To let his plan, whatever it was, fall apart while I hunted down the target and incapacitated Ford in whatever way necessary. I needed to win this thing, now more than ever.

But here I was, heading away from the tourist locations, where I would most likely be able to catch up with the target, and heading instead deeper into the business district to meet with Zane.

I shook my head. *Ridiculous.* I had no way of knowing

if he was even capable of taking care of the tracking issue, except that he said that he could, and I believed him.

I *wanted* to believe him. And that was incredibly dangerous. No matter how fiercely he proclaimed otherwise, he had changed. He'd been seconds away from attacking Ford, a cry for help at best and a suicide attempt at worst.

I didn't know what to make of that, but I needed to find out.

Plus, as grateful as I was to find Zane alive, there had to be a reason for what St. John had done beyond compassion. And I couldn't figure out what that would be. Whatever it was, I did not want it to bite me in the ass when I was least expecting it.

Hole in One was exactly where Zane said it would be, though on the opposite side of the street. I darted through a gap in the traffic and slipped inside, gritting my teeth against the brush of so many bodies in close proximity.

Zane was nowhere in evidence at the front of the restaurant, as far as I could determine, and his height usually made him fairly easy to find, so I wormed my way in deeper.

It was possible that I'd arrived ahead of him, in which case it seemed wise to stake out some small piece of real estate where we could talk in relative privacy. A crowd would certainly help hide us, but it also made having a conversation without being overheard trickier.

Then again, anyone bored enough to eavesdrop on us today would likely assume we were (a) crazy or (b) working a bizarre creative writing project.

Ha. I wished.

In the far corner, I found a small, secluded seating area: a single row of three tables with chairs instead of the more prominent booths in the front by the windows.

Two out of the three tables were occupied. At the closest, a college-aged guy demolished a bagel while he thumbed through something on his tablet, his lips moving as he read. The woman at the second table with the painfully tight ponytail was glaring at her phone, her coffee forgotten in her annoyance.

I started for the last table in the row, which also offered the advantage of the corner. I could put my back to it and know that no one would be sneaking up from that direction, unless someone decided to leap over the ordering counter and come through that way.

That seemed like something Ford might do. But not today, I hoped.

As I passed the second table, the woman with the phone looked up suddenly. Her gaze passed over me from head to toe, lingering an extra second on my hair and my face, with frank curiosity.

"Wait," she said, holding out her free hand, palm out, as if to prevent me from passing her by.

Her interest immediately set off an alarm in my head. Nothing about her seemed inherently dangerous, though, except that she was sitting up straighter and paying more attention than she should have been.

That, in and of itself, wasn't exceptional. Occasionally I'd had strangers—women, usually—stop me before. It never failed to send me in a panic in Wingate. But running would have broken Rule #4, keeping my head down and being as inconspicuous as possible, so I'd stood my ground, trying to keep my shaking from being obvious.

It had always turned out to be innocuous. Most of the time, they wanted to know if that was my natural hair color, and if not, who did it for me. Sometimes one of them would cluck over my thinness and ask, "Isn't anyone feeding you?" as if I were a stray animal.

I'd always given the answers as quickly as possible. "Yes, it's natural. And yes, I'm fed well at home. I just have a small frame."

Responses that would ring true and encourage no further dialogue.

So, more out of habit than intention, I paused, those old phrases leaping to mind in preparation.

But then she spoke again. "Ariane," she said with a big smile. "Right?"

My field of vision narrowed to the woman's face, panic blocking out everything else. The intense interest in her expression was familiar in a very specific way. I'd seen it from Dr. Jacobs repeatedly, every time I'd achieved another level of accomplishment in his experiment. It was an eagerness born of the desire to obtain, to own.

This woman, whoever she was, knew not only who I was but *what* I was. Worse yet, I couldn't get anything from her thoughts, which meant she'd had training and knew exactly what to expect from me.

Suddenly, the air felt suffocating, the warmth and smells that had seemed so pleasant a moment ago now seemed to cling to my face, like plastic pressed against my nose and mouth.

Get out. Now. A scene in here with all these people, that would only draw more attention to me, which was the last thing I needed. I didn't know this woman, but if she knew me, that could only mean that she was somehow involved in this mess.

I spun around immediately to return the way I'd come.

"Don't." As if she'd anticipated my reaction, the woman's hand landed on my arm before I got more than a step, jerking me to a stop.

NO. Even before I consciously made the decision to defend myself, power rose up in me and flooded outward, surrounding her.

The pressure of her hand on my arm lessened as she loosed her grip and tried to pull away. But she wasn't going anywhere.

I turned to face her, holding her frozen.

The tips of her fingers twitched against my forearm as she struggled to free herself. "I'm not going to hurt you," she whispered, her eyes wide as she stared at her hand and then at me.

"No," I agreed. "You're not."

The college student guy at the table in front of us turned to glance back with a frown, evidently sensing the tension.

"Leave," I said, making sure he heard the threat implied in my tone.

His eyes bugged, but he didn't move.

I stared him down. It didn't take much effort to make full-blooded humans recognize that something wasn't quite right and that they should listen to the tiny voices in their brains screaming at them to run away.

College guy scrambled up out of his seat, grabbing his bag and his iPad, leaving his half-finished bagel behind.

There. That was better. One less witness for whatever I did next.

"Ariane!" I heard Zane's voice, breathless, behind me. Out of the corner of my eye, I saw him move around the bakery racks toward me.

"What are you doing?" He approached, his hands out as if to keep me from making a sudden move.

"She grabbed my arm," I said flatly, in the same tone I would have said, "I don't like her." The two were equivalent in my mind.

"I see that." Zane sounded wary. I glanced at him, his face even more flushed, his eyes still oddly dilated. He looked . . . ill. That's what had bothered me before. He and Adam, they both looked like they were on the third day of a virus. That had to be a side effect of their alteration. I wondered if it was permanent. Would he always be on the verge of being sick?

How could that possibly be good for him? Would it eventually work its way through his system?

The woman grimaced, trying to shift within the field of my power, drawing my attention to her again. I squeezed a little tighter as a reminder that she was not the master of her own destiny at the moment.

She gasped. "I wasn't . . . I just wanted to stop her from leaving."

"Ariane doesn't like to be touched," Zane said, edging closer with caution, as if I might suddenly lash out at him as well.

"Noted," Justine said through clenched teeth. She watched the two of us, her mouth set in grim lines.

"Are you okay?" he asked, inching toward me, and despite the fact that I still didn't know what was going on, part of me trembled in anticipation of his nearness.

"Yeah," I said. His dilated eyes were alarming at this proximity, just a sliver of the blue-gray left around the edges, and the knuckles on his left hand were bruised and bloodied. "Are you?" I asked.

He waved his hand dismissively. "I'm fine."

I didn't quite believe him, but for the moment there were greater worries. "What about the trackers? Did you—"

"It's taken care of," he said, waving my words away. "I gave my phone and tag to Adam."

I frowned. "Adam? How—"

The woman cleared her throat loudly, calling our attention to her. "Excuse me. Now that we've established that you're both well and full of cozy puppy feelings, do you think we can move on to releasing me from this lovely little bear trap you've created?" Her smiling eagerness had subsided to a general crankiness that pleased me.

Zane shifted uncomfortably. "Can you let her go?" he asked me.

Can I? Yes. Would I? Not yet. "Why? Who is she?" I asked.

A look of exasperation crossed the woman's face. She didn't like that we were discussing her as if she weren't here. But, wisely, she said nothing.

"This is Justine," Zane said, raking a hand through his hair. "She's who I brought you here to meet."

I stared at him and took a step back, all my fears returning and my stomach sinking with dread. "You planned this?" I asked, working to keep my voice level. I'd worried that Zane had been changed by whatever St. John had done; I'd never considered that they'd somehow convinced him to switch sides.

He nodded, and my heart fell.

"She's government like the others," I spat. It was stamped all over her, now that I knew to look for it. The hardness in her expression that suggested she was used to getting what she wanted. I'd seen it at times even in my father, who was accustomed to giving orders to teams beneath him both at GTX and in his former military life.

"No, not like the others," Justine said quickly.

Zane shook his head. "She's not. She's been working with Emerson—Dr. St. John—to try to reach you and get you out."

I raised my eyebrows. "Right." As if there could be a fairy-tale ending to this one, a winged godmother—albeit a seemingly grumpy one—appearing out of nowhere to grant my fondest wish.

"Just hear her out," Zane said. "Okay?" His strangely dilated eyes met mine, pleading with me. Then he held his hand out, palm up, a gesture of peace . . . or a reminder of our first "date." When I'd first trusted him and taken his hand. I wanted to have that same sense of trust again.

But I couldn't bring myself to let go of my suspicions and take his hand. Not yet.

Listening, however, felt manageable. "Fine." I released the field around Justine, and her hand dropped off my arm, but with no force to counterbalance her weight, she toppled forward.

She caught herself and straightened up, glaring at me as she rubbed her wrist like the blood circulation had been impeded. Oh, please.

Zane lowered his hand without looking at me. I couldn't feel his hurt, not anymore, but I could see it in the new stiffness in his posture.

"I'd ask you to sit," Justine said to me mockingly, "but I wouldn't want you to take it as a threat."

"You spend your life in a cage with people poking and prodding at you," I snapped. "Then let's see how you interpret someone making a grab for you."

"Fair enough," she said, picking up her coffee cup and setting it upright. "But it seems as though maybe you've gotten used to some kinds of poking," she added darkly, eyeing the two of us.

It took a second for the double-meaning to click.

My mouth fell open. Had she seriously just said that?

"Jesus," Zane muttered, his cheeks flushing a deeper shade of red.

She waved one hand dismissively as she wiped up the puddle of coffee with a stack of napkins. "Don't get your panties in a bunch. It was a joke." She shoved the soggy napkins aside and leaned forward in an all-business manner, her hands folded neatly on the table.

"Here's what you need to know in brief," she said, "since we're all on borrowed time here. Zane is correct. I've been working with Dr. St. John for the last seven years."

That matched what Dr. Jacobs had hinted at, that perhaps Emerson St. John had colored outside the lines. Interesting. But whatever had compelled him to break the bounds of confidentiality to enlist this woman's aid, it had clearly not been an objection to the morality of the program. He had, after all, "created" Adam and saved Zane with his invention.

"The contract that St. John and the others are all hoping to win is being offered by a division within the Department of Defense, to greatly simplify a complicated history," Justine continued. "I'm part of a . . . competing organization."

Zane glanced at me. "Department of Homeland Security."

Justine glared. "I can't say much about the particular situation," she said to me, choosing her words with care. "But I'm sure the concept of limited funds, overlapping responsibilities, and competing priorities is one you understand."

I eyed her speculatively. "A turf war would be the vernacular, I believe."

She gave me a tight smile. "We prefer to think of it as two strong organizations vying for the opportunity to protect the people of this country in whatever way necessary."

I shrugged. Either way, it meant the same thing. She was in this because whomever she worked for wanted to screw over the other guys. Maybe it was about protecting people; more likely it was about money or credit or a tweaked ego.

And the Department of Homeland Security, if Zane was right about that, was indeed a separate entity from the Department of Defense, and it didn't require a stretch of the imagination to believe that they might not always be, what was the saying, two peas in a pod.

It sounded good. Whether it was true remained to be seen.

"They're interested in using you for strategic military strikes, high-profile targets where anonymity and death by natural causes might be a benefit to them." She shrugged. "Ordinarily, we would agree. But we think you might have more value as a resource, a tool of sorts instead of a weapon."

"They have documents, tech—" Zane began.

Justine shot him a dark look for the interruption. "Zane is correct. We have inherited from various other agencies a cache of documents and a warehouse of evidence gathered from a variety of 'incidents.'" She paused, giving me a significant look. "Particularly the one taking place in a desert around seventy years ago, give or take."

Wait, was she telling me they had the remains of the ship from Roswell? I felt light-headed suddenly. That was where I'd come from. Well, that was where the DNA donor that Jacobs had used to create me had come from. Supposedly. That ship, or whatever was left of it, might tell me more than I'd ever known about that part of my heritage. Even if it didn't, just touching it, being in the same room with it, would be more of a connection to those beings than I'd ever had before. It was a gray area, no pun intended, in my life that I'd never thought would be further defined.

And here it was, being offered up with zero fight. Mine for the asking.

I needed to sit. I pulled the seat out across from Justine and collapsed into it.

Zane reached over and grabbed a chair from the table behind us and sat next to me.

"Why?" I asked, my voice cracking.

Justine smiled, a gleam of excitement in her eyes. "We recognize that whatever information can be gleaned from what was left behind might be valuable in the event our . . . visitors return, not to mention in the further advancement of our own sciences. But the technology appears keyed to their genetic code, a portion St. John wasn't able to successfully implement with his virus."

"So Zane and Adam don't have it," I said slowly, "but you're hoping I do."

"Yes," Justine said, turning her hands palms up, as if to say, "It's that simple." "All you have to do is say yes."

But looking down at her empty hands, I couldn't help remembering, from my early "learn to be human" studies, that the handshake had originated as a way of proving that you weren't holding a weapon. Which only meant that people had to find other ways to hide their intent to harm.

"So, you want to, what, take me away from all of this and stash me in a basement somewhere, surrounding me with stacks of paper and a broken-down spaceship?"

"No," Justine said. "In exchange for your willing assistance, we're prepared to offer you a life, free from their overview. You'd be able to live on your own, go to school, if you wish. You'd have a new identity, of course, and a protective detail."

I fought to keep the shock from showing on my face, the faint pinging of alarm in the back of my head growing louder. Another of my father's lessons—be careful of someone offering too much and not asking for enough in return. There's generosity and then there's sleight of hand. Look at this over here, so you don't notice what we're doing over there.

"What about *your* overview?" I asked.

She waved a hand dismissively. "I assure you, you'd find it quite innocuous. We'd assign an agent to act as your guardian until you are of age. And you'd be required to check in on a regular basis with your findings. Other than that?" She shrugged. "Your life is your own. We have no interest in holding you prisoner." She gave me a tight-lipped smile. "That hasn't worked well for us in the past."

A reference perhaps to Guantanamo Bay? Interesting that she would class me with potential terror suspects.

"Here." Justine reached down into a briefcase I hadn't noticed before and slid a blue file folder across the table to me.

Pages from a color printer spilled out. The first page was a real estate listing for a beach cottage, a rental with a for sale option, some place called The Outer Banks in North Carolina. The second was a printout from a school website, featuring a low-slung brick building with a smiling bulldog as a mascot on the sign out front. The other pages appeared to be information about the town.

"And Zane?" I asked, tracing my finger against the water in the picture of the adorable cottage. I'd never seen the ocean. But with this place, I could walk out onto a porch and watch the waves roll in every morning. If there was a place on Earth the exact opposite of my tiny cell at GTX, this was it. Wide open, no restriction. Hell, there wasn't even any land on one side of it. Just blue, blue water.

"If you wish," Justine said with that open-handed gesture again. "We can't pull him right now without creating a connection between your disappearance and Emerson St. John. But we'll protect him, and once the trials are finished we can have him relocated to join you."

Zane flashed a grin at me. *This* was what he'd been hiding, his reason for entering the trials.

I tried to return the smile, but it felt sick and crooked, hanging there like a broken mirror. So this Justine was offering me a new life, a new house, a new identity. Almost everything I'd ever wanted, the only exception being that it came from someone else, rather than something I'd created for myself, which meant it could always be taken away.

Still, here was the easy exit I'd been hoping for my whole

life. All I had to do was walk away. Dr. Jacobs surely wouldn't hurt the surrogate who'd given birth to me if I weren't around to witness it. There would be no point in that.

But I just couldn't shake the feeling that saying yes would be like stepping out onto a lake that wasn't quite frozen through. Everything would seem fine, until the cracks sounded, loud and sharp.

Then it would be too late.

CHAPTER 8

Zane

ALTHOUGH I'D TECHNICALLY ONLY KNOWN ARIANE FOR a month—on speaking terms, at least—I'd been in school with her for years. And from that, I could tell she was quiet, thoughtful, deeply internal. Still waters, that's what my mom would have said about someone like her (ironically enough, my mom being the one who would know exactly *why* that was the case).

But I always got the sense that so much more went on inside Ariane's head than you could ever read on the surface. And when I'd woken up in Emerson's lab and realized that the occasional pops of static and random words in my head were from other people thinking and feeling, my first thought had been of Ariane, that maybe now I'd get a chance to really understand her.

But as it turned out, even reading minds, poorly as I did, didn't help. Ariane was as much a mystery to me as ever, whether that was because I wasn't good enough at hearing her or she was just better at keeping her thoughts to herself.

At the moment, she was studying Justine as if the mysteries to the universe were written in the fine lines by her eyes or the long-faded freckles across the bridge of her nose.

Justine shifted uneasily under Ariane's gaze. "I need a decision quickly," she said. "We don't have much time to get this arranged."

Ariane remained silent, still just watching, and worry flickered to life in me.

"It's a chance," I whispered to her. "The best chance we're going to get. You have to take it."

Ariane turned to look at me then, sorrow and regret etched in her face. Then she straightened her shoulders, steeling herself, and returned her attention to Justine. "What do you really want?" she asked Justine, her voice cold and calm.

Crap. "Ariane," I began.

"I don't know what you mean," Justine said flatly.

Ariane raised her eyebrows. "No? I think you do. My heritage might mean I could have some connection to the technology, but that's assuming whatever you've managed to save isn't broken beyond repair. I might not be completely human, but that doesn't mean I was born with an advanced degree in alien engineering." She turned to me. "And as for any documents they might have found, I don't speak the language. I was born here, remember? And that's if they even have a written language. Why would an advanced society rely on such rudimentary methods?"

"You don't know that," I said, trying to keep my voice calm. I needed her to see that while it might not be a perfect choice, it was, in fact, a choice.

"There's more to it," Ariane said with complete confidence

and more than a hint of fire in her tone. "They're offering too much for too little gain." She turned her attention back to Justine. "And what about Ford and Carter? What about the trials?"

Justine's mouth tightened into an unhappy line. "They will continue as they are now. So will the trials."

"You're not going to do anything to stop what Laughlin and Jacobs have been doing," Ariane said, folding her arms across her chest.

"That is not our primary concern," Justine acknowledged, after a pause.

Disgust twisted Ariane's expression. "I bet."

Frustration flashed across Justine's face, and she looked to me with a raised eyebrow, as if to say, "What are you waiting for?"

I stood quickly, my chair shrieking across the tile floor. "Can we have a minute?" I asked Justine, but I was already moving away before she nodded.

Ariane followed me without protest to the edge of the seating area, near where the line of waiting customers coiled.

"What are you doing?" I asked, as soon as we were far away enough to be out of Justine's earshot.

She regarded me solemnly, her expression giving me nothing. "She's offering too much for—"

"For too little, yeah, I know." I waved the words away impatiently. "So what? I doubt they're going to pit you against another alien/human hybrid and recommend killing off the competition." Okay, mainly because there weren't any other alien/human hybrids, as far as we know, but the point still held. And there was always the frying pan into the fire concern, but at a certain level of heat, it didn't really matter, did it? Taking the chance was better.

Ariane avoided my gaze. "Maybe, maybe not."

"Are you serious?" I raked my hands through my hair. "Look, I know this isn't easy for you, that maybe you feel like you don't deserve something more than whatever half-life you've been able to cobble together, but you do. You deserve this."

That seemed to light a fire in her. She stiffened. "Do you think I don't want to say yes? Do you think I'm eager to turn her down?" Her eyes were bright with anger and unshed tears.

"I don't know, maybe!" I said, frustrated and working hard not to shout. I could feel the attention of the crowd a few feet behind us. Even if it's conducted in whispers, a fight is a fight, and everyone recognizes the universal body language.

Ariane's expression softened, and something in her seemed to shift from questioning to acceptance. "We can argue about what I deserve or don't deserve endlessly. You don't know everything that I've done, Zane." She dropped her gaze to the floor.

"If this is about the entry qualification for the trials," I said in a quieter voice, "you know that doesn't count. Just because Jacobs forced you to—"

She looked up sharply. "He didn't. That's what I'm trying to tell you. I . . . needed to be here to end this, so I did what I had to do to get in." Shame and regret colored her features, but she met my eyes, daring me to argue.

I eyed her skeptically. "You killed someone. Just like that." I snapped my fingers. "Dead. Permanently." It wasn't that I doubted her ability to do exactly that—she could, easily—but I *knew* her.

She hesitated. "He . . . is alive now," she allowed, her jaw tight. "But that might not have been the case if my attempts at CPR had failed or—"

"That's what I thought," I said with no small amount of satisfaction. "You would never—"

She held up her hand, cutting me off. "It doesn't matter. The truth is, even if her offer is on the level, it will last only as long as they want it to. I have no leverage, no power," she said slowly, calmly, as if speaking to a toddler in a tantrum. "The second they're done with me or when someone new takes charge of their organization, I'll be turned over to Jacobs or sold off to the highest bidder. Or worse."

I wanted to protest, but I could feel the truth of her words hanging heavy in the air between us. And yet, none of that mattered. "But, Ari, if you go along with it, even just for a while, it's safer than what you have right now. It'll get you out of the trials. And it'll give us time to come up with a more permanent solution. Please." I could feel her slipping away from me even as she stood there.

I edged closer and grabbed her hand, feeling her cool fingers in mine. But she didn't respond. She didn't pull away, but neither did she fold her hand into mine.

She took a deep breath and let it out in a shaky exhale. "I can't. Ford and Carter—"

"Ford is more than capable of taking care of herself. I have the scars to prove it," I said.

"It's not just them," she said. "You haven't seen what I have."

She glanced at Justine, who was unabashedly watching and likely doing her best to eavesdrop. "At Laughlin's, he has a hallway. He calls it his 'gallery.'" She swallowed convulsively. "Glass boxes embedded in the wall, holding the bodies of all the hybrids who died before Ford and Carter. They're just floating there, all their suffering on display." I felt ill. How close had Ariane come to being in one of those display cases? I imagined her pale hair swirling around her face, her eyes open and unseeing.

The image was so real, felt so possible, it sent a shudder through me, and I couldn't stop myself from pulling Ariane toward me. She came willingly, wrapping her arms tight around my back, her fists clutching at my shirt. The warmth of her body reminded me that she was here, that she was okay. But it all felt so tenuous.

"If I don't end this now, that's what will keep happening," she said, her words muffled against me. "How many more of those will Laughlin fill?"

She pulled away from me, her hands releasing my shirt. "Winning will give me an opportunity to catch them with their guard down," she said. "Then I'm going to do whatever it takes to end it. All of it. There won't be any more hybrids after us. No more Project Paper Doll. No more experiments."

The cold determination in her voice took me aback. She'd made her decision already.

"And no more running," she added, with a weary smile that looked something like relief.

With a sudden bolt of clarity, I understood what she was saying. She didn't intend to survive. She'd decided. She would die in the process of destroying Jacobs and Laughlin, maybe even Ford and Carter, if they got in the way. And she'd accepted that as her fate, as payment for the chance to finish what others had started.

"No," I said, my voice breaking. "No," I tried again. "You don't have to do this. You don't have to . . . sacrifice yourself." I couldn't look at her right then, so I shifted my gaze to stare at the scarred and dented wall instead.

"Hey." She gave me a sad smile and reached up to turn my chin toward her. "Do you really think Ford's going to do it?"

"Screw her," I snapped. But the invective lost some of its sharpness with my voice thick with unshed tears.

"Besides, do you think you're really one to lecture me about sacrifice?" she asked with a knowing look.

"I told you I'm fine," I said with as much certainty as I could manage. "Better than fine, actually."

The doubt and worry in her eyes made my stomach hurt.

"What did they do to you?" she whispered.

"They saved me, made me better," I said.

Her mouth tightened. "You're putting yourself at risk again."

I clenched my fists, wanting to hit something, anything. "Because it's my fault." The words spilled out of me, like an infection in a long-standing wound. "I did this. Jacobs would never have gotten ahold of you if I—"

"No," she said fiercely, grabbing the front of my shirt and shaking me. Or trying, anyway. Powerful as she was, I was still taller. "Listen to me: this is not your fault. It was always going to be this way." She shook her head. "I just didn't want to see it. We might have had a few minutes of peace here and there, but we would have always been afraid, running or hiding. It just took me a while to understand that."

"Is everything okay here?"

The interruption startled me, and I turned to see a guy in a dark suit hovering nearby, outside the boundaries of the waiting line.

Ariane leaned around me to stare at him in that unnerving way she had. "We are fine," she said, leaving no room for questions with her crisply enunciated words. It was just short of telling him to go screw himself.

He backed off immediately and returned to the line, his hands up in surrender. I felt a flash of pride. That was my girl.

"You can't just give up. You have to fight," I said, closing my hands over hers, trapping her close to me.

"What do you think I'm doing?" she asked. She pulled her hands out from under mine and slid them up to my neck, raising up to her tiptoes.

I bent down to meet her, wrapping my arms around her back, resisting the urge to pick her up and carry her away somewhere safer. I wanted to shift time and space until we were back in my truck that first night, after the activities fair, when it was just us and so much simpler.

The familiar smell of her, lemons and the outdoors mixed with hotel soap and shampoo that I recognized from my own shower that morning, made my chest ache.

She brushed her lips across my cheek, near the corner of my mouth but not on it. "Please, get out of here," she whispered. "Ford is right. I can't split my attention." She looked down, hesitating. "If you . . . if you love me, I'm asking you please to leave."

Ariane kissed me, her mouth hard against mine. Then, before I could respond, she slipped out of my arms and eased past me.

I swallowed hard. "Ariane. Don't, please." But that was all I could do, words were all I had to offer. I couldn't stop her, and she'd hate me forever even if I could.

"Wait," Justine said sharply, loud enough to be a shout, startling me. I'd forgotten she was there.

Ariane froze.

Was this where Justine signaled her entourage of henchmen to grab Ariane?

I spun to face her and whoever was coming, ready to do whatever I could to fight them off. But I saw no sign of anyone but Justine and the now lessening crowd of coffee seekers.

Justine reached down and produced another file folder from her briefcase, this one red. "If you're so keen on self-sacrifice, Tucker, maybe you should look at this first before you throw yourself off the nearest available cliff," she said, holding it up.

Justine, who'd obviously been listening in to as much as she could hear of our conversation, certainly had a way with words.

And yet, when I glanced over my shoulder, Ariane had stopped.

A desperate kind of hope sprang up inside me. I wasn't sure if it was what Justine had said or something Ariane had detected in her thoughts, but whatever it was, it worked.

For the moment.

Ariane turned slowly, with a frown. "What is that?" she

asked, tipping her head toward the folder, suspicion written on her face.

"Why don't you come and see? You were convinced I was hiding something." Justine flapped the file at Ariane.

I glared at her. "And you were." I wasn't surprised, exactly—more annoyed that she'd waited until the last second to speak up.

"Sorry," Justine said to me offhandedly. "This is need-to-know. And you didn't need to know."

Ariane edged closer, and Justine stretched across the table to hand her the folder.

She took it with obvious caution, still watching Justine as if expecting some kind of trap.

Looking over Ariane's shoulder, I couldn't see anything all that intriguing about the file. No seal, no official "top secret" stamp across the front. It looked just like a normal folder with maybe twenty sheets of paper inside. Which was, most likely, the intent. If you think about it, announcing something as top secret in inch-high letters in a screaming red font doesn't do much for the whole "secret" part of it.

Ariane flipped open the folder front, revealing a thin stack of pages.

"Going old school?" I asked.

Justine shook her head. "Digital can be . . . slippery. Harder to contain."

What they were trying to contain, I wasn't sure. I couldn't really tell what I was looking at.

The top few sheets appeared to be transcripts from a conversation. No, a series of conversations, on different dates and in different cities. Milwaukee, Chicago, Phoenix. And a few company names I recognized. American, United, Southwest.

"Air traffic control?" I asked with a frown.

"Talking to pilots," Ariane murmured. She skimmed the pages, and I caught glimpses of phrases. "Can you please confirm identity of aircraft?" "Do you have traffic for us at two o'clock?" "Are you seeing what I'm seeing?" "Negative." "Holy shit."

And then, blurry and indistinct images I recognized only from messing around with Google Earth. Satellite pictures. A grayish blur highlighted in each of the photos with red circle.

"These are reports of UFO sightings over Milwaukee, Wisconsin; Chicago, Illinois; and Phoenix, Arizona," Ariane said, sounding unimpressed. "Eyewitness accounts."

"Surely you've heard of the Phoenix Lights," Justine said with just a hint of condescension.

Ariane shrugged. "People have been seeing UFOs for years." She pursed her lips in a tight smile. "Centuries, if you believe that guy with the big hair on TV." She held the folder out to Justine.

But Justine kept her hands neatly folded on the table. "Yeah, well, these are real," she said, mocking Ariane's casual tone. "Confirmed through airport radar and our own satellites. And not a weather balloon among them," she added lightly.

Ariane went still, a new alertness running through her like electricity. I could feel it from where I stood. "That doesn't mean anything," she said, but she didn't sound quite as certain as she had a few moments ago.

"And yet, don't those locations seem significant?" Justine pressed.

It took me a second to see it. “Milwaukee and Chicago. It’s near you, near Ford and the others,” I pointed out quietly. Phoenix was the outlier that I couldn’t make fit, but the other two were dead-on. That couldn’t be a coincidence.

Justine gave me a nod. Then she looked to Ariane. “It seems, my dear,” she said, “that our visitors are looking for something very specific.” She paused. “You.”

CHAPTER 9

Ariane

I STARED AT THE FOLDER IN MY HANDS UNTIL IT BECAME an unfocused red blur.

That was the fantasy, wasn't it? Every orphaned or abandoned or unhappy child dreamed of her "real" family showing up to claim her. Taking her away from the horror of her current life, whether that was being forced to eat her vegetables before dessert, or being bled and broken as a laboratory experiment.

The difference being that, in this case, we weren't talking about a previously unknown aunt from Omaha or even a minor member of royalty in some unheard-of country. (That was a key factor in most of those stories, a subgenre I'd discovered during my exploration of fiction. The rescuing relative was also usually wealthy, possibly famous, and preferably gruff with a soft heart that had been hardened by tragedy or loss.)

No, when it came to me, we were talking about an advanced civilization from light-years away. An entirely different planet, species, everything. And they were here for me, supposedly? That made no sense. Why? How did they even know I existed? It wasn't like I was someone they'd lost along the way.

My fingers felt numb and thick on the file. "I don't understand," I managed to say.

With a hint of weariness, Justine gestured to the chairs we'd abandoned.

Zane slid a glance at me, and I nodded. Even if this was a trick, a joke of some kind, I wasn't leaving now without the punch line.

We sat again, and Justine leaned forward, her expression sharp with intensity.

"The government has been tracking the incidents for years. Most of them, as you so astutely pointed out, are the result of witnesses mistaking experimental aircraft or a weather phenomenon as something . . . extraterrestrial. Occasionally with the assistance of mind-altering substances, including what they've cooked up in their own distillery." She rolled her eyes. "Or worse."

"But . . ." Zane prompted with a hint of impatience. He was on the edge of his seat, as if he might try to pull the words from her faster.

"When we inherited these files, it was one of our analysts who noticed the pattern." Justine gave a dismissive sniff for all those who'd missed the connection, likely the FBI and possibly the CIA as well. "The only confirmable instances were those in the last fifteen years or so, in those locations. Then we received information from a knowledgeable source inside Project Paper Doll." She said this last bit carefully.

"Emerson St. John," I said.

She gave me a tight, enigmatic smile.

Zane snorted. "It's him. He ran out of funding faster than the others. He said as much."

I nodded. That was consistent with what Dr. Jacobs had suggested.

Justine scowled at both of us. "Regardless, it became obvious that the most active locations were also those we knew to have the only living sources of extracted tissue." She cleared her throat. "And the size and general shape of the craft at each of these sightings match that of the recovered ship from . . . the desert." She gave me a significant look.

A shiver slid over my skin, and I resisted the urge to run my hands over my arms to warm them. This had nothing to do with a physical change in the temperature.

The recovered ship from the desert. Justine was being cautious, not using buzzwords that might catch attention from even the most casual listener. But she meant Roswell.

Justine was saying not simply that humans had evidence of recent extraterrestrial visitors but that these visitors were likely from the same place as that original ship. The ship that had carried the source of my nonhuman DNA once upon a time.

My breath caught in my throat. My people. Whatever they were, whoever they were. The other half of my heritage. They'd been here, and not that long ago.

"Have you had contact with . . . them?" Zane asked, his face paler than even his new normal. The idea made him uncomfortable, despite the extraterrestrial bits currently transforming him into this new version of himself.

Or maybe because of it. It was one thing to be okay with genetic changes on a theoretical level, but it was another to be confronted with the reality of a ship full of black-eyed, gray-skinned telepaths hovering in your sky at night.

"It's been attempted," Justine said, avoiding our eyes and studying her hands.

Another cagey answer. I couldn't get much from her thoughts, but I could put pieces together from the obvious gaps in her answers. "Meaning either you lack sufficiently advanced technology to speak to them, or they lack sufficient interest in hearing you."

"*Us*," Justine emphasized, pointing first at herself and then at me. "Remember, you were born here. You are as much one of us." She nodded fiercely, as if confirming the answer to an unspoken question.

I sat back, startled. Her approach was the exact opposite of Dr. Jacobs's, who had sought to make it very clear that even a little alien-ness invalidated my humanity, made me lesser.

"But I'm not *quite* one of you, or else I wouldn't be useful for whatever it is you need, right?" I asked. She wanted me, specifically me, for something, and whatever it was, she'd gone through a lot of trouble—and possibly a lot of money—to get to me. Another thought occurred to me belatedly. "Why didn't you just ask Dr. Jacobs about me? I'm sure he would have been happy to sell to the highest bidder."

She shook her head. "This is an off-the-books operation. We can't have any record of it for the DOD to find, for *anyone* to find." She paused. "And as I'm sure you are aware, Dr. Jacobs is far too interested in public accolades and fanfare. We couldn't take the chance of trusting him."

"Because if it blows up right now, it's officially the DOD's project and it'll be the other guys' responsibility," I said, finally getting it.

She nodded. "Exactly."

"Wait, wait." Zane held up his hands, stopping the conversation. "I have a question. About the . . . about *them.* If they've been coming here, looking for Ford, Carter, and Ariane, how did they know where to find them? And what's in Phoenix?" He paused. "Or should I say, who?"

A secondary lab, a beta site with a backup copy of the research, including one or more hybrids? It wasn't unrealistic that Laughlin or Jacobs would take that precaution, though this was the first I'd heard of it.

"It's a little more complicated than that," Justine hedged.

"Of course it is," I muttered.

"What I told you earlier was correct," Justine said. "The technology recovered from the desert—"

"Roswell," I snapped, suddenly weary of her circumspection. It felt like another polite term to cover up an ugly truth. Like saying, "Native American Relocation program" instead of "rampant colonization and displacement and abuse of an indigenous people." Or "economically advantageous labor force" instead of "slaves."

"Just say it," I said to Justine. "Roswell."

"Fine," she said evenly. "The technology recovered from *Roswell* has a genetic component," she said. "From what we can tell, it would likely form a connection with individuals from that background, for control, communication, everything. Our scientists are hypothesizing that it's related to the way their society is structured. In the same way we might use voice command with our phones or cars, these vehicles are likely responsive to telepathy."

Because that is their . . . our . . . the primary mode of communication. It made sense. They created their tech to meet their needs. Humans have buttons on their phones because they have long, skinny digits that can push the designated numbers. If they'd had tentacles instead, the tech would have developed in some other way to accommodate that physicality.

"In any case, that genetic portion of the technology is likely detecting Ariane and the others. A specific brain wave pattern or some genetic kind of marker that their ship has programmed to pick up." She sighed. "We aren't sure. It might be that they're searching for those who were lost all those years ago, or it might just be chance."

"And Phoenix?" I asked, still envisioning a lab underneath the desert sands, another pale-skinned, white-haired child stuck behind a glass wall. Alone.

Justine tugged her sleeves down, absurdly interested in the evenness of sweatshirt cuffs. "A storage facility."

I gave a sharp laugh. "What, no Area Fifty-One?"

"That's DOD territory," she said. "Not us." She shook her head. "We presume that something within the wreckage may still be active in some way, though no one here has been able to detect it. It may be, again, that telepathic component."

I eyed her carefully, searching for the telltale signs of deception. She spoke clearly, concisely, and without hesitation. She was uncomfortable at times, but nothing indicated that she was lying. Then again she would be better at it than most, wouldn't she?

"Everything you've shown me could have been easily falsified," I said, nodding my head toward the folder. "Created to convince me for your own purposes."

Justine raised her eyebrows. "You want proof?"

"Ariane . . ." Zane murmured, and I wasn't sure if it was in warning or concern.

"Fine," Justine said. "I suppose that should work both ways."

I didn't understand exactly what that meant, but I didn't like the eager, speculative gleam in her eyes.

I watched as she tapped on her phone for a few seconds. Then she spun it to face me.

"Here," Justine said.

The screen was black with a white triangle—the traditional "play" symbol. With a sense that I was stepping out into water that was likely way over my head, I touched the play symbol and immediately pulled my hand back.

At first, there was nothing. Faint static and some small rustling noises in the background made a little sound-measuring needle flutter, but barely.

"I don't hear anything," Zane said, frowning. "What—"

Cold. Pain. Alone. Alone. Help. Damage.

Cold. Pain. Alone. Alone. Help. Damage.

The needle never moved, but the words somehow broke through the static in my head that was a permanent part of my existence, all the human thoughts being broadcast around me. Except they weren't words so much as sensations screaming in my head and sending waves of chills across my skin.

"Shut it off!" I said, clapping my hands over my ears, an

instinctive and completely illogical response to something that was likely a frequency my brain was detecting rather than my auditory nerves.

Justine gave a triumphant grin. "They weren't sure it would work. It's new technology, a broad spectrum recording, but—"

Zane reached over and slapped at the phone, cutting the sounds off instantly. "Are you okay?" he asked me, his eyes wide.

I had to wait a few extra seconds for my teeth to stop chattering. "It's . . . Something's wrong." I shook my head and wrapped my arms around my middle. "A distress call, maybe, I don't know." I'd never felt anything like that inside my own mind before, like a finger rising up out of nowhere to poke at the gray matter around it.

Zane stared at me, and I winced a little on the inside. I was, once more, just a little *too* alien.

Justine cleared her throat. "If I may continue?" Without waiting for us to respond, she said, "We would like you to interact with the artifacts and to look at the accumulation of reports on the incident and of the various tests run on the tech. See if you can think of something we haven't."

That's what she'd meant by documents, not sheaves of paper on which my relatives had jotted down interstellar directions or something. So, no written language, or at least not one the humans could perceive as such. I'd been right about that.

"Or see if something speaks to me, you mean," I said. "You want to see if the wreckage responds to me. If I can hear it, then maybe it can hear me."

"That is one of our interests, yes," she agreed, but there was the lingering feeling of words unspoken hanging in the air.

A new weapon or a better engine, most likely. That's what they were hoping for out of this mess, I could almost guarantee it.

"And what are your other interests?" I prompted. Because so far, this was exactly what she'd asked me to do before breaking out the recording from hell.

"Our primary interest in your assistance is in communication," she said.

"You want to talk to them?" Zane sounded alarmed. "Are you sure that's a good idea? I'm thinking they might be kind of pissed." He slid me a questioning glance.

I nodded. That was my take as well. And part of me wanted to see it—Dr. Jacobs sucked up screaming into a vortex of light to a ship where he'd be punished for all that he'd done.

I smiled grimly at the mental image of the good doctor trapped in a giant maze, where one lever would bring the alien equivalent of cheese; and the other, death by some vaporizing ray.

Yeah. I could live with that.

"We want to be able to talk to them," Justine said. "Learn from them. Offer an exchange of information and culture in what could be a major turning point in human history." She sounded almost excited for a moment. Then her gaze dropped to her hands. "And, of course, we'll want to explain our efforts to preserve their culture and species in the best way we knew how," she said primly, tipping her head toward me.

I couldn't help it; I laughed. "*That's* your story? That's the rationale for why I exist?"

She nodded. "Yes. And we hope it will be yours as well."

"Oh." It clicked finally. Duh, Ariane. I couldn't believe I'd been this slow to catch on. "You want me to be your mouthpiece, to stand in front of them and speak in official bullet points."

Zane looked horrified. "You want to just offer her up? You don't know them. You don't know what their reaction might be to—"

"We want her to communicate with them," Justine corrected. "*If* they return. It's been three years since the last incident. They were within a hundred miles of Ariane and the others and never attempted to make contact."

"As far as you know," Zane said, furious.

"But someone is thinking it might just be a matter of time, and if they do come back, you want someone to be able to tell them that you're A-OK here," I said. "Good folks. Not worth blowing up or conquering."

Justine nodded reluctantly. "Yes."

Well, at least now her motives were making sense.

"What makes you think they'd listen to me?" I asked. "They might consider me every bit a freak as you do." And I wasn't particularly eager to hear from them, if it was at all like what I'd just experienced from a simple recording.

She looked unsettled for the first time in this conversation. "We don't know what they'll do," she admitted. "We hope, if or when they decide to make contact, it will be a peaceful encounter, one that could be mutually beneficial."

"But it's your job to prepare for the worst," I said.

"This is, for better or worse, your home," she said quietly. "I'm hoping you'll want to do everything you can to save it. And the people you love."

"That's low," Zane said to her in disgust.

He was right. And yet what Justine had said was not untrue. Even if I could try and convict Dr. Jacobs as a jury of one, could I do that to an entire planet?

I listened to the dozens of people around us, their voices clamoring. Laughing, talking, placing orders, and arguing with spouses or coworkers on the phone. They were alive. With their own dreams and destinies.

There were good things here: peanut butter, french fries, music, art, puppies and kittens, orchids, high-quality denim. And good humans, too. Not just Zane and my father, but thousands of others I'd witnessed acting out of kindness, in person or on video clips.

Full-blooded humans could be the most shortsighted, self-serving, hateful beings (see the comments section of any blog post ever), but they also rushed into burning buildings to save strangers, raised orphaned animals (and little alien/human hybrid girls) by hand, and held the door open for the person behind them.

The dichotomy was difficult to wrap my brain around, but it was one of the things I loved most about that half of my heritage. That people capable of extreme ugliness could also do such amazing things.

Justine was right; I couldn't, wouldn't, leave them to their fate if I could have a hand in saving them. It was my home and these were my people, as much as whoever might show up in a flying saucer at some future point.

Besides, oddly enough, this arrangement Justine was suggesting might also provide the leverage I'd been missing before.

I felt a flicker of excitement, maybe even hope, for the first time in a long while. They wanted to use me, but I could use them right back. After all, they were counting on me to provide a good report, when and if it was needed, and I would be willing to do that only under certain circumstances. Namely, find a way to end the trials and then leave me and mine the hell alone until the day those ships show up again.

"Why me?" I asked.

Zane turned in his seat to stare at me in disbelief. "You're not seriously considering this?"

Come on, Zane, don't make me get into this now.

I spoke as calmly as I could. "We're talking about saving the people I care about." Truth, but also what Justine would want to hear.

MY GOALS HAVEN'T CHANGED, ZANE. I'M JUST GOING ABOUT IT A DIFFERENT WAY. I thought the words at him as hard as I could. *I'LL EXPLAIN LATER.*

His head jerked up, as if he'd heard a distant shout.

I gave a tiny warning shake of my head. *DON'T REACT.*

"Ford was the first candidate we considered, but she was deemed . . . inappropriate," Justine said loudly, another of her less-than-subtle efforts to steer the conversation back on track.

"Translation: she hates humans and you're afraid she'll encourage them to blow this place up," Zane said. "And Carter won't do anything without her."

"My point is that if you think those ships are looking for us, don't you think they'll search out Ford and Carter too?" I asked. "It's kind of hard to spin the story if you're not controlling all the sources."

"We'll cross that bridge when we have to," Justine said

vaguely, which was totally a pat on the head, filler for an answer she didn't yet have or perhaps didn't want to share.

I raised my eyebrows. "But in the meantime, the trials continue. That girl, the target, dies. And Laughlin keeps making hybrids."

With a sigh, Justine squared her shoulders, likely preparing to give a speech about collateral damage and broken eggs being a requirement for omelets or whatever.

But Zane spoke first, frowning. "What girl? What are you talking about?"

Startled, I glanced over at him. "The girl. You know. The one in the packet they gave us."

He sat up straighter. "No, it was a guy. Adam said it was a dude."

A chill slid its way down my spine. "Are you sure?"

He nodded slowly.

"Did you see the pictures yourself?" I asked.

"No, but I know what Adam said," he insisted.

"Maybe Adam said that to confuse you, in case you decided to actually compete," Justine said with impatience. "What difference does it make?"

Possibly a huge difference. If they'd provided us with separate targets, that changed everything. If we each had our own target, that would mean there could be multiple "winners," which meant there was more to this test than they were saying.

I put the red folder down on the table, pulled my assigned phone out of my pocket, and tapped the screen until I had the pictures I'd taken of the hard-copy photos from the envelope. "Here. This is her." I handed the cell to him.

Zane took it and thumbed through the images, his brows drawing together in confusion.

"This is not who was in our packet," he said.

"If you didn't see it—" Justine began.

"Because Adam would have said something," Zane said sharply. He handed me my phone. "I recognize that girl," he said to me. "I spent weeks sharing a room with Adam. She's in a couple of the family photos he had up in our quarters at the facility. It's his sister."

CHAPTER 10

Zane

"SEPARATE TARGETS," ARIANE SAID TO JUSTINE, WITH the air of someone confirming plane crash fatalities. She stood, shoving her phone in her pocket, a new urgency to her movements.

"I don't understand," I said, frustrated. Something big was going down, but I didn't have enough of the pieces to see the whole picture. It was like being half-blind in a world of people with X-ray vision.

"You didn't know?" Ariane asked Justine.

"Not my area of concern," she snapped.

"Hey," I shouted, no longer caring if I drew attention. "What is going on?"

"If each of the competitors has a separate target," Ariane said, "then this isn't the contest. They could each take out their target and be successful. It doesn't eliminate anyone."

"So, that means . . ." I pressed.

"There's another stage," Justine said.

"Likely direct confrontation between the candidates," Ariane said.

Justine hesitated, then nodded. "That would be my guess."

Ariane smiled bitterly. "And what better motive than vengeance?"

"Vengeance," I repeated, still not getting it. Until, suddenly, I did. "If they pulled Adam's sister into this as your target . . ." Words failed me, but the thought echoed through my head. If they'd pulled Adam's sister into this, odds were that the other two targets fell into the same category. Family. Friend. Someone who meant something to another candidate.

I stood. "Give me your phone," I said to Ariane, my heart pounding out a panicked rhythm. My mom. Quinn. Had they just gotten out of this mess only to get sucked back in?

Reluctantly, she shook her head. "Jacobs and the others, they're monitoring it. If you start making calls, they're going to know that you're not where your tracker is and that we're onto them. Right now, those two things are our only advantages."

I looked to Justine.

She leaned away from me, her fingers curling around her phone protectively. "No," she said, her mouth a tight line. "It's an expensive piece of equipment with access to highly sensitive—"

I lifted my hand and mentally *pulled* the phone from her. It slipped free from her grasp easily enough, landing in my palm with a slap. But it was screen-locked, of course.

Justine's mouth fell open in protest.

"Code?" My face felt like it was on fire, and the lights overhead flickered and sizzled, like grease in a skillet. Black spots swirled in my vision, and the room tilted, the wall falling away from me. Nope, that was me.

I scrabbled for a hold on my chair.

"Okay, it's okay," Ariane said with the calmness that was so much at the core of who she was. She grabbed my arm and held me steady. "We're going to figure this out," she said soothingly. "We don't need any lights exploding here." The teasing lilt to her voice was a bit forced, but I appreciated what she was attempting.

I tried to smile. "No, that's your specialty." But blood ran, warm and bitter, down my nose and into my mouth before I closed against it.

Her forehead pinched with worry, Ariane snagged a napkin from the holder on the table and handed it to me.

"Give him the code," she said to Justine.

I held out the phone, and Justine, after a long pause, reached out to type in a code and then hold her index finger to the screen with a sigh of disgust.

With the napkin pressed against my nose, I punched in my home number, the phone at the house in Wingate, my fingers shaking enough that I misdialed twice. Finally, I got it right.

I didn't have any other number for my mom. But I was hoping that if Quinn was still there recuperating, she might have stayed with him.

Right as the phone started to ring, it occurred to me, very belatedly, that this wasn't going to be an easy conversation. They all thought I was dead. Or, missing, best-case scenario.

Guilt sat heavily on my chest. Yeah, I'd been acting under orders, keeping it a secret so that it wouldn't jeopardize everything. But I wasn't going to be able to explain that—or, anything really—to their satisfaction. My mom might understand, given her experience with both Jacobs and Laughlin, but that did not mean she wouldn't be pissed, especially when she found out I'd stayed on voluntarily.

"Do you have any pull to stop this?" Ariane asked Justine quietly, as I counted off rings, imagining the phone on the kitchen wall echoing through a quiet and empty house.

Two . . . three . . .

My stomach clenched.

"Two separate departments, remember?" Justine said. "So, no, not without revealing our involvement."

Four . . . Oh God, someone should have picked up by now.

"Hello?" My mom answered the phone, sounding wary.

I exhaled loudly in relief. "Mom."

An audible gasp. "Who is this?" she demanded, her voice shrill.

I grimaced. "Mom, it's me."

Next to me, Ariane went very still.

"Do you think this is funny? To pretend to be my son?" she hissed.

"It's me, Mom! I promise." I closed my eyes, frantically searching for something to say that would prove it to her, something that would stop the pain and hurt in her voice. "When I was five, I got the Millennium Falcon for Christmas. But the decals, they were from the wrong box, some My Pretty, Pretty Princess or Barbie thing. And Quinn let me put all the stickers on before telling me." Han Solo had had a glittery ride, despite my best efforts to peel everything off.

A woman in line peered through the bakery rack of to-go items to frown at me. Shit. I needed to remember to keep my voice down. I waved at the eavesdropping woman, and she flushed and turned her attention to her phone.

My mom choked on a sob. "Oh God, Zane, where are you?" She drew a ragged breath, one I could hear as clearly as if she were standing next to me. And the guilt in my chest increased until it felt like I couldn't breathe.

"Are you okay? What happened? They couldn't find you at the hospital, but—"

"Mom—"

"—I knew you had to be there. I saw you get shot." Her voice broke. She was crying.

"Mom," I tried again. "I'm okay, I promise. Please . . . please stop crying." I winced at the jagged sounds from the other end of the phone. "I need you to listen to me. I only have a few minutes."

"What?" She sounded confused, her voice thick and ragged. "What do you mean? What's wrong?" Suspicion darkened her tone. "Just tell me where you are. We'll come get you and—"

Oh boy. My mom wasn't stupid; she was going to catch on quickly. "You're there at the house," I said. "Is Quinn there with you?"

"Quinn?" she asked, startled. "Yes, he's here."

"No, I mean, can you see him?" There was no way I was going to get by with that question, but I had to know. Before, when GTX had taken him, it had been days before we knew it because everyone simply assumed he was at school and doing his thing.

"Zane Alexander Bradshaw," she said through clenched teeth.

I flinched

"You're still mixed up in that mess, aren't you?" she demanded.

"Mom, I can't talk about it." I fidgeted, refolding the napkin and pressing it against my nose. The bleeding was slowing now. "I just need to know if you're all okay."

"Zane, God, if I'd known what I was doing all those years ago, I never would have gotten involved. And I'm sorry that you were pulled into this. That was never my intention. But you are done now. You are coming home." Her voice was iron, reflecting her will. If she could have reached through the phone and yanked me back to Wingate, she'd have done it.

I shifted my weight uneasily. "I can't."

"It's because of that . . . girl. She's with you?" Her tone was carefully neutral.

But that was enough to trigger my temper. I turned away from Ariane, even though I knew she'd be able to hear, anyway. "She's not 'that girl,'" I snapped. "Her name is Ariane. And my choices are mine."

"You're in over your head," she said. "And you don't know what you're doing."

I crumpled the bloodied napkin up, trying to find a clean side. If only she knew. But her dismissive tone set my teeth on edge. As if she'd done so much better?

"Mom. I just need to know if you guys are all right. People's lives are at stake. Including mine," I added, though I wasn't sure if that would help or just make things worse.

"Quinn's on the couch," she said icily. "I can see him from here."

"And Dad?" I pressed. I couldn't imagine that they'd risk messing with him, but I had to know for sure.

"At work," she said. The "of course" was implied.

"Good." I relaxed slightly. "But don't let anyone in, even if they look . . . official. Okay? In fact, maybe just leave town for a while." Theoretically, no one should be coming after them. The trials were already in process. But better safe than sorry.

"I realize you care about her," she said. "And that's . . . admirable."

And there she went again, ascribing my feelings for Ariane to charity, as if Ariane was something lesser that didn't deserve to be loved, just pitied. I had to grit my teeth to keep from shouting at her. How I felt about Ariane had nothing to do with pity or even sympathy. I admired the hell out of her, thought about her constantly, and hoped to see her naked at some point. That was definitely not compassion.

"But I'm not losing my son," my mom said fiercely. "I've spent the last few weeks thinking you were dead. I'm your mother, and it's my job to protect you, even if it's from yourself. If you're not home by tonight, I'll be forced to take measures that you won't like."

I gave a tired laugh. "Mom. If you're threatening me, you're going to have to get in line."

Justine cleared her throat loudly behind me. I glanced over my shoulder. She gave me the "cut it" signal, a finger across her throat.

"I've got to go." I hesitated. "I'm sorry. About everything. I'll be in touch again, when I can."

"Zane, no! Wait, please. Just tell me where you are," she begged. "I can help you, please! I have contacts who—"

I lowered the phone from my ear and disconnected the call, even as she continued to plead with me, which tore at my heart.

"They're okay," I said with effort to sound casual, collected. "Everyone is present and accounted for." I stuffed the bloodied napkin in my pocket, not sure what else to do with it.

"You were a last-minute surprise, as designed," Justine pointed out. "They were counting on Adam participating. Odds are that they didn't have time to find someone and get them in place for you, but they were curious enough about St. John's approach to let you in." She hesitated, glancing at Ariane. "Or they were counting on motivating you in another way."

Meaning Ariane's death would serve equally well to provoke the need for vengeance, assuming I survived Round One.

"She didn't know you were alive," Ariane said, startling me.

"My mom? No," I said grimly. "I couldn't tell her. I couldn't tell anyone." I handed the phone to Justine.

Ariane closed the distance between us abruptly, startling me. She wrapped her fists in the front of my shirt and pulled herself up on her tiptoes, her lips brushing the bottom of my chin before I realized what she was trying to do.

I bent down, and her mouth was on mine, open, warm, and insistent. Aggressive, almost. Everything else faded into background buzz. She wasn't waiting for me; she was taking charge, and it was hot.

Justine cleared her throat loudly to get our attention. It was gross and an obnoxious tick in her behavior, but it worked.

Ariane pulled away a few inches but still close enough that I could feel her breath against my skin. "Thank you," she whispered, before releasing me.

Except I wasn't quite ready to let her go. I caught her hand and linked my fingers with hers.

She smiled at me, and I couldn't stop my goofy grin in response.

"Plenty of time for all of that later," Justine said, her mouth pursed in disapproval. She pointed to Ariane. "We need to get you out of here." She turned to me. "And you need to meet Adam for the switch back."

Next to me, Ariane went still, her only motion to bite at her lip, a familiar gesture I recognized, and with a sinking heart I realized exactly what was coming next.

"I can't go, not now," she said. "They may not have Zane's family, but they have someone. For me. For Ford."

At that she looked at me, and the same thought pinged through both of us. "Carter," she said.

I nodded. There just weren't that many people that Ford would give a crap about. None, actually, except him. And how convenient that he was here, anyway. Ford had said that Laughlin had removed him from the premises. I wondered if that was true or if that was simply what Laughlin had told her to keep her from finding out what was really going on.

And Ariane . . . she didn't have many people left in her life—not that there'd been that many to begin with. But knowing Ariane, it wouldn't matter. If it was someone she'd met once, that would be enough. She couldn't let even a stranger suffer on her behalf. That just wasn't part of who she was.

"You can't end the program," Justine said. "All you can do

is bring everything down around your ears. And then you're putting the rest of us in jeopardy." She shook her head.

"These people don't deserve to die," Ariane argued. "Carter and whomever they took because of me."

"You're missing the big picture here," Justine said with frustration.

Ariane stiffened. "Everyone keeps talking about that. As if the here and now doesn't matter. If every life matters, then every life matters."

Justine's gaze narrowed in on Ariane, her posture shifting, shoulders straightening, her hands coming up to rest on the table above her phone. "Is this your final say in the matter?" she asked in a cool, neutral tone.

My pulse picked up, reacting to the new tension in the air. I couldn't hear Justine's thoughts, but I could feel the change. The low-level hum cranking up another notch or ten.

Justine was going to do something. And she wasn't alone. I could feel it. The buzz in my brain was too much for one person.

Then it dawned on me. The line behind us, all the cranky, corporate coffee-seekers. Crap. How many of them were Justine's plants? I'd never even thought about that. She wasn't going to have black-clad security personnel, like Jacobs and Laughlin. She'd have agents in suits, blending in nicely with all the accountants and bankers in here.

I fought the urge to swing around and count the number of faces turned in our direction, watching too intently. The only slight advantage we had was that, in order to keep their cover, any agents in the restaurant were forced to blend in. Stand in line. Sit at the booths. But that wouldn't last.

WE'RE SURROUNDED. I thought at Ariane, concentrating on projecting the words clearly.

Next to me, Ariane cocked her head, listening. To me, or the others. "Is that my final word?" she repeated to Justine. "No. This is." She looked to me. "Over the counter."

I was still processing that when she moved, boosting herself over the counter and into the area with the bagel shop employees, who seemed equally surprised by her sudden entrance.

Oh. I was supposed to be following her.

I jumped the counter, but not nearly as smoothly, catching a rack of potato chips with my foot and knocking it to the ground.

"Hey!" One of the gape-mouthed employees recovered enough to shout at me.

Ariane ignored it, ducking the grasping arm of a manager and slipping around the three cashiers at their stations to push through a low swinging door, set at counter level.

I stayed as close as possible on her heels as we pushed out into the main room.

I could hear Justine shouting, and, out of the corner of my eye, I saw several figures move with purpose, fighting their way toward us, not just lurching out of our way or jumping back in surprise.

The same people who would now be chasing us.

"You realize we're running from our one chance to get out of this alive," I said as we plowed out the door and onto the crowded sidewalk, jostling shoulders and elbows as we went. Protests and curses surrounded us, and I heard more than one cell phone clatter to the concrete.

Ariane slowed a fraction. "You can go back. You should. I've never wanted anything for you but—"

"Shut up. I just needed to state the obvious." If there was one thing the last month had taught me, it was that I would regret not sticking around for the ride. I would regret not trusting Ariane.

She looked at me, concerned.

"But if we die in an alien attack a year from now, because they're blowing up cities and shit, I'm going to be kind of pissed. Just so you know," I said, pulling even with her.

She shook her head. "That won't happen."

The certainty in her voice was reassuring.

"We'll have met our fate long before then," she said, and picked up the pace.

Oh, good.

CHAPTER 11

Ariane

FIRST OBJECTIVE: DITCH OUR TAIL.

"You know, it would help if you weren't dressed like a human highlighter," I said over my shoulder to Zane.

Zane gave me an exasperated look as he dodged a tourist family clogging his half of the sidewalk. "Not a lot of choice in my clothes, Ariane."

I'd figured. He'd protested vehemently when I'd made us both dress up in the Linwood Academy uniforms to infiltrate the school and meet Ford and the others. He was not, I knew, fond of khakis.

In spite of everything, I grinned. I had absolutely no idea what was going to happen, how we were going to untangle ourselves from this mess, but for just one moment, the joy that Zane was alive and okay—or mostly okay—and we were together overrode the panic and anxiety.

"Please tell me you have a plan," Zane said, drawing up next to me.

I dared a glance behind us. The crowds of people that helped hide us also made it difficult to keep tabs on the agents pursuing us. But I caught a glimpse of pumping legs and dark suits. They were still there. "I have a plan," I said.

"Do you really have a plan, or are you just saying that because I told you to?" He gave an out-of-breath laugh that still managed to convey his uncertainty.

"Come on," I said, taking a left at the next intersection, another major thoroughfare. We weren't likely able to outrun anyone chasing us; there just wasn't enough open space to get up sufficient speed. But they had the same problem when it came to catching up to us.

I wished I'd had time to memorize more of downtown Chicago.

It seemed the roads ran on a grid, which was good. As long as I kept us out of a narrow alleyway or a semideserted street, we might have a shot of losing our pursuers temporarily, just long enough to double back on them.

I spied what we needed, up and around the corner ahead. Bright gold lettering on a sign—THE SHOPS AT NORTHCROSS—and four stories of windows with glittery eye-catching backdrops. It appeared to be a mall, laid out vertically instead of the sprawling horizontal mass I was more familiar with. Still, it would work for what I had in mind.

"This way." I darted into the street, cutting through traffic in the middle of the block. The fastest route to any destination is a straight line.

However, the collection of cabs and personal vehicles in the street disagreed. Loudly. Squealing brakes, honks, and screamed curses followed my path.

"Jesus, Ariane, be careful!" Zane shouted behind me. He sounded far more winded this time.

I slowed once I was on the sidewalk on the other side. "Are you all right?" I asked when he reached me.

"I just . . . I'm not . . ." He waved away his attempt at an explanation, concentrating on catching his breath. His face was flushed from exertion. "Let's just go."

I nodded, but made sure to keep a pace closer to his as we headed up the block.

Even without his words, I was pretty sure I understood what was going on. The virus gave him enhanced strength and stamina, not to mention nifty powers that were similar to mine, but it was also fighting his body. Or his body was fighting it. Either way, not the best condition to be running flat-out with adrenaline pumping.

"We're almost there," I said, touching his arm. "Just a little farther."

I looked back to see three agents closing in. My cross-traffic maneuver had saved us time and given us a clear view of those chasing us. Two men and a woman were currently attempting to navigate through the traffic. The woman was in the lead, and absurdly, I felt a brief flash of pride in that.

I dropped back a step or two behind Zane so I could guide him. If this was going to work, I needed him ahead of me.

"See the mall up ahead, on the right?" I asked Zane, keeping my voice down. "About a quarter of the way down the block on the cross-street. Don't move your head, just shift your eyes." I didn't want to telegraph our next move to the agents.

"NorthCross? Yeah, I see it," he panted. "I didn't know you hated the highlighter shirt that much."

"It's got to go," I said. "But that's not our main purpose."

The sidewalks were crowded here, but in front of the mall, clusters of people loitered. Even better, they appeared to be roughly our age. Camouflage. Not enough, but it was a start.

"We're going to get lost in the crowd," Zane said. "Right?"

"Something like that, yes."

According to my father's training, the best way to lose a tail on foot is to simply give them what they want, what they're expecting to see. Human beings track based on sight. And when they track in a crowd, they fixate on a single characteristic that makes their target stand out.

I knew the agents would be zeroing in on my hair and/or Zane's bright yellow shirt. We could split up and confuse them momentarily. But I didn't want to take the risk of separating from Zane.

So a different tactic would be required.

"Head in and straight for the back," I said to him as we crossed the street, thankfully with the light this time, dodging tourists, strollers, and people walking with their heads bent over their phones.

"What if there's not an exit?" Zane asked.

"We're not looking for the exit." We needed a distraction, sleight of hand on a larger scale. "We're coming back out the front," I said grimly.

He turned slightly, raising his eyebrows at me in disbelief.

"Trust me," I said, sounding more confident than I felt. God, I hoped this would work.

We threaded through the people on the sidewalk, forced

to slow down because there was simply no room to run. I could feel the agents gaining behind us.

I pushed Zane ahead of me through the glass double doors, following on his heels.

Instantly, it felt like the walls were closing in around me. It was so dim inside compared to the brightness of outside. The air was cool—air conditioners working overtime to deal with the unseasonably warm temperature outside—but heavy with the scent of body spray and new clothing. And the crush of bodies, while exactly what I'd been hoping for, was more unnerving that I'd anticipated.

I blinked, forced to wait for my eyes to adjust even though I kept expecting to feel fingers locking onto my shoulder.

Gradually, the dark blobs in my vision turned into recognizable objects and features. The mall was a tall, narrow structure, open in the center with an escalator to access the stores on the upper floors.

"There." I pointed to the escalator. "Behind it, not on it."

Zane nodded, still too out of breath to argue or question me.

As we passed a storefront, I focused and *pulled* a deliberately tattered and torn hoodie in dark blue off a hanging rack near the front, praying it wouldn't have a security tag attached.

The sweatshirt slipped off the hanger and moved through the air toward my hand, without a sound, like someone had thrown it to me. Which was, I expect, exactly what the middle-aged guy who got whapped in the face by a trailing sleeve thought was happening.

He glared at me, his mouth open as if he was going to

protest. I stared at him until he dropped his gaze, disconcerted.

"Here. Put this on." I pushed the sweatshirt into Zane's arms.

He shrugged into it while I kept searching for the other things we needed.

"Hood down," I said. "We don't want to look like we're hiding."

"Then what exactly are we doing?" he whispered to me, shoving the hood back. He zipped the hoodie up, covering every inch of yellow except for a tiny vee in the front.

"Helping them see what they expect to see." Concentrating again, I pulled a pale green knitted cap off one of the display mannequins in another store, possibly with less precision than I should have. The blank-faced dummy, her plastic mouth frozen in an exaggerated duck-face pucker, wobbled and then fell sideways, clattering to the floor loudly as I yanked the hat out of the air. Fortunately, everyone was too busy looking at the fallen mannequin to notice the levitating hat or me grabbing it.

I snapped the price tag off and wrestled the cap over my unruly hair. Then I took the lead, heading behind the escalator.

It was practically deserted back here, with most people diverting to the escalator instead. The sudden openness of the space was a shock that felt like exposure.

Zane moved closer to me, hiding me with his body. "Ariane, they're going to see us. . . ."

"We won't be here long enough," I said, relieved when I spotted the last item on my mental checklist. If I'd been unable to find it, I would have come up with an alternative.

Shattering store windows, making the lights overhead explode, something. But this—a fire alarm box on the rear wall—was much more convenient.

"Ariane." Zane tipped his head toward the exit in the far corner, the glowing green sign beckoning.

"No, that won't help. Can you check for them?" I asked Zane. He'd be able to see over the crowds much easier than I would.

He turned, leaning out. His whole body stiffened.

"They're here. They haven't spotted us yet, but—"

Without stepping out from my sheltered position behind the escalator housing, I raised my hand to direct my power and *shoved* at the protective glass over the alarm with my ability.

It gave easily, the broken bits raining down on the floor with a distinctive patter of clinking that signaled danger.

Before anyone could come investigate, I sent the pull bar on the alarm down with another flick of power, scarcely more effort than a thought. And the system responded with bright flashing lights and a piercing wail that rose and fell, grinding against my eardrums.

"Now. Move." I grabbed Zane's hand, unsure if he could hear me over the noise, and pulled him out with me on the opposite side of the escalator. The agents wouldn't, I hoped, be expecting to see us facing them.

On the main part of the floor, everyone appeared frozen in place, some still in midstep and gesture, their faces turned up toward the ceiling, startled and confused. This was the freeze part of the fight-or-flight response. It wouldn't last long.

Maybe once, people would have waited for someone to

give them directions or indicate that it was a test. But now, everyone was trained. Or traumatized. An alarm in a crowded public place, in a large metropolitan area, meant trouble, possibly terrorism, and no one was waiting around to be a victim.

A couple of girls shrieked, the noise rising above the alarm, breaking the group paralysis. Like a single organism, the crowd throbbed and surged toward the doors at the front.

Those closest to the doors were pushing, to get space, to get out. The ones in the back, running to join the others. No one was getting left behind.

The agents were on the opposite side of the central space, forced there by the press of bodies moving in the opposite direction. But they were still watching, shouting at each other.

I tugged Zane with me, keeping my head level and showing no obvious signs of distress, other than the ones everyone else was making. This was the trickiest part. If the agents recognized us in the crowd, we wouldn't be able to get free before they caught up with us.

We merged in with the others, first on the edges and then on the middle, the flow pulling us along, like driftwood on the ocean. Or so I would imagine, if I'd ever seen the ocean.

My heart pounding, I waited, anticipating the ripple in the crowd as agents pushed toward us, ordering people out of the way.

But everyone continued to funnel outside without disturbance. After a few minutes of jostling, with Zane using his elbows and size to make space for us, the doorway loomed in front of us, and it seemed like we might just make it.

I bit my lip. Had we gotten away with it? I couldn't tell

for sure, unable see a damn thing besides all backs, sides, and elbows surrounding me.

I looked up at Zane, catching his attention by squeezing his hand.

"Do you see them?" I mouthed. Speaking aloud wouldn't help with the noise of the alarm, and I was unwilling to rely on our intermittent ability to communicate by thought.

Zane craned his head to look back, then he turned to me with an admiring grin. "Two of them are looking around, checking stores," he said near my ear so I could hear him over the alarm. "The other one is heading straight toward the back exit."

I nodded, relieved, my shoulders sagging with it. Give them what they expected—a distraction, an attempt to evade—and then use it against them. Yet another of my father's lessons that had saved me.

I felt a pang in my chest at the thought of my father. Was he out there somewhere? Lured into town under the guise of some request from his former employer, the military? The Committee had made it pretty clear that the target, well, targets, were not being held captive, had no idea they were being hunted.

My father was one of the smartest people I knew. He would have avoided any hint of GTX or Dr. Jacobs. But if the army had found him and asked him to come here for one made-up reason or another, I wasn't sure he would say no. His loyalty ran deep.

Even to a child that wasn't his, wasn't even wholly human.

I pictured him as I'd last seen him, watching me run from GTX, his face grave but proud.

And my imagination immediately transformed that image into a photo, slipping free of a manila envelope and falling into Ford's hand. I wondered if they'd given him to her intentionally, knowing that her appearance would disarm him. Possibly long enough for her to kill him.

My free hand contracted into a fist reflexively, fingernails digging into the palm of my hand, the bite of them a reassuring reminder that I was alive and free and there was still time to stop Ford and save my father.

Assuming he was even here. It was possible that they'd found someone else.

Next to me, Zane picked up my tension, whether through the grip of my hand on his or something more ephemeral, like the whisper of a stray thought. He bent down with a worried look. "What's wrong?" He glanced around, searching for a new threat.

"Nothing. We're fine," I said, forcing a smile.

And we would be. As we crossed out in the bright sunshine, I refused to let myself consider any other possibility.

CHAPTER 12

Zane

OUTSIDE, ARIANE KEPT US WITHIN THE CLOUD OF OUR fellow evacuees, leading me through as they milled around, using them as cover for as long as possible.

"Where are you supposed to meet Adam?" she asked when we reached the corner, moving swiftly to the right so that the buildings would block us from view. "And when?"

The sharpness in her expression was a little alarming. This was Ariane on a mission, certain, unrelenting, and not entirely human. Or, not human in a way that I'd seen in everyday life. She was focused but distant, a contradiction but the truth, regardless.

"You think Adam's going to help us?" I asked. "He's as douche-y as he looks, trust me."

She shook her head. "If Justine thinks about it, she'll realize that's our only move. We need to beat her there."

I hesitated. "We were supposed to meet at an alleyway, not far from Hole in One. I can show you where it is, but I don't see what—"

"They wouldn't have assigned Carter as Ford's target. That means he's yours. You didn't look at the packet, but Adam did. He can tell us what it said about Carter, or what he remembers of it, at least," she said, her words clipped, maybe because we were moving so quickly but more likely because she was just in that warrior mode. "We find Carter, and he's the key to Ford."

Now I got it. "Because they're connected. Or will be, once they're in close enough proximity." I frowned. "Does it work that way?" I pictured Ariane and myself walking around the streets of Chicago with Carter out in front of us, like a human . . . well, an alien/human metal detector set to a unique frequency to find his missing comrade.

"I don't know for certain. Do you have another plan?" Ariane asked with no hint of humor.

I held my hands up in surrender, which brought her hand, still held in mine, up as well.

She looked over, startled, and a faint smile flickered at the corners of her mouth before disappearing beneath that hardened veneer.

"I'm supposed to meet him in . . ." I searched, looking for an indication of the time. No watch, no cell phone. A flashing bank sign with the time caught my eye down the street. 10:59. "Sixteen minutes."

Ariane raised her eyebrows.

"What? I thought it might take some time to convince you to listen to Justine," I said with a shrug.

She nodded, her mouth twisting. "I can't imagine why."

"For the record, I still think it was a good option," I said quietly.

"It . . . was," she admitted. "I might have gone. I would have had some leverage, and it would have been nice to see what they had, maybe even meet . . ." She shook her head, then shrugged, her thin shoulders moving stiffly. "But it's not possible."

And where did that leave us at the end of all of this? I guess that was something to worry about *after* we survived, assuming that we did.

Following an extended and circuitous route, which involved some doubling back, we reached the block with the designated alleyway with a few minutes to spare.

After establishing that no one appeared to be watching, Ariane led the way to a Starbucks that was perched midway down the block.

The air-conditioning attacked with a wall of freezing air as soon as we stepped in, and I shivered, despite the heat and the hoodie Ariane had given me to wear. This feeling of constantly being sick, or on the verge of it, was wearing.

"Here. Sit." Ariane gave me a push toward one of the tall chairs at the front of the store, where a counter against the windows overlooked the street. We'd be able to see Adam approaching from either direction.

"I'm fine." I waited while she paid for two bottles of water at the register.

Bottles in hand, she nudged me toward the tall chairs with her elbow, and this time I followed the suggestion.

When I sat down, sideways in the chair to keep my face in profile to the street, the room shifted, tilting a little. I grabbed the edge of the counter, bracing myself on it to regain my balance.

Alarmed, Ariane set the waters down on the counter immediately and moved toward me, grabbing my shoulder. I reached down and pulled her closer between my knees, locking my hands behind her back.

"What did you do?" she murmured, rubbing my arm, distress showing on every line of her face. Gone was the impassive and clinical soldier she'd been on the street only a few minutes ago.

It was a rhetorical question, but one I felt compelled to respond to. "I'm fine," I repeated.

She reached up and laid her hand across my forehead, fingers cool against my overheated skin. It felt so good that I closed my eyes for a second, leaning into it.

When I opened them again, she was watching me, worried.

"You look like a Smurf in that hat." I tugged gently at one of the strands of her pale hair that had escaped on the side.

Her eyes went wide, and her hand fluttered away from me and up to the knit cap without touching it. "It's green. I believe their predominant color is blue. And their hats are white."

I loved that she took her pop culture/human studies so seriously. "So . . . an alien Smurf."

Her eyes grew shiny with tears suddenly.

"Ariane, I'm sorry," I said, panicking. "I didn't mean—"

She put her hand across my mouth, muffling my words.

"Hi," she said. "I don't think I've had a chance to say that yet." She smiled, which made a tear slide down past her nose to hang on the edge of her upper lip.

I pressed my mouth in a kiss against her palm before tugging her hand down. "Hi." Then the goofy grin that she always brought out in me broke through, despite my efforts to fight it. My face actually felt strained, stretched from it.

"I thought you were dead," she whispered, her breath hitching.

My smile faded. "I know, I'm sorry. It was the only way."

"Is this permanent?" Her gaze drilled into me. "The changes."

"Yes . . . well, maybe." I shoved away thoughts of the boosters of virus I needed too often. "It depends on how my body reacts to the virus. It was a little more . . . sudden for me than for Adam. Emerson is still tinkering with it." That was a mild way of putting it.

She looked down. "I'm so sorry for what happened, Zane. I never meant for you to be caught up in the—"

"It was my fault," I said flatly. "I was the one who called Jacobs. You had a plan, and I ruined it."

"We've been over this. You were trying to save me. You did the best you could, the *only* thing you could do," she said with a fierceness that was supposed to convince me of her words.

But all it did was remind me of the inadequacy of my actions. I'd wanted to keep her alive, and the extent of my power in that situation had been to make a phone call and get her captured by the slightly lesser of two evils. Yep, *that* had been my best.

Not anymore.

Ariane reached up, touching my cheek lightly with her fingertip, her eyes searching mine. "What happens if you stop?" she asked. "Can it be stopped?"

"What do you mean?"

"Can he . . . Emerson"—she hesitated over the name as if it were foreign or the first time she'd said it—"reverse the effects?"

I jerked back, as if she'd suggested physically taking something away. "Why would I want to do that?"

She looked at me, her gaze focused at a point between my forehead and the back of my skull. She was trying to read my thoughts.

"Stop," I said sharply.

"You needed it to save you, and you have no idea how sorry I am about that. But you're okay now, and you don't know what the consequences might be," she said, pleading.

Actually, Emerson had been pretty clear about those after I'd woken up in the lab. The long-term effects were unknown, obviously. It wasn't like there were years of studies and research behind this with human test subjects. If my body eventually accepted the changes, I'd be fine, more or less. If not . . . well, that's when things would get significantly bloodier.

"You've seen Adam," I said to Ariane lightly. "He's the first test case. That's pretty much as good as it gets. Though, you're right, the asshole personality is definitely an unwanted side effect."

But she wouldn't take the joke, her mouth a flat, unhappy line. "It is changing you. I've never seen you so quick to fight."

"Maybe because I would have lost before," I pointed out.

"You don't need this," she said. "You don't need to—"

"I don't need what? The ability to actually make a difference? To help? To be something other than a useless lump of human?" The frustration in my voice came through loud and clear, even to me. My whole life I'd been second best, doubted, unable to do anything right. But Emerson had changed all of that. "Right now, I admit, I've still got the training wheels on, but give me a few more months and I'll have it down."

"Down for what?" she demanded. "What will this do for you, except make your life more difficult and possibly shorter?"

"You don't understand," I said. "This is the first time I've had the chance to contribute in some way."

Backing away from me, she raised her eyebrows, the rest of her face a careful blank. "Is your ego so fragile that you cannot accept help in a situation that you never should have been in in the first place?"

"I could ask you the same thing," I shot back.

"This has nothing to do with helping me," she said. "This is about you risking your life to become something you're not."

"Yes, because you're so comfortable with who you are," I muttered, and immediately regretted it.

She stiffened. "Maybe not. But I am who they made me. I wouldn't choose it."

I was tired suddenly, of this fight, of fighting with her. After all of this, with everyone else after us, we were going to turn on each other?

I met her gaze straight on. "And I wouldn't choose who I was, either. That's the problem."

"But *I* would," she said softly. "That guy, he made me laugh. He showed me a world I didn't even know existed.

French kiss cookies and Puppy Chow and Rachel Jacobs covered in shaving cream and shrieking. Having a life, being normal." She edged closer, touching my chin. "When I was stuck in the house, hiding behind my father's Rules, that was all I ever wanted. It was like everyone else lived in a different reality than the one I was in. And I couldn't get there, just had my face pressed against the glass, watching. Until you came up to me in the hall that day, looking so tired and angry. You wanted my help, wanted to bring me into that other reality." Her eyes were shining with emotion, gratitude, love—I couldn't pin it down, nor did I want to. It was rare enough that I didn't want to diminish it by trying to classify it.

"I hate to break it to you, but I'm not sure you got an accurate picture of regular life. Rachel coated in shaving cream wasn't exactly a weekly event," I said, my voice gruff.

"No?" she asked, her mouth curving with amusement. "That would have been too much to hope for, I guess."

I reached out and pulled her toward me, her forehead resting against my collarbone. Her breath fluttered through the thin fabric of my T-shirt where the hoodie was unzipped, and I could feel it against my skin. It made my heart beat that much faster. She was here and real, after weeks of wondering if I'd ever see her again. I wanted to keep this moment under glass, preserve it forever just like this, but I couldn't let it go, couldn't stop the doubts from eating at me.

I bent my head over hers. "But the thing is, normal is just another word for average," I whispered in her ear, running my hands down her arms, careful of the fragile bones beneath. "Another word for nothing." That was it, my deepest fear: that my father was right about me.

She moved back, narrowly avoiding a collision with my jaw. "No, it's not," she said firmly. "Everyone's version of normal is something different. And if you think it's so bad, then consider what lengths people go to pretend to be normal." She looked down, her pale lashes like snowflakes on her flushed cheeks. "For some, it might even be their highest aspiration."

And by tearing it down, I was tearing her down, spitting on what mattered to her, what she valued.

"Okay," I said. "I get it." I wasn't sure I could believe it for myself, but I understood why she did.

Her shoulders relaxed a little, and she eased in under my chin, resting her head against my chest.

I fought the urge to lift her up and pull her onto my lap, just to have her closer. "Ariane, even if you get to Ford, then what?" I asked. "You save all the people they've set out as targets, they'll just set up and start over." And kill Ariane for messing up their plans.

"I don't know," she said softly. "I'm still trying to figure that part out."

I waited for her to straighten up and remind me that we were in public and in no position to be taking a time-out, but evidently the connection that simple touch afforded was comforting to both of us.

But then she shifted, pulling away from me with a swiftness that spoke of urgency.

I tensed. "What's wrong?"

"He should have been here by now," she said, her brows drawn together in concern.

It took me a second to click out of the moment and understand what she meant. Adam. He should have arrived at the alleyway not long after we got here.

I twisted in my seat, making sure to keep a hand on the counter for balance. She was right. Adam wasn't out there.

My chest tightened with anxiety as I ran through scenarios for his delay. Traffic accident, sudden relapse from the virus in his system, the Committee figuring out that we'd tricked them.

Or, worse.

"What if Ford found him?" The words spilled out before I could stop them. Adam had been more than confident in his ability to take on Ford and Ariane, before he'd been sidelined, despite everything that I'd told him. He wouldn't have run from a fight, no matter how outmatched he was. An impulse I was beginning to recognize in myself. Was that volatility a side effect of the treatment, perhaps? I pushed that thought away.

Ariane frowned. "She wouldn't see him as competition. She's looking for you. That's who she believes is representing St. John."

I raised my eyebrows. "Are you honestly telling me that if they somehow crossed paths, she wouldn't take the opportunity to eliminate him, just in case?" And Adam's arrogance almost guaranteed that he'd underestimate her and lose.

Ariane bit her lip, thinking, though I was pretty sure I already knew the answer.

"It's a huge city," she said. "The odds are against it. But if Ford saw him, she would likely—"

A low hum filled the air, cutting out only to return a second later. It took me a moment to identify it. The phone in Ariane's pocket, pressed between us. I could feel it against my leg, a vague tickle that I would not have likely even noticed in other circumstances.

She took a step back, fumbling in her pocket to pull the phone free.

A list of texts lit up the home screen.

"I didn't think to check it until now," Ariane murmured. "I didn't feel it before."

"Running for your life does tend to take up a lot of attention," I said.

She looked up from the phone just long enough to roll her eyes at me.

Though I was looking at it upside down, I could tell that all the messages came from the same blocked number and contained the same demanding, condescending tone.

Keep moving. What are you doing?

Why are you stopped? You're nowhere near your target.

Remember what's at stake, 107.

Clearly, Dr. Jacobs had mastered the art of the nastygram. But it was the last one that really caught my attention.

The others are closing in. You're going to lose!

"They're tracking the targets too." Damn. No one had ever said anything about that. But then again, they'd also kept the whole multiple targets thing to themselves as well, so the lack of transparency on their part wasn't really a surprise.

It was a problem, though. That meant Jacobs would be able to tell when Ariane wasn't making progress, or whatever he deemed as acceptable progress. I pictured two glowing dots on a computer screen, moving closer or farther from each other. This morning, Ariane had pretty much done nothing more than go in very large circles. And if they had a contingency plan, some kind of backup in place in the event of rebellion or a hybrid gone wild—I pictured military snipers positioning themselves on nearby rooftops—then she might be in very real danger.

"Ariane, I think we might need to keep moving," I said, glancing over my shoulder to the buildings across the street. I couldn't see the roofline because of the angle, but suddenly it felt ominous that it was hidden from view. Like maybe we'd walked right into conditions ripe for a trap.

But Ariane didn't seem to hear me, focused on the messages still. " 'The others,' " she said slowly.

"Yeah, I don't . . ." I stopped as her meaning filtered through, and I felt a sudden stab of cold. " 'The others,' as in more than one. More than Ford." That could only be one person. Crap. "Adam."

"He has your phone and vitals tag," Ariane said with a nod, letting me know she suspected the same thing. "And he saw the contents of the packet, the pictures of Carter."

I shook my head, even though the sinking feeling in my gut told me more than I wanted. "He was just supposed to be out there, moving around, pretending to be me, so they wouldn't realize I was with you." It had been Justine's call to use him as a decoy instead of bringing in someone else on our secret.

"Jacobs could be lying," she said. "Just to motivate me."

It was possible, but all I could see was the look on Adam's face when Emerson told him that I was going to the trials in his place. It was the same expression I'd seen from him every time I'd failed at using my new abilities or simply not succeeded as quickly as he had. Disgust. Envy. Hate.

"No," I said. "Adam's got something to prove, and I think he's using us to do it. He *wants* to be their guy. Badly."

I shook my head. "If he accomplishes the mission while I 'fail' . . ."

"He's hoping the Committee will honor success over anything else, including that you were chosen as St. John's official candidate," Ariane said. "Actions speak louder than words."

"Exactly."

"Which means Carter is in danger." Her expression was grim. "Along with our plan."

CHAPTER 13

Ariane

"If Adam finds Carter and kills him, we lose our connection to Ford and whomever she's hunting," I said, trying hard to focus on the practical, the logical, against the wave of emotion inherent in the thought of Carter, with his shy smile and his iPad and his desire to keep attending school, dying.

My chest ached at the idea of impending loss; there were so few of us. Living, anyway. We were like a small, oddly shaped family. No branches on our tree, just strands of DNA binding us, like the old-fashioned paper dolls for which our project had been named. Always tied together by our similarities, unable to escape them.

"But I'm more worried about what Ford will do," I added.

"I thought you said distance keeps them from actively connecting," Zane said.

"Yeah, but if he dies, if the bond is completely and permanently severed, I can't imagine that she won't sense that,"

I said. Even if it was just an absence where previously there'd been . . . something. If so, she'd certainly recognize the feeling; she'd lost other members of her group. Nixon. Johnson.

"You're afraid she'll lose her shit," Zane said.

"I think if Carter is gone, she's got no reason to keep from lashing out," I said. When Nixon died, she threw SUVs around and killed at least one of Laughlin's security team. With Carter, the last member of her family and her motivation for trying to succeed, I could only imagine how much worse it would be. I wasn't sure *any* human would be safe around her at that point, let alone one who had been designated as a target.

Whomever she'd been assigned would die, and it would be ugly. There would also likely be additional civilian casualties, anyone who got in Ford's way once she'd pulled herself together after the temporary disorientation from Carter's death.

So, no, this particular row of dominos could not be allowed to fall, never mind that I had no idea how to stop it.

I squared my shoulders. "Did Adam say anything else to you when he looked at the packet?" I asked Zane. "Anything that might tell us where he'd be going to find Carter?"

"I didn't even know the target was Carter," Zane reminded me, his mouth tight. "Not then. Just that it was a guy."

I let out a slow breath, anxiety crawling over my skin like an itch that I couldn't scratch. I wanted to be moving, to be doing something. But taking action now, without a plan in place, would be useless at best and reckless at worst.

The situation was spinning out of my control. Which was, of course, an illusion, because it had never been within my control. But at least in the beginning I'd been expecting a direct confrontation, honor in a death I chose, one while fighting rather than one of futility.

That was still an option, I realized with sudden grim clarity and a sinking feeling.

In a logical evaluation of our situation, our objective against available information and options, we were, in the common vernacular, screwed.

We didn't know where to find Adam, Carter, or Ford. We didn't even know whom they'd selected as a target for Ford, but it had to be someone who meant something to me.

And no matter how I approached that particular problem—find Adam before he hurt Carter so I could stop Ford before she reached her target, all without running out of time—I couldn't see a way through.

But there was, as my father had always taught me, more than one way to view a problem. If I couldn't achieve my objective with the information I had, then maybe it was time to reevaluate my objective.

What *could* I do?

We did have one piece of solid intel: I had the location of Jacobs, Laughlin, St. John, and the Committee.

I imagined them all lounging in some suite within the hotel, drinking and eating whatever luxuries room service could deliver, with occasional glances toward the computer(s). In reality, based on Dr. Jacobs's texts, they were likely hunched over laptops, watching the blips of our various tracking devices on-screen, like it was some kind of important sporting match.

That image rekindled the fury in my gut. They were

using us, and even worse, using us against each other. It wasn't even a fair fight.

Maybe it was time someone brought that unfair fight to them.

"Whatever you're thinking, I don't like it," Zane said darkly.

I blinked up at him, startled. "I didn't think you could hear me that clearly—"

"No, not from your thoughts. It's on your face," he said. "What's going on?"

I sighed. "Zane—"

"No," he said in a tone that brooked no argument. "The last time you had that look, you pretended to be Ford and sneaked into Laughlin's facility, otherwise known as certain death."

Either he could hear more than he realized, or he was just getting better at figuring me out.

"You're thinking about going back to the Manderlay, aren't you?" He stood, swaying before catching himself. "No. Hell no." He shook his head. "The second they see you start that way, they'll have someone on you. You have to know they have a contingency plan. Jacobs is already threatening it." He gestured to the phone in my hand and the messages on it.

"I can ditch the vitals monitor," I protested. "Make someone wear it and then put the phone in someone else's bag—"

"And maybe get that person killed if they send someone to shoot you from a distance because you're not following orders and tracking down your target?" he demanded.

"What else would you have me do?" I asked, trying for calm. One of us had to be.

He raked a hand through his hair. "I don't know, maybe take time to consider that throwing yourself on this particular bomb isn't the way to go?" He glared at me. "You're always so quick to sacrifice yourself."

"Says the guy who endured multiple doses of an as-yet mostly untested virus that changed his DNA, to enter a competition where he might die," I shot back. Staying calm was not so easy when I could feel his agitation, and my own frustration was growing. Why couldn't he just let this go? Accept it as part of the deal, a price that had been agreed upon before I was born, to be paid in the future.

"Yeah, and look how pissed you were with me for that," he said. "And you want me to just throw my hands up and say 'Oh, well' while you walk in to your own execution?"

His expression softened and he reached out and touched my cheek, his thumb brushing over my mouth. "How am I supposed to do that?" he asked in a pleading tone that sounded like he genuinely wanted me to help him find the answer.

I forced a swallow past the sudden lump in my throat. "I know it's not fair, but I can't put my personal feelings ahead of—"

He dropped his hand, his face shuttering. "And why the hell not?" he asked. "You're a person too. Don't you get to choose what you want? Why does it have to be you?"

"Because there's no one else!" I shouted, and immediately regretted it when the bubble of low-level noise in the coffee shop shattered into shocked silence and I felt the few other customers staring at us.

"Or maybe you just think you deserve it," Zane said quietly into the void.

I blinked at the unexpected tears that welled in my eyes.

"You are more than someone's experiment, more than Dr. Jacobs's brain child," he whispered fiercely. "You have a right to want things for yourself, Ariane, to see yourself as a person. How do I get you to believe that?"

I turned away from him, unable to hide how closely his words had come to striking the vulnerable center I tried so hard to hide. "What do you want me to do?" I asked again.

"I want you to fight," he said.

"But I—"

"And not by giving yourself up," he added.

I turned to face him. "Again, I'm very open to suggestions," I said through gritted teeth. "But I don't see another option when they have all the information, all the power. You can't just tip the balance in our favor by wishing it, no matter how noble your motives." I couldn't keep the sneer out of my voice, even though he didn't really deserve it. I was as frustrated with myself as with him. "We're the underdogs here, remember?"

He scowled at me. "I'm not suggesting that we—" He paused, a strange look crossing his face. "Maybe, maybe not." A faint smile pulled at the corners of his mouth.

"What's that supposed to mean?" I asked with wariness.

He sat in his chair again, his entire posture changed now, confidence pouring through the cracks. "You could do exactly what they're expecting you to." He gestured to the phone still clutched in my hand. "You have Adam's sister. You can track her."

"I am not going to kill on their orders again," I said. I'd done it once because it was a necessity; that was not the case this time.

He made an exasperated noise. "No, I'm not saying that. But they'll be watching you. Seeing you track her and find her will keep them off your back temporarily. If you're dead, you can't save anyone," he said rather pointedly.

"And then?" I prompted. Part B of this had to be damn near spectacular to make any kind of difference.

"You do what they're expecting you to do, and then you turn it around on them," Zane said with a grin.

Which was exactly what we'd done to Rachel in what felt like another lifetime, but I failed to see what that had to do with our current dilemma.

But Zane wasn't done. "Adam had family pictures of that girl at the lab. I think the odds are pretty good that he'd answer a call from her." He raised his eyebrows in a triumphant smirk.

I went still. "You have the number for the phone they gave you?" I asked breathlessly, the words tumbling over one another in my hurry to get them out. "Why didn't you say so?" We could just call Adam and . . .

"No, but I know Adam has his own phone. One he used to stay in touch with his family. He had it at the facility."

"Dr. St. John let him keep his phone?" I asked in disbelief.

Zane shrugged. "Adam is a volunteer. It's not like he was going to try to plan an escape. As long as he didn't talk about the 'mission' in specifics, I don't think Emerson cared."

"But that doesn't mean he has it on him now," I pointed out. "He's got yours instead."

"He didn't when he left the hotel this morning, and I'm sure Emerson was checking in with him before we met up," Zane said. "Therefore, odds are, he's got his own phone on him."

"So, you have his number?" I asked.

"Nope," he said cheerfully. "But I know someone who does, and so do you." He grinned.

Now I could see what Zane had. I felt the first glow of excitement, of possibility.

"The odds are against us," I warned him. "We're running short on time."

Zane just smiled. "So, what's the plan?"

CHAPTER 14

Zane

THE BAD NEWS WAS THAT ADAM'S SISTER WAS IN A city of three million people and thousands of tourists. The good news was that my girlfriend—was it okay to call Ariane that? We'd never officially discussed it, but I thought there might be some kind of automatic boyfriend/girlfriend status conferred once you've almost died for one another—had scary skills.

After pulling her phone from her pocket, she tapped the screen, flipping through various applications as I watched upside down. Then she landed on one very familiar icon and tapped it with complete confidence.

"Wait . . . you follow her on Twitter?" I stared at her. "How? When?" As far as I knew, the packets containing target information had been handed out only last night.

"The documentation they provided gave me her first name—Elise. After that, it was just a matter of interpreting contextual clues from the provided pictures. I tracked her through her university, Michigan State, and her sorority to get her last name, and then I used social media to create a false profile to follow her." She shrugged. "I'm 'Brittany Pearson' as far as Elise knows."

I gaped at her. It was scary, frankly, exactly how good Ariane could be at this stuff. This girl, Elise, would have died today if Ariane had so chosen.

She frowned. "What?"

"Nothing. I'm just glad you're on my side," I muttered.

Ariane returned her attention to her phone. "Now we just need to find out what she's been posting in the last hour or so. She doesn't use the location check-in function, but she's been posting to one of the photo sites. I found her account there as well. Apparently, she won the annual all-expenses-paid trip with five friends from the Midwest Fine Arts Council, if such an organization even exists, to visit the city for the weekend." Her tone held bitterness. "Just enough to make it impossible for her to say no but not enough to make her wary enough to stay away."

"Tempting, but not too good to be true," I muttered. The Committee knew what they were doing.

Ariane stiffened suddenly.

"What's wrong?" I looked at her phone, expecting to see something horrible, like a photo of trials-related violence or an "account deleted" notification.

She shook her head, her mouth tight. "I think I just figured out who the Committee selected as Ford's target."

Meaning the person they thought Ariane would fight or seek vengeance for.

"Who?" I asked, mystified.

"Before I left GTX, Rachel was talking to me—"

"Rachel Jacobs?" I asked in disbelief.

"It's a long story," Ariane said with a sigh. "But she mentioned something about Cami winning a shopping trip. She's here in the city today."

"You're kidding." If the Committee had selected Rachel as someone Ari would care about, then maybe we weren't in as much trouble as we thought, because clearly their research skills sucked.

She shook her head. "It didn't occur to me before, because they were clearly attempting to select people who were of emotional interest to the candidates. I'm not sure how Rachel qualifies for me, but I think it's a good possibility. . . ."

"Ford and Rachel inhabiting the same space," I said, trying to imagine it. Rachel would think Ford was Ariane, which meant she'd be her typical abrasive self. I doubted Ford would handle that with anything like the patience Ariane had demonstrated. "That's going to go bad, and quickly."

"My thoughts exactly, which means we have another reason to hurry." Ariane turned her attention to her phone, skimming through Elise's posts. "Elise was at the Museum of Science and Industry as of forty-five minutes ago." She turned the screen toward me, and I vaguely recognized the white sprawling building in the picture. "Lake Shore Drive." She clicked her phone off and returned it to her pocket, moving swiftly. "I should have more than enough money for a cab, assuming we don't encounter traffic difficulties. . . ." She hesitated. "Are you . . . how are you feeling?"

Her dark eyes searched my face.

I forced a smile. "I'm fine." I could handle a cab ride, no problem. And a museum? That didn't sound too taxing.

The problem with our plan became very, very clear as soon as the cab pulled up to drop us off in front of the building.

"Wow. It, uh, didn't look this big in the picture," I said.

Ariane looked up from her phone, where she'd been attempting to find out information for the layout. "It's one of the biggest museums in the country, apparently," she said, sounding displeased, as if the museum had done this deliberately to aggravate her.

I fought the urge to laugh.

Ariane paid the cab driver, her actions awkward and uncertain, indicating the newness of the activity for her, and then we got out.

The museum, with its towering columns, sat in the center of an expansive lawn, the lake a bright blue pool to the east. All the skyscrapers that made up downtown Chicago had been left behind for this vast openness that felt out of place in the middle of the city. Hundreds of people swarmed up and down the museum sidewalk and steps. In the grass, families were having picnics or eating bag lunches. Crowds of elementary-aged school kids, tourist groups with cameras, and even groups of people on Segways flowed around us.

And that was just on the outside. This place looked so huge, I couldn't imagine how many more people were already within.

"Any chance 'Brittany' could message her and suggest meeting up out here?" I asked.

"She just happens to be in Chicago the same day as Elise,

the very next day after following her on Twitter?" Ariane shook her head, her mouth in a tight line. "It would be too suspicious. And if she thinks Brittany's . . . what's the word?" She paused, flipping through her mental dictionary. "A creeper. If Elise thinks Brittany's a creeper, she might block me."

It was funny sometimes, hearing slang come from Ariane. She used the words with such precision, unlike everybody else, like someone from another country who was still adapting. She'd been living outside with the rest of us humans for ten years, but she'd spent her first few years in near isolation, with only adult scientists for company. And then just her father for the years after that. Occasionally her unusual childhood showed, especially when she was stressed.

I was lost enough to notice and to find it kind of cute.

"So we're going in?" I asked, forcing my attention back to the matter at hand.

"Not that way." She gestured at the main entrance. "Admission for both of us will take almost half the money I have left. There has to be another way in."

She headed off to the side of the museum with the confidence of someone for whom locked doors were no deterrent. It didn't take long to find a loading bay and next to it a regular door, which, when opened, led into a narrow hallway with offices at the far end.

"What about cameras?" I hissed.

She nodded, a tiny motion. "I'm sure there are. Act normally, move quickly, and try to find a way onto the main floor," she said under her breath.

"If anyone asks, you're Jan Peterson's son and I'm your girlfriend," she added.

Aside from the quick burst of warmth I felt at hearing her call herself my girlfriend, that statement raised more panic in me than it allayed. "Who is Jan Peterson?"

"Hopefully someone who works here," she said over her shoulder as she started down the hall.

"Shit," I muttered. "You're kidding me with this, right?"

But she wasn't, and in this very rare instance, luck evidently decided to give us a pass. Before I could ask what would happen if we encountered someone who actually *knew* a Jan Peterson at the museum, she'd found a door labeled MUSEUM FLOOR.

A security badge scanner, a black plastic square with an ominous red light at the top of it, held a place of prominence on the wall next to the door. Well, that was a problem.

But Ariane ignored it, and with a quick motion of her hand by the door, the lock retracted with a loud snap.

I held my breath as she pulled the door open. The light on the scanner stayed red, but no alarms sounded.

Ariane's enhanced skills and training were no match, though, for the sheer size of the museum and the number of visitors. As soon as we stepped into what turned out to be a small side corridor, the noise crashed over us. When we reached the main floor, it got worse. It wasn't anything bad, just people shuffling around in every direction possible, talking and laughing.

"Can we page her?" I asked as we merged into the crowd, trying to watch for Elise and keep from getting run over. "They have to have something like that here, right? For lost kids and stuff?"

Ariane pulled her phone from her pocket, checking for

Elise's latest posted whereabouts. "Likely. But who will we say is calling?"

"I don't know, her brother?" I asked.

"Is Adam his real name?" Ariane asked, looking up from her phone.

I paused. "Uh . . ."

"And what do we say when she arrives and finds that there is no phone call from her brother? Instead, there are two strangers who want her to call him for reasons that won't make much sense."

I made a face. Fair enough.

"Come on." She frowned at her phone. "It looks like they're still near the aviation exhibit, if we hurry."

And that began the world's worst game of hide-and-seek. First, there was no hurrying at all, anywhere. It was like trying to run underwater. Second, Elise was a freaking ghost. She'd post a picture or a status update, referencing an exhibit or display or, hell, a "cute" shirt she saw someone wearing (she wasn't the most discriminating of posters), and we'd arrive at the designated location, out of breath and surrounded by the irritated people we'd pushed past, and never catch so much as a glimpse of her. We were always a step behind.

And Elise and her friends seemed to have the attention span of spider monkeys, leaping from one thing to another with no discernible pattern.

Under other circumstances this might have been fun, wandering the exhibits and people-watching, but with each passing moment, I could feel time slipping away and Ariane growing more and more tense.

The text messages from Dr. Jacobs, which had shifted

from berating to glowing encouragement once we'd actually started trying to find Elise, had stopped.

That couldn't be good, but I was, at least, pretty sure that Jacobs wouldn't have been able to resist screaming at Ariane if Ford or Adam had succeeded in eliminating their targets ahead of her. Which likely meant they were having as much trouble, or more, finding their people. I doubted Carter had any kind of social media presence for Adam to use against him, and I was pretty sure Ford wouldn't know what to do with Twitter if it bit her (and biting Ford wouldn't end well for anyone or anything).

We'd lost a lot of time at the beginning, but we now had more up-to-date information on Elise's movements than the others would for their targets. We were okay, maybe even ahead of the game.

But when I'd mentioned that, Ariane had not seemed all that reassured.

Or maybe she was still recovering from the exhibit we'd stumbled across upstairs. I was.

The Pre-Natal Development exhibit consisted of twenty-four fetuses and embryos, at various stages of development, in glass display cases. It was kind of creepy and weird and a little sad, especially considering that, if they'd lived, some of those babies would have already died from old age. They'd been at the museum since the 1930s, according to the signs, but they were still perfectly preserved. You could see their eyelashes, even. It was like they might open their eyes at any second and start crying to be freed from their glass boxes.

It had chilled me.

But Ariane's reaction had been more severe. She'd frozen

in place, oblivious to everyone around us. "It's like this at Laughlin's. He has displays of all the previous models. . . ." Her voice had broken, as if she might start crying. And I'd never seen her so pale, the color draining from her face until she really was gray.

I'd pulled her out of there, her hand, thin and so cold, in mine. She'd been much too quiet ever since.

Now, at the start of our second hour at the museum, we were sitting on benches near the main entrance. Perhaps Ariane was following the principle that you were more likely to be found by someone—or to find someone—by staying in one place. Or maybe she was taking pity on me. I hadn't asked for that, but I was definitely grateful. The trials had only officially started five hours ago (nineteen hours to go), and my whole body ached, and I had chills, off and on. The virus battling my still-adapting immune system. No nosebleeds in the last couple of hours, but I hadn't tried to use any of my new abilities recently, either.

I wasn't sure what would happen if I did. If I'd been at the hotel, I bet that Emerson would have been hovering nearby with a worried frown and a thermometer in hand.

Unwilling to think about that too much, I shifted uneasily. "I still think we should consider paging Elise," I said. "We can always walk away as soon as we see her coming. Then at least we'll have a visual on her. A chance to identify her in the crowd." That was something else I was worried about. People in real life, three dimensions, could look very different from flat photographs. If Elise's hair was shorter or pulled back or something, I wasn't sure that I would have picked her out of the crowd.

Before Ariane could respond, her phone chimed. She'd set it to alert her whenever Elise updated her feed. She clicked on the notification. "'Heading to Millennium Park. Gotta see the Bean. So excited!' They've left. But they're not there yet. Let's go." She bolted up as if the floor were spring-loaded beneath her.

I followed her outside to the cab stand, and when a yellow taxi stopped in front of us, Ariane lurched for the door, yanking it open.

"Take us to the park as you would take tourists," she commanded as I pulled the door shut.

She sounded so stilted. I kind of doubted the driver saw either of us as natives, especially now.

"You kids are new to the city, eh?" he asked, glancing at us in the rearview mirror.

Ariane stared out the side window, studying the traffic and the taxis around us, leaving it to me to answer.

"Something like that, yeah," I said. The TV screen embedded in the seatback in front of me flickered and sputtered, spitting out the occasional words "missing," "bioethics violation," "Chicago," "scandal." Must have been the local news, though it was kind of early for that at just after two in the afternoon.

"Uh-huh." The cabbie's gaze flicked from me to Ariane, lingering longer on her than it should have.

I couldn't blame him. Her knitted hat had slipped back, revealing more of her pale hair, but more than that, it was her posture that spoke of something other. Her back straight and formal, she was rigid with tension, sitting forward in the cracked and worn leather seat as though she might be ejected from it at any second and have to scramble to regain her footing.

It wasn't normal. At all.

I looped an arm over her shoulders and leaned back in the seat, pulling her with me. *HE'S STARING.* I focused on the words, putting effort behind them and trying to imagine them floating through the air to her. *YOU NEED TO RELAX.*

She stiffened and then sagged into me, her head resting on my chest, a deliberate act rather than one of true ease. I could still feel the steel rod of fear running through her. "I can't fail, Zane," she whispered. "If we can't find her, then nothing changes."

"I know, it's okay. We'll find her, I promise." A promise I had no business making, but what else was I going to say?

I tugged her hat into place. The wisps of hair that had escaped, now more than before, formed a halo of white-blond that framed her face, drawing even more attention to her unusual coloring.

Brushing the strands off her forehead, I tried to smooth them into place beneath her cap. But they refused to cooperate, curling and kinking in absurdly illogical directions, tangling around my fingers.

I winced in empathy and attempted to free myself without hurting her. "Sorry. I was just trying to help, but I . . . I think it has a mind of its own."

A startled laugh escaped her. "You wouldn't believe how many hours I used to spend trying to get it to look . . . right." She made a face. "Never quite managed it."

"It's beautiful," I said, my voice gruff. I felt like the

biggest doofus saying it, but she deserved to hear it. I just wasn't used to the whole giving or receiving compliments; I hadn't had much practice with it.

She looked up at me. "Thank you." She reached out and touched my chin carefully, the tips of her fingers catching on the stubble. Then she stopped, turning her head to the side, her gaze going distant. I recognized the look. She was hearing thoughts, most likely those of our driver.

When she turned to face me, her expression had shifted to something more calculating. "You're right. He is curious. Perhaps we should give him a reason to turn his attention elsewhere," she said under her breath.

She raised herself up on her knees and pressed her mouth against mine, her tongue sliding over my lower lip.

Whoa. In the cab? With the driver right there . . . Oh, who cared?

I caught hold of Ariane's waist, holding her steady against the motion of the car and pulling her closer.

She framed my face with her hands as she kissed me, and her breasts brushed against my chest in a way that sent shock waves through me.

I could feel the edge of her hip beneath my grip on her waist and, listening to temptation whispering in my brain, I slipped my thumb beneath the edge of her jeans.

Her breath caught, and she shifted abruptly, moving to sit in my lap. Which made things so much better and so much, um, harder.

I moved away from her mouth to trail kisses down the side of her neck. And she tipped her head back to let me. The skin of her throat was so soft, and she smelled so good.

God, if we could just have twenty minutes alone . . .

The cabbie cleared his throat loudly—we were getting a lot of that lately—and Ariane pulled away.

"Almost there. You're missing all the good stuff." He gave an awkward bark of laughter. "Or maybe not, eh?"

"The park is nearby?" she asked. Then she slid off my lap and onto the seat, as if the last few minutes hadn't happened. Her cheeks were flushed and her breathing faster than it had been, both of which sent an odd burst of pride through me.

I let out a slow breath, not able to make the shift as quickly.

The cabbie pulled up to a sidewalk, across the street from signs for the Art Institute. "Here. Millennium Park." He gestured grandly at an expansive stretch of manicured grass and gardens.

Ariane sat forward in her seat. "And where is the Bean from here?"

"Oh, for that, you'll need to head north and a little west, away from the lake. . . ."

I tuned out the driver's directions, concentrating on calming the blood pounding through the various parts of my body, which was made all the more difficult because I could still feel Ariane against my side and smell the fresh lemony scent that would forever in my mind be associated with her. I'd probably have a hard-on every time I smelled dishwashing detergent for the rest of my life.

As I stared out the windshield, trying to focus on something, anything else, a cab that had pulled to a stop ahead of us caught my attention. Five girls were piling out, laughing and tripping over each other in their giddiness. One girl, in particular, stood out. Her hair, some shade between brown and blond, was pulled up in a ponytail, and she wore a green shirt. One that might have been the shade used by Michigan State.

"Ari." I nudged her. "Look."

She straightened up and tilted her head to see around the driver.

"Is that her?" I asked under my breath.

Moving swiftly, Ariane shoved her door open. "Yes."

"Hey, hey," the cabbie protested. "The fare?"

Ariane paused long enough to thrust a handful of bills through the plastic divider without counting them.

I hung back for a second, just to make sure it was enough. Though, if it wasn't, I didn't have more funds to cover.

"You guys on a scavenger hunt or something?" he asked, handing me a bunch of singles through the divider.

"Yeah," I said to the cabbie, "and we just found the team we have to beat." I pulled out a couple bills and gave them as a tip.

With one last curious glance at me in the rearview mirror as I slid across the seat and out the door, he gave a nod. "Good luck with . . . whatever."

Yeah, that sounded about right.

CHAPTER 15

Ariane

ELISE AND HER FRIENDS LINKED ARMS, LAUGHING AND chattering, as they walked into the park. They paused just long enough to crowd together and take a picture of themselves on someone's phone—I couldn't tell whose from this distance.

One of them shrieked upon reviewing the photo, and they went through the routine again, wobbling as they squished closer.

I felt a squeeze of envy in my chest. Of all the emotions I expected to feel upon actually seeing the girl who was supposed to die at my hand today and who might now be the one person able to help me save lives, envy was not one of them.

But there it was, just the same.

"Hey." Zane caught up with me, out of breath. Then he frowned. "What's wrong? You look . . . sad."

"Sometimes I just miss what might have been." I tipped my head toward Elise and her friends.

He followed my gaze and nodded in understanding. "Doesn't mean you can't have it, Ariane. Just not right this second, maybe." He flashed me a smile.

"Okay." I took a deep breath. "Let's do this."

"Wait." He caught at my sleeve. "We can't just walk up to them and start talking about alien assassins and conspiracies and government agencies."

"Really?" I asked. "And that was going to be my opening line, too."

He sighed. "Fine. I deserved that. My point was that we should have our story straight."

"And what should that story be?" I asked.

He frowned. "The cab driver said something about a scavenger hunt. We could use that. Tell them we need to get points for, I don't know, getting a stranger to let us use their phone."

"I was thinking we could tell her the battery ran out on my phone and just ask to borrow hers for a minute." We wouldn't be able to say much to Adam because they'd all be listening, but that would be the case, regardless.

Zane opened his mouth and then closed it with a rueful smile. "Oh. Okay, yeah, that could work."

"Simpler is usually better," I said, and because he looked so crushed, I stood up on my tiptoes and kissed him quickly, though it was more on his jaw than his mouth, because that was all I could reach.

He looked startled, then pleased.

I drew in a deep breath. "Excuse me," I shouted at the girls ahead of us, lifting my hands to my mouth to help funnel the sound. "Hey!"

It was a bizarre feeling to shout with the intention of drawing someone's attention to me; I'd spent so many years working for the opposite. It made me feel exposed.

A couple of the girls turned around to look; neither of them were Elise.

Nor were they looking at me, I realized. The taller of the two girls leaned down to whisper to the shorter as they stared at Zane, and they both giggled. I felt a distinctly familiar buzz of interest from them.

Crap.

"Um, I think you're up," I said to Zane.

"What?"

"This is going to go better if you do the talking." I gestured ahead of us to where all five of the girls had now stopped and were facing us. Elise was in the dead center, smiling, looking on mildly interested as her two friends on the end laughed. She resembled her brother mostly in her coloring, honey-colored hair, and brown eyes.

Zane made a face. "I'm not really very good at that kind of thing—"

"They're not particularly interested in your words," I said tightly. One of the girls, the tall one with the gorgeous dark skin, was very loudly wondering in her head if I was his girlfriend and how *that* had happened.

My meaning sank in and the color in his face rose. "All right," he muttered.

Visibly summoning effort, he jogged over to them, and I followed at a slower pace.

"Hey, sorry to bother you." He gave them an easy smile, which all of them immediately and reflexively returned. I gritted my teeth against the gnawing jealousy. Of course they would smile at him. This was his world; these were the type of girls that should be flirting with him.

"I was hoping we could borrow your phone for a minute," he said, mostly to Elise, because of course that's whose phone we needed.

But it was the tall girl who volunteered hers. "Here. You can use mine." With a flirtatious smile, she flipped the thin, ornate braids of her hair behind her shoulder and produced her phone from the pocket of her very short shorts.

I tensed, ready to step in, but to Zane's credit, he didn't so much as blink. "Actually, it's really dumb," he said with an apologetic smile, "but we're on a scavenger hunt and we need to borrow the phone of a girl in a green shirt."

Elise swung her bag off her shoulder but hesitated.

Zane held up his hand in the Boy Scout salute or whatever it was. "I promise, we're not calling China or a 900 line or anything. We just need to check in."

Her friends nudged her, whispering endorsements. I held my breath, but then Elise shrugged, digging into her bag and pulling her phone out of a deep side compartment.

"You look so familiar," the tall girl said to Zane as he stepped forward and took Elise's phone. "Have I seen you somewhere?"

I barely kept from rolling my eyes. *I am here.*

The little blonde next to the tall girl with braids, her partner in staring at Zane, nodded. "Teri's right. I know I've seen you before." She frowned. "Are you on TV or something?"

Oh my God, seriously? Zane was handsome, there was absolutely no doubt about that. But weren't they laying it on just a little thick?

"No, sorry," he said, concentrating on Elise's phone.

The blonde frowned at him. I could *feel* her certainty and confusion. This was not flirting, or not *just* flirting, anyway. She really believed she'd seen him somewhere, and recently. She was mentally flipping through her day, trying to place his face.

A small ribbon of dread began to uncoil in my stomach. I had a bad feeling about this.

"You don't remember where you saw 'him,' do you? I mean, he's always wanted to look like someone famous," I said.

Zane raised his eyebrows at me, but I ignored him, concentrating on keeping my fake smile intact. I was good at pretending to be normal, when it involved being quiet and staying out of the way. Engaging people and getting them to give me information through regular social discourse, however, was *not* one of my specialties.

The blonde stuck her lips out in exaggerated pucker of thoughtfulness. "No . . . Maybe . . . no." She pulled out her own phone from a sparkly bag strapped across her chest and scowled down at as she scrolled through images.

Zane turned to me and tilted the screen so I could see the list of names. There was an Adam in Elise's contacts. No last name.

I nodded.

He hit send and held the phone up to his ear.

The ensuing silence in our little impromptu circle lingered too long, well past the comfortable point, even for me.

Fearing that would only draw more attention to whatever Zane would say on the phone, assuming Adam even answered, I tried to fill the gap. "So . . . you're having fun in the city? Where have you been already today?" I figured that would be a safe topic of conversation.

But the blond girl was still frowning over her phone with the braided hair girl. The other two girls were already bored, talking amongst themselves and rolling their eyes with great enthusiasm at something.

Elise bobbed her head in assent. "Yeah, it's been great. We've hit the usual places. Museums, Wrigley, Willis Tower." She shifted her weight uneasily, glancing between her friends and Zane, who was holding her phone captive.

His head popped up sharply. "Hey, man. It's Zane," he said quickly. "Don't hang up." He gave me a thumbs-up gesture, which I took to mean that we'd reached Adam and that it was the correct Adam.

I let out a slow breath of relief. Thank God.

There was a long pause on Zane's end, and I abandoned all pretense of conversation with Elise and/or her friends.

"No, it's not what you think, okay?" Zane said, still trying to sound casual. "But this . . . scavenger hunt is more complicated than what we were told. The targets are different for everybody. We need to meet up and . . . get a game plan together." Zane sent a questioning look to me, and I nodded quickly.

Even though Zane's words weren't anything conspicuous, the tension was building. Even the girls, who had no idea what was going on, could feel it, fidgeting as they waited.

"It's not a trick, and I don't care that you took my place," Zane said. "But there are some things you should know. You need to stop what you're doing and we need to meet."

"You know, guys, we really need to get going," Elise said to her friends, but in a loud voice that was meant for us.

Then something Adam said made Zane blanch.

Oh no. No, no, no. I knew all too well what that might

mean for Carter. For Ford. For all of us. "Give me the phone," I said.

"No," Elise protested, reaching out as if she might try to intercept, even though she was on the other side of Zane.

Zane turned away from me, keeping the phone out of my reach. "Yeah, fine. You're more qualified. Done. Agreed. Just tell us where you are," he said. "We'll meet you."

My temper sparked to life. "Zane," I said through clenched teeth. "Give me the phone."

Suddenly, the blond girl shrieked, making me jump. "I knew I recognized him!" She shoved her phone, face out, at her friends.

As she did, I caught a glimpse of Zane's face, an image of his school picture from last year like they'd scanned it from the yearbook.

Or gotten it from his parents.

Oh no.

"It's the guy from the news," the girl continued. "On the screen in the cab? Remember, the mom worked for those companies and then they abducted him or whatever, and Teri said that, hell yeah, *she'd* abduct him." She paused just long enough to look in Zane's direction and blush, though he was still distracted, his back to them as he talked to Adam.

I moved swiftly, darting around Zane and snatching the phone out of the blonde's hand for a closer look.

"Hey!" she said with a pout.

It was indeed Zane's school picture, with a blue banner beneath it that said MISSING, PRESUMED ABDUCTED. And it was part of the Breaking News section of the ABC 7 site.

TONIGHT: Research Assistant in Alleged Chicagoland Bioethics Scandal Speaks Out; Accuses Former Employers of Abducting Her Son.

My heart sank.

There was a promo video, posted an hour ago and just fifteen seconds long. The still of it was Mara Bradshaw sitting in a chair, looking small, old, and tired, the silver in her hair lighting up extra bright beneath the television lights. And oddly enough, she was wearing a school sweatshirt supporting the Mustangs, even though Wingate was home of the Hawks.

How had she managed this so quickly? Zane had spoken to her only this morning. Unless it had been something she'd been planning already. I supposed that was possible. Still, something about it seemed strange. And it was definitely dangerous. Very dangerous. For her and us.

I reached back and yanked on Zane's sleeve until he turned. "What?"

I held the screen so he could see it.

He paled, his hand with the phone slowly dropping to his side. "She said she'd do something. I . . . I didn't think it would be that."

I hit the button to play the video. Better to know what we were dealing with.

"Oh, there were questionable practices at both companies, GenTex and Laughlin Integrated. I was involved in unauthorized human testing, experimenting on children," Mara said in response to an unheard question.

I couldn't breathe. She was really doing it. Talking about the lab and what they'd done there. I felt as if someone were tearing my clothes off in the middle of a public arena. Or lifting me up so I could see the sun for the first time. It was a horrible mix of exposure and relief that made my stomach churn.

There would be no going back from this. Not for Mara. Not for me, either. The risk now would no longer be being recaptured but what lengths Jacobs and Laughlin would go to keep us silent or make us disappear.

"Tonight on ABC Seven," the voice-over announcer said, "one woman's story of her years at two area corporations and the consequences of her speaking out against their alleged infractions."

"They took my son so I'd stay quiet," Mara continued.

Well, not exactly. But that was an interesting spin on the story.

The screen flashed to Chief Bradshaw outside the Wingate Police Department. He looked both angry and like he hadn't slept in weeks. "I can confirm that my son is missing. He was last sighted in the company of employees from these corporations. We have witnesses."

So Mara had been working on this angle before today. Interesting. I wondered what Mara had done to make the chief cooperate, or if he'd just finally figured out that Dr. Jacobs wasn't God.

The video ended with a tag about joining them at ten P.M. for the full story. Nothing about aliens, at least. Then again, accusing her former employers of kidnapping her son was already on the edge of crazy. Mentioning extraterrestrial DNA would likely have pushed this story off the mainstream news and into the tabloids, where it would have done no good.

But it was still Mara blowing the lid off of everything at the worst possible time. Or the best, depending on how you looked at it. Dr. Jacobs and Dr. Laughlin were probably crapping kittens right about now, with this airing right in the middle of the trials.

A tiny insane part of me wanted to laugh, imagining their confusion and rage, and relishing it. But Mara's decision to go public had only made things worse for us as well.

Zane glanced over at me. "We're screwed. If my face is all over town right now . . ."

I nodded, my neck so tight with tension I could hear it creaking.

"I think we should call the cops," Teri interjected, reminding me of their presence. "She could be in on it." She nodded at me. The five of them clustered closer together, staring at me.

"Does she look like someone who can keep me anywhere against my will?" Zane asked, trying for a joking tone to defuse the situation.

"So . . . are you guys like star-crossed lovers on the run?" The blond girl asked with a hopeful smile.

"Emphasis on star," I said before I could stop myself, the absurd urge to laugh returning.

"Something like that," Zane said.

"Can I at least have my phone back now?" Elise asked, her expression troubled.

"Yeah, I'm guessing that scavenger hunt thing was bull." Teri sounded offended.

Zane looked down at the device in his hand, obviously having forgotten about it. "Oh. I don't know if—"

"Wait," I said, a vague, niggling concern bursting forth from the dark corner of my brain as a full-fledged and ugly worry.

I fumbled and pulled my phone from my pocket and clicked the home button. The screen was as blank as the last time I'd checked. No missed calls, no texts, angry or otherwise.

A slow creeping dread rose over me, like sinking into a tub filled with cold water.

There was nothing from Jacobs.

"Give it to me," I said to Zane.

He hesitated, which told me all I needed to about Carter. "Ariane . . ."

I swallowed hard. "I need to talk to him. Now. I think we've got a problem. Another problem," I amended.

Zane handed me the phone this time without argument. But the call had ended.

"Hello, can't you use your own phone?" One of the formerly bored girls snapped at me.

"I'm going to see if I can find security or something. Come on." Teri turned on her heel and started deeper in the park.

I ignored her, every passing second somehow confirming my worst fear. "It's Ariane," I said to Adam when he picked up.

"It doesn't matter what scheme the two of you have cooked up." Adam sounded out of breath but alarmingly cocky. "Like I told him, you can't distract me with this crap. It's bullshit. And messing with my sister? How did you even find her? That only shows what kind of amateurs—"

"When was the last time you heard from St. John?" I demanded.

"What?" he asked, confused.

"Have you been in contact with St. John or any of the others?" I asked.

"Yeah, they confirmed my target."

Carter. My heart gave a painful throb, but I forced myself to focus. "When was that?"

"I don't know, about an hour ago."

"Nothing since?" I pressed.

"I . . . no. I'm still waiting for further instructions." He sounded puzzled and much younger suddenly. "Why?"

"Listen to me," I said quickly. "This is not a trick or a ploy to get ahead. I think we're in trouble."

"Like I care about what you guys—" Adam began.

"All of us," I hissed. "We're exposed. Someone went to the media. The game is up."

At this point, Jacobs and company only had two choices: try to hide the evidence or destroy it.

And we—Adam, Zane, Ford, Carter, and me—*were* the evidence.

They'd invested millions of dollars in us. But if they were caught with us—living proof of illegal experimentation on humans, extraterrestrial life, and years of government deception—the damage would be far worse than anything you'd see on a balance sheet.

They were going to burn it down and salt the earth, just to be safe. They had to.

"But that's what I'm trying to tell you. It doesn't matter. I won," Adam crowed in my ear. "I found my target; the deed is done."

Even though I'd suspected that already, hearing it was

much, much worse. "You killed Carter?" I asked, my voice cracking. Carter with his shy smile and his earnestness. He hadn't deserved this, not that kind of death, not this kind of life.

Adam made a sound of disgust. "I did my—"

There was a strange, loud pop, and then a rustle of clothing and a loud clattering as if Adam had dropped the phone and it bounced a couple of times before landing.

"Hello?" I asked, a chill skittering over my skin. "Hello?"

There was no response but the wind moving over the microphone for a few seconds and the faint sound of people talking and laughing.

"Hey, hey, buddy, are you okay?" A tentative male voice, not Adam's, came through the cell, but it sounded distant, as if the guy was near the phone but not speaking into it directly.

Then a woman started screaming, panicked and screechy.

I jerked my head up at the sound. It wasn't just coming through the phone pressed against my ear but through the air as well. Fainter but still recognizable.

He was here. Adam was in the park somewhere. Or, at least, that screaming woman was, and I had a very bad feeling I knew what that meant.

I ended the call, taking the extra step of deleting it from the list of recent numbers, and then turned in a circle until I could pinpoint where the noise was coming from. There, from the northwest, the direction the cab driver had told me to go to find The Bean.

"Stay here," I ordered Elise and the others, and tossed her phone to her before bolting in the direction of the screaming woman.

"Ariane?" Zane called after me, and I could hear the alarm in his voice, but I couldn't stop to explain. Not now.

Even though we were outside, I could feel the walls closing in on us. Which was ridiculous. If I was right, I never ever had to worry about being captured again. I should have been far more worried about the faint, imaginary tickle of a target painted on my back.

I weaved my way through crowds rather than taking the clear, open space to run. And to my surprise, I reached my destination unharmed.

The Bean sat in a large, open plaza ahead of me with picnic tables lining one side.

I saw Carter first, his pale hair a bright spot in the sun.

Still wearing his Linwood Academy uniform, he was stretched out on one of the picnic benches, his arms crossed over his chest as if he were sleeping, taking a break from playing tourist and basking in the sun. But the only movement came from the wind ruffling his hair. Anyone who bothered to look and really *see* would be able to tell that something was different, not right. The spark that meant life was missing.

"Ariane," Zane said breathlessly as he arrived at my side. "What—" He stopped, his attention arrested by the scene unfolding off to the right, about 100 yards away from Carter. No one else had noticed Carter yet. They were too preoccupied with a more obvious bit of drama playing out.

The woman whose screaming had led me here had finally subsided to a quieter hysterical sobbing, but a small crowd had gathered. And yet in the true way of it, no one was getting too close (though several were recording the whole thing on their phones), except one guy on his knees who was attempting CPR.

Zane stiffened suddenly, and I knew he'd seen it . . . him. "Oh my God, is that—"

I jerked my head in a nod. "He must have been hanging around, waiting for instructions after . . . after Carter."

Through the gaps in the crowd, Adam was plainly visible on the ground, his face turned skyward, his immediately identifiable bright yellow shirt now stained an equally bright red, blood seeping out beneath him and spreading out like thin angel's wings.

And yet, no one was panicking, no one was running away. His assassination had been subtle, handled with the utmost discretion. He would be seen as a victim of random violence in the park, not a target of any kind. Unless you happened to know better.

"We're definitely in trouble," I said.

CHAPTER 16

Zane

ADAM WAS DEAD. SHOT, IT LOOKED LIKE. OR MAYBE stabbed. *Oh Jesus.*

There was so much blood. I could smell it from here on the breeze from the lake, that strong metallic scent that coated the back of my throat. I'd smelled it only once before . . . when I was dying. That scent brought back an instant and visceral flash of the fear and intense bone-quaking vulnerability I'd felt in that moment.

Had Adam felt the same thing? Had there been enough time for him to realize that all of the blood and confidence were draining out of him? He'd been so sure he was better than everyone else who was competing, better than me.

He was right in that, at least. He'd had more time, more practice, with his new skills. But it hadn't saved him.

Adam was dead, and all of his strength and abilities *had not* saved him.

I blinked, feeling myself wobble as the realization ricocheted through me. Adam had behaved as though he were invincible—which I guess I thought meant maybe I would be too, once my treatment was finished—but Adam was wrong. There was always going to be someone who was faster, stronger, or smarter to defeat you. And in this case, that someone had found and soundly defeated Adam.

But who? Guns, or knives, weren't Ford's natural inclination. And they definitely weren't sanctioned parts of the competition. Discretion was supposed to be key.

"Come on." Ariane pulled hard on my sleeve. "We need to get out of here. Now."

"But . . ." I looked back at Adam, alone in a crowd of strangers. I didn't like him, but just leaving him there felt wrong.

Then, as I turned to face her, I caught a glimpse of white-blond hair and a too-still form on one of the picnic benches.

It was Carter, laid out like one of those statues on old tombs in England our Ancient History teacher had shown us in class, the ones of the really old knights or whatever.

"Ariane," I said softly.

Her empty expression didn't change. "Move with them." She tipped her head toward a gaggle of elementary-school-aged kids, laughing and tripping as they passed about twenty feet away from us. They were running circles around their weary-looking adult chaperones, all of them oblivious to the death near them.

After a moment of hesitation, I hurried after them to catch up, one more adultish figure on the edges, and Ariane joined me.

At my side, Ariane slipped her phone from her pocket, dropped it to the ground, and crushed it beneath her heel, pausing just long enough to stomp a couple extra times to be sure.

I stared at her. All this time she'd been so careful to keep up the illusion of participation in the trials. But destroying the phone meant they'd immediately know something was up. "What are you doing?" I asked in a hushed voice.

She didn't answer, just reached down the collar of her shirt and pulled the vitals monitor off her chest, the adhesive giving way with a reluctance that I could hear and taking layers of skin with it, I knew from experience.

But Ariane's face remained impassive as she folded the plastic edges together, the middle giving with a snap before she discarded it as well.

"They're cleaning house," she said. "I believe that's the expression."

"What does that mean for us?"

"Mara called out Jacobs and Laughlin. The Committee can't take the risk that someone will find us and tie them to the program. They waited until Adam took Carter out, and then they shot him. And we're next."

Instinctively, stupidly, I hunched my shoulders. As if that was any protection from a bullet.

"The trials are over. They'll get rid of us so we can't be evidence, and then they'll just restart the program later," she said.

"Isn't that kind of a good thing?" I asked cautiously. "If we can just avoid—"

"We won't get out of this alive," she said.

"So what now?" I asked, fighting the urge to turn and search the rooftops.

"We need to get out of sight, reevaluate, figure out a new plan." But the grim set to her jaw told me more than I wanted to know. She wasn't sure there would be a new plan.

"What about Ford?" I asked.

"I don't know," she said.

Seeing Ariane so uncertain like this was enough to make me feel as if the world were tipping and I needed to find something to grab hold of to keep myself from flying off into space.

"Will Elise and her friends be okay?" I asked.

She paused, the faintest hesitation in her response. "I don't know. I think so. They're fully human, and they don't know who sent them on the trip. Carter is . . . They let Adam kill him because he's like me and that saved them the trouble. Two deaths, one bullet." Her voice was choked with justifiable bitterness.

"Ari, I'm sorry." I wrapped my arm around her shoulders, pulling her closer.

She slipped out from under me. "Not now. They might be looking for a couple, especially if they know Adam took your place."

I tried to tell myself that she was right, not to mention still reacting to Carter's death and this new, incredibly messed-up situation we'd just found ourselves in.

But I still felt a flash of frustration. If she was right, she wasn't the only one who was going to die. And maybe, just maybe, she wasn't the only one still trying to adjust.

Dying once, technically, had not made the prospect of a second go-around any more appealing.

We joined the streams of people, moving toward the

shopping on Michigan Avenue. It was relatively easy to feel sheltered by the number of people around us, but that was an illusion.

"What exactly are we looking for?" I asked, more for something to say to ease the agitation I could feel growing inside me, like my internal organs were all set to vibrate.

"I'm not sure yet. Maybe that." She pointed to a banner in the distance. ULTA HOTEL: LUXURY SUITES. OPEN DURING RENOVATION!

"Another hotel? Are you serious?" I asked.

"We need a place to keep our heads down for more than a few minutes at a time without attracting any attention. I'd consider breaking into a condo building, but the odds of us being identified as outsiders are much higher in that case," she said.

The elementary kids and their teachers peeled off at the next intersection, heading for the next block up while we continued down Michigan.

Ariane picked up the pace to attach us to a quartet of elderly people.

By crowd surfing in this way, never by ourselves, always on the heels of a larger group, it took us longer to reach the hotel.

I found myself imagining a cover story for us with each group, as if that helped project a cover over us. With the old folks, I was a dutiful grandson and she was my reluctant, kind of rebellious girlfriend. When we joined a group of city kids, clearly cutting through on their way to somewhere much cooler, we were cousins (from opposite sides of the family) from the hopelessly dorky suburbs. With the three nuns, in full black-and-white garb, we were two trouble-making students who couldn't be left alone with the others on the class field trip, therefore requiring direct nun supervision. I didn't actually know if that was how it worked in a Catholic school; I was just guessing.

Ridiculous, yeah, but it made me feel better.

Then finally we were crossing the street to reach the main entrance for the Ulta. The signs of renovation were more obvious now. Scaffolding lined the structure on the lower levels, and two huge green Dumpsters were filled to overflowing with chunks of drywall and other debris.

"Okay," she said, as we headed toward the doors. "Just follow my lead."

"Uh . . ." Before I could ask what that meant, she was crossing the threshold into the lobby.

Then, to my surprise, she grabbed my hand and beamed up at me.

I started to respond, smiling reflexively, before I noticed the flatness in her gaze. That's what people talk about when they say someone is (or isn't) smiling with their eyes. She was faking it.

"It's not that expensive? Daddy will get it for me?" she said in a singsongy voice that pitched upward at the end of the sentence, like a question.

Ariane was, as always, an amazing mimic when she wanted to be, thanks to all those years of observing the people around her, and right now she sounded exactly like Cassi Andrews from our school. Cassi had never, in all my years of knowing her, stated anything with confidence. She was like a contestant on a perpetual game of *Jeopardy!*, where everything must be phrased as a question in a breathless surprised voice. A flake, in short, and the furthest thing from Ariane's true nature.

I struggled to play my part equally well, though I wasn't exactly sure what, or who, I was supposed to be. "Okay, if you say so."

Lame. Very.

But no one, including the staff behind the oversized registration desk, paid us much attention beyond a polite nod, acknowledging our existence.

She headed to the elevators, moving excruciatingly casually when I wanted to run. "The only question is blue or green? I mean, I know that blue totally sets off my eyes better, but you know it can't always be about that, right? Sometimes I've got to consider my hair, which, I think, means green?"

I had no idea what the hell she was talking about. A car, a dress? Possibly jewelry. Or maybe she was just talking, prattling to fill the space with talk that would fit the part she was trying to play. "Uh-huh," I said. "Of course."

She pushed the up button for the elevator and turned to face me with an excited squeak that was entirely phony. "Obvious solution! I'll just get one of each!" She clapped her hands excitedly, and I almost laughed in spite of everything because it was just so not her.

Inside the elevator, faster than I could blink, she pushed the buttons for the first seven floors. Roughly the same floors that, from the outside, appeared to be under construction. That much I had figured out. Beyond that, I had no idea.

"Oops, more time alone with you!" She caught my hand

and pulled herself closer to me, rising up on her tiptoes. "Just go with it," she said in a whisper I could barely hear a second before she pulled my head down toward hers and she kissed me.

Uh, okay.

But she wasn't entirely with me. When I wrapped my arms around her, pulling her up and helping to support her weight so she wasn't wobbling on her toes, I could feel the tightness in her whole body. Usually she sort of went soft and boneless—not bragging, just reporting the details—but right now, it was like trying to cuddle with a metal support beam. She was still on high alert, no matter how convincing her performance of "relaxed and flirty," and her body was giving her away.

Not to mention that every time the doors opened, she was distracted enough that her tongue stopped, which was driving me crazy in an entirely different way.

She was paying attention to the levels we were passing, perhaps counting off floors without turning around to check. I wasn't sure what she was looking, or listening, for. But I was more than happy to help her in this way.

"I think this is us," she said brightly, and turned to peer out onto a floor that reeked of new carpet and paint. The light fixtures gleamed so brightly, they were almost blinding.

"Nope, guess not." She smiled up at me, her cheeks flushed and her mouth pink and slightly swollen.

"Too bad," I murmured, and pulled her back to me.

Three floors later—or possibly four—Ariane paused again and glanced over her shoulder when the door opened.

I followed her gaze. From what I could see, the left side of the hall looked normal, if a bit dusty. Footprints and wheel marks from a luggage cart were outlined in white in the dark-green patterned carpet, with larger crumbs of drywall sprinkled throughout.

The right side, though, was sectioned off in plastic, and faint sounds of hammering and sawing came from that direction. This floor was definitely under construction.

She tugged my hand and led me off the elevator to the left, just as the doors started to close.

The hall split again and she took us right, down a dim corridor with glossy wooden doors and plaques bearing suite numbers above what appeared to be . . . Yep, those were doorbells.

"Stay close to me, and keep your eyes down," she said quietly.

The first light overhead blew before I had a chance to ask what she meant.

I ducked instinctively, my free hand flying up to protect the back of my neck.

She moved swiftly, the bulbs popping and raining down on us as we passed, and then she let go of my hand to stretch her fingertips toward either wall. Door locks snapped open on both sides of the hall, even as the lights on the key card scanners remained a stubborn red.

Glass from the lightbulbs crunched into the carpet beneath my feet as I followed her.

Once she'd reached the end of the hall, she backtracked to the second-to-last room door and waved me inside, the motion tight as though it were painful.

She shut the door with care behind us, even as I heard the

first confused guests open their now-unlocked doors and call out into the darkened hall.

"What's going on?"

"Hello? Is someone there?"

"The goddamn power's out again."

Ariane held her position at the door, while I hesitated just inside the largest hotel room I'd ever seen. It was, from what I could see, three rooms. A living room with a huge flat-screen and a big sectional couch. Beyond that, I caught a glimpse of a dining table and chairs, and then, through a set of black-framed French doors, a big white corner of a bed.

"What—" I began.

She shook her head, holding her finger up to her mouth. A second later, her shoulders sagged as if she'd been holding her breath and finally exhaled, and the lock snapped into place on our door with a loud clack.

The same noise sounded in the hall, moving away from us, a series of muted thwacks that got quieter, like someone running past and hitting each door as he passed.

She'd forced open the locks on all the doors in this section and then released them. And I had no idea why.

I shifted my weight but kept quiet as the sound of heavy footsteps and the squawk of a walkie-talkie came through the door. "I'm on seven," a man's voice said just outside our door.

Security, it had to be.

I jerked back as if he could somehow see me through the door. Ariane caught my wrist, giving it a warning squeeze.

"I don't care what you were working on," the man said, annoyed. "You had to hit something with the electrical.

I've got twelve doors that misfired here and broken glass everywhere."

The doorknob rattled; someone checking to make sure it was locked. Even though I knew it was, my breath caught in my throat.

The walkie-talkie chirped again, a softer female voice asking a question, but the words were indistinct.

"Yeah, I don't know," the security guy answered. "Locks are back on line now, but you've got to get someone up here to clean up the mess." His voice sounded farther away. He was moving on. The further rattle of doorknobs confirmed his location.

"Hey, are the lights coming back on or what?" a loud and irritated voice, no doubt one of the guests, demanded.

The security guy answered, his voice low and soothing, and Ariane edged away from the door, moving past me and deeper into the suite.

She peered cautiously around the corner into the dining area, which, when I followed her, also turned out to have a freaking kitchen in the opposite corner.

That didn't seem to impress her, though. She paused only to grab several snack items from the honor bar basket sitting on the counter, then she kept moving toward the bedroom.

Getting us away from the door, I realized.

"What was that about?" I asked, tagging along after her. Just inside the bedroom, there was a doorway to a huge bathroom with a marble floor, a tub that would easily seat six, and a television in the mirror. Holy crap. On the bathroom counter, a silver tray next to the sink held any and every kind of personal item you might need—shampoo, toothpaste, mouthwash, cotton balls, a disposable razor, even condoms—in discreet packaging with the hotel's logo.

Behind me, Ariane closed the French doors, shutting us off in the bedroom. "I couldn't have them checking the room individually for someone breaking in. You're the one who taught me that they can tell when the room locks are triggered on an unregistered room."

I blinked. She was right. When we'd stayed in that crap motel on the way to my mom's house. That felt like a lifetime ago.

"So you picked a floor that was under construction, figuring they'd blame anything strange on a malfunction or short circuit or something." It was freaking brilliant. I felt a burst of warm pride in my chest. No, *she* was brilliant.

"You need to eat," she said, pushing a package of pretzels into my hands with a frown. "You're too pale."

With my adrenaline pumping, I'd managed to push the shaky, unsteady feeling caused by the NuStasis battle in my body to the back of my mind. But now, when I felt relatively safe once more, it zoomed back to the forefront of my awareness.

I sat on the corner of the bed and opened the pretzels, eating a few in the hopes of a blood sugar boost. "Ariane."

"I'm not sure what to do," she said quietly. "I don't know if there's anything *to* do."

The warmth in me drained away, leaving behind a cold emptiness. It wasn't her words so much as the defeat in her voice. That was not something I was used to hearing from her. Ever.

"The Committee, I'm sure, is long gone," she said.

"Laughlin, Jacobs, and St. John have probably been sent to their respective companies to consult with lawyers and prepare some kind of defense or statement."

Emerson was gone? I felt a tiny spurt of panic. My condition hadn't stabilized yet. How soon would I start to see symptoms of my body rejecting the virus and its changes?

"We have virtually no money, no ID." Ariane lifted her shoulders in a helpless shrug. "We can't run, and hiding will only work for so long. Whomever they've tasked with finding us will eventually succeed. It's a matter of days, maybe only hours. The government has resources we can't beat and access we can't avoid."

She sank down on the opposite side of the bed, drawing her knees up to her chest. "I don't know where Ford is, even if she's alive. I have no way of tracking her down." She looked small and vulnerable and, even worse, uncertain for the first time since I'd met her.

"We'll go to the news," I said, sounding more confident than I felt. "The same place my mom—"

"The Committee will have thought of that." She shook her head. "They'll never let us get close. There's too much risk. I . . ." She stopped, her gaze going distant.

"What?" I glanced behind me reflexively, half-expecting to see a SWAT team bursting through the door behind me, but it was still just the quiet and empty suite.

She looked at me, fierceness burning her gaze. "You can."

"I can what?" I asked.

"With the focus your mom put on you, they might not want to take the risk of hurting you. You're likely a secondary target. If one at all." She stood again, warming to the idea.

"It would only add credence to her claims if they kill you."

I winced, but she didn't notice, her brain in full strategy mode, kicking up possibilities.

"They'll throw Jacobs to the wolves as long as it doesn't come back on them, and right now this is a simple bioethics case, corporate misbehavior. Not a government conspiracy. If they hurt you, it might inspire someone to dig deeper," she said, pacing again.

"Okay," I said slowly. "But what's to stop him from telling his side of the story, talking about the contract and the alien DNA and Project Paper Doll?"

She stopped and gave me a bitter smile. "He won't. As it is, he'll be lucky if he escapes this with his company intact. If he tries to pin any of this on the government, they'll bury him. If you go to the police and tell them who you are, they might be able to protect you. Particularly if I provide a distraction and lead away whomever the Committee sent after us," Ariane said. "I'm a much higher priority."

"Always bragging," I murmured.

"No, it's just that I would give it all away." She gestured at herself, her body, the alien DNA hidden within. "Even a simple blood test would show there's something wrong—"

"—different," I interjected.

"—with me," she finished. "Your tests will show an unknown virus, I'm guessing, but nothing as conclusive."

Until I collapsed bleeding from my eyes or something. But I wasn't going to mention that. She didn't need another thing to worry about.

"So, I run for the police while you distract." I didn't love that plan, but at least it was a plan. Better than wandering the streets waiting for a bullet. "What are you going to do, pull more fire alarms? Break more lights?" I asked, teasing a little, feeling incrementally better just seeing determination flaring in her eyes again.

"Whatever it takes. I'm something of an expert by now," she said, teasing in a confident tone, but beneath that, I could hear something that sounded like sadness.

CHAPTER 17

Ariane

ZANE NARROWED HIS EYES AT ME, SUSPICIOUS. "Ariane . . ."

I ignored him, my heart pounding at pretending this was like every other strategy moment we'd shared. "So, listen, give me twenty minutes before you try to leave the hotel, okay? That should give me enough time to implement Phase 1." Which sounded really good but meant nothing. I fully intended to be a distraction as long as possible to give him safe passage, but I had no illusions about my own fate. The second I stepped outside, I was dead. Actually, I was dead already, it was only a matter of time until the bullet—as yet unfired—caught up with me. The best I could do was make sure Zane stayed alive.

But if he knew what I was up to, he'd be angry and upset, and I'd have to try to explain the inevitable, which was an endless debate that we didn't really have time for. The fact was, I'd known all along that if I refused to become what

Dr. Jacobs wanted me to be, if I resisted the Committee's desire to make me a weapon, then death was the most likely outcome.

I'd accepted it a long time ago. In fact, during my first six years in the lab, I'd thought more than once that I would die there, in the dark and alone, for not obeying Dr. Jacobs. Then, during the three weeks I'd been there after being recaptured, I'd wanted to.

Instead, I'd gotten the gift of a life outside for ten years and then the discovery that the boy I loved was still alive. All in all, it was an acceptable deal, both times.

"So you're going to get to the police, tell them who you are, and back up your mom's story. That will help shut Jacobs and maybe Laughlin down," I continued, forcing myself to keep eye contact with Zane, as if nothing were wrong.

"But you're going to meet me," he said, frowning, searching my face for reassurance.

Pain arrowed through my chest. "Of course." I smiled at him, even as my throat tightened. "I don't know exactly how long they're going to keep you in protective custody, so it may be a while before I can reach you. I'll try to get to the same police station today. But if not, go back to Wingate. Stick with your mom. She's your safety net."

His expression troubled, he nodded.

It was only his confidence in my abilities and skills that let him believe I could pull this off. I appreciated the support, as misguided as it was, because it let me get away with a lie for the greater good.

This plan wasn't just about Zane surviving, even though that was the biggest, most obvious benefit. We couldn't stop the government from starting up the project again at some point, but if Zane went along with his mother's story, he might be able to keep Jacobs and Laughlin from participating in it.

It wasn't the same as destroying Project Paper Doll, but if I could keep them from doing to someone else what he and Laughlin had done to me, Ford, Carter, Nixon, and countless others, then my death would be worth something.

Not that Zane would agree.

He looked at me, skeptical, unsure, his shoulders stiff with tension. Even though I was blocking as hard as I could, trying to keep any stray feelings or thoughts from reaching him, he wasn't an idiot. "I swear to God, Ariane, if I get home and you're not there—"

"I'll be there. Promise," I said over the lump in my throat. It was easy to make commitments that I had every intention of honoring if my heart was still beating.

I inched closer, and when he didn't move away, I slid my hands up his chest and stood on my tiptoes to wrap my arms around his neck, clinging and breathing deeply in the familiar scent of him. I couldn't say good-bye, but I could take a moment, just this one, for me, for us.

Zane would recognize it for what it was afterward, and that would have to be enough.

After a second, Zane's arms came up around me, lifting me off my feet and holding me so tight I couldn't breathe. And I wouldn't have had it any other way.

I buried my face in his neck, and I could feel his breath warm at my collarbone and the lightest brush of his mouth against my skin. It sent a frisson of electricity through me, and the whole world stopped.

I wasn't sure who moved or touched or what changed, but the tenor of the moment shifted lightning fast, like someone had flicked a switch from loss to wanting.

Zane's breathing picked up, his chest moving against mine, and I could feel his heart pounding, hard.

Acting on an instinct that I didn't know I had, I pulled myself tighter against him, wrapping my trembling legs around his waist.

He made a noise somewhere between a groan and exhalation of surprise before sliding one arm around my hips to help support my weight. With his free hand, he pulled the stupid cap from my head, which I'd almost forgotten I was wearing, and tangled his fingers in my hair, tilting my face to slant my mouth against his.

His tongue delved into my mouth, tangling with mine. This was not the tentative, explorative kiss of before. No hesitation, no uncertainty. It was as if he were trying to convince me of something or stake a claim with his conviction.

And still, it was not enough.

I squirmed against him, and his hands tightened on my hip and in my hair, but it didn't hurt.

Feeling that odd frantic energy growing in me, I wedged my hands between us, fumbling for the zipper on the hoodie I'd insisted he wear.

My questing fingers got caught in a loop of the stupid hoodie string, and I couldn't free myself without the patience or willpower to slow down, so I yanked it out, sending the sealed plastic end up to hit us both in the face.

"Shit," I muttered.

Zane laughed against my mouth, a low vibration in his chest that I felt everywhere, but he didn't stop. He shifted both of his hands to my hips and took an off-balance step and then another to the bed before turning and sitting, bringing me tighter against his lap.

I broke off then with a gasp. The sensation was more intense than I'd expected, echoing through me.

He went still, his fingers just under the edge of my shirt where I could feel them warm against my waist, almost teasing with the lightness of his touch. And then he started to pull away.

"Don't . . ." I said, breathless.

Zane immediately froze. "What's wrong?"

"No, don't stop," I clarified, impatient and pushing the words out, all muddied with desire and half-garbled, before pressing my mouth to his again.

With his help, I wrestled his arms out of the hoodie sleeves and let the garment drop immediately to the bed and started tugging his T-shirt over his head.

He lifted his arms to help me before his hands returned to my hips, hitching me closer, which drew sharp breaths from both of us. Resting my hands on his shoulders, I took in the sight before me. This intimacy, seeing this side of him for this reason, it changed everything.

His skin was smooth under my hands and darker than mine; it would be difficult for it not to be. His chest and arms had curves of muscle from years of lacrosse that sent a shiver through the very human part of me. The gunshot wound that he'd survived only through Emerson St. John's intervention had left a faint, puckered pink circle on his abdomen, barely visible above the line of his pants.

Color rose in his cheeks at my scrutiny, but I couldn't help myself. I'd seen him without his shirt before, or rather, with his shirt unbuttoned. But this was different. It felt *different.* We weren't in a grungy bathroom, fumbling for a few minutes before someone or something interrupted.

It was like being invited into this new world that I'd only caught glimpses of before.

"This looks painful." I touched his chest just below his collarbone, carefully outlining the triangle-shaped patch of raw skin where the vitals monitor had been attached, staying clear of angry redness.

He grimaced. "Yeah." His gaze flicked to the same spot on my chest, hidden by my shirt. "Bet yours isn't much better."

I recognized the unspoken question for what it was, and my heartbeat sped up. A flare of anxiety went off in me. He'd seen me without my shirt before as well, but it had been in the context of bandaging an injury to my arm. Taking off my shirt in front of him now meant more. Intention was everything.

I pushed my worry down and reached for the hem of my shirt and pulled it over my head quickly before my self-doubt could get the better of me. He'd found me plenty human enough before, there was no reason for that to have changed just because everything else had.

The heat in his expression sent a ripple of relief through me. His eyes were dark in the dim room, but it was more than that. *I'd* put that look on his face—my body, my skin, my not-entirely-human self.

Zane reached up, slipping a fingertip beneath the strap of my bra and sliding it down my arm, away from the similar triangle-shaped injury on my chest. That light touch made me tremble and catch fire at the same time. I wanted to close my eyes to focus on it, but I didn't want to miss anything.

"Yours doesn't seem as bad," he said, his voice hoarse.

"Fast healer," I reminded him, the words half-catching in my throat.

He leaned forward, slowly, as though he feared I might stop him, and placed his mouth on the edge of it, his breath skating over the skin between my breasts.

And that broke something in me, my fear or my willpower, I didn't know which.

I fumbled for his hand on my hip, dragging it up and beneath the stretchy fabric of my bra. The warmth of his skin against mine, the all-too-pleasant friction of his slightly rough hands against sensitive flesh, shattered the last of my functioning synapses and stole my breath.

Zane inhaled sharply and then reached with his free hand to release the catch in the back of the garment.

And then there was nothing between his skin and mine, and it was everything that I'd wanted. But long before I was ready to give up that sensation, he turned, carefully shifting me off his lap and onto the bed.

I started to protest until he moved with me, crawling up next to me, his knee between mine.

His mouth covered mine as he settled over me. The weight of him, which could have been suffocating or heavy or frightening, just felt right. It was *Zane.*

Instinct surfaced in me again, and I pushed up against him with my hips.

"Jesus, Ariane," he gasped. "You're killing me." But from the way his mouth continued to wander over my collarbone and breasts, he meant that in a good way, I was fairly sure.

"Don't stop," I whispered. I wanted this, wanted him, and I was so, so afraid that he'd change his mind. That I would be judged and found lesser, not enough. Or that he'd have an attack of good-guy conscience, worrying that I was making a decision under duress. When, in my life, hadn't I been under duress? But this wasn't about that. This was about what I wanted, what *we* wanted. A tiny piece of freedom of our own making. And I didn't want to leave without this memory . . .

"Ariane," he murmured against my throat.

. . . I wanted to have this to take with me, when I was gone. Maybe I wouldn't have the memory for more than a few hours before I no longer existed. But I wanted it for those minutes.

"Ariane," he said again, more urgently, pulling himself up on his elbows, and holding himself over me until I looked up at him, my eyes stinging.

He framed my face with his hands, brushing my hair away from my flushed face, his gaze searching mine. "I won't. Unless you say so, I won't stop. I promise, okay?" Even without being able to read my thoughts, he knew what I was worried about, and his eyes were asking the question that was really at the core of all of this, which was: *Trust me?*

And I did.

CHAPTER 18

Zane

ARIANE WAS TUCKED UNDER MY ARM, HER SKIN BARE against mine, and it was an amazing, unreal feeling. I'd never felt that close—literally or otherwise—to anyone.

She was quiet, her breathing was slow and even, but the high from that moment kept me from completely dozing off.

So I was mostly awake when she slid out from under my arm, taking care not to jostle me.

She hadn't been asleep, then. Her caution might have read as concern for my well-being, an attempt to let me rest. But there was a furtive quality to her movements as she got dressed.

The faint clutch of dread that had started when Ariane first suggested her plan of splitting up grew more intense in my gut.

I waited, but she didn't wake me. Didn't run a hand over my shoulder or whisper my name.

That's when I knew. She'd wait until the last second to

tell me she was leaving, so I wouldn't have a chance to ask many questions before she disappeared for good.

I listened to the soft sounds of her feet on the carpet, hoping, praying I was wrong. But when the whispers of fabric moving gave way to the faintest squeak of hinges on the bedroom doors, I couldn't stay still any longer.

I sat up, fury making my pulse pound. "Were you going to tell me? Or just let me figure it out when you never showed up?"

She froze in the doorway, the truth written in her stiffened posture.

"I don't know what's going to happen," she said, turning to face me.

"No, but you've got a good guess. You promised. No self-sacrifice."

"I promised I would try," she corrected gently. "And I will."

But she didn't believe she'd succeed. And that right there said it all.

I should have known. I grabbed my clothes from the floor and got dressed, motions jerky with anger and hurt.

After all we'd been through, together and separately, this was how it was going to end. Her death would facilitate my life (for a little longer, anyway) and perhaps I'd get a chance to prevent GTX and Laughlin Integrated from doing to someone else what they'd done to her and the others. But for the size and scale of the sacrifices we'd made, particularly Ariane, that payoff was a joke.

It was just wrong.

But I knew what she would say if I pointed that out—life

isn't fair or balanced, especially not where she was concerned. Because of who she was and the circumstances of her creation, she had even fewer expectations of the opportunities the rest of us took for granted. Life, liberty, pursuit of happiness, all of that.

And maybe that assessment was accurate, but that didn't mean it was *right*.

Gritting my teeth in frustration and to keep all my angry but useless words in, I grabbed the remote from the bedside table, clicked on the television, and found one of the local stations, which was on commercial.

"Zane," she said quietly as she moved toward me, her hand raised in a pleading gesture.

I braced myself in anticipation of her touch, her cool fingers against my skin, and she must have read that because she stopped abruptly.

"It's after six," I said. "The news is on. I'm going to check to see if there's more from my mom."

"I have to go, but I don't want to leave it like this," Ariane said, sounding helpless but resolved. "I don't know what to say to make you believe. That's why I—"

"It's back," I said, nodding at the television, where the news had returned from commercial. I didn't want to hear any more explanation, another round of rationalizing. I got it. This was for the best, and nothing I could say or do would convince her otherwise. But that didn't mean that I couldn't hate it with every cell in my body.

I knew what she was looking for; she wanted me to be okay with it. To say that I understood and I was okay with the actions ahead of us.

But I wasn't. Maybe she was the more pragmatic, rational one of the two of us, or she was simply channeling that side of herself. Either way, I couldn't give her what she wanted.

We stood silently through an update on interstate construction and the resulting traffic congestion, an on-scene report from the site of a house fire with fatalities, and discussion of a suicidal jumper off the top of a building right near Millennium Park (the photo was not of anyone I recognized). No mention of a shooting or bodies discovered *at* the park, though. Either the reports hadn't reached the media yet, or the Committee had worked hard to cover up their cover-up.

"I want you to know that I wouldn't change anything," Ariane said, but I kept my eyes focused on the screen. "Not even the end. It was worth it. All of it. Especially you." She was close to tears; I could hear it in her voice.

Fighting the urge to turn and gather her up, I stared hard at the television through rapidly blurring vision as the anchor introduced another clip from the featured story coming up at ten.

They cut to a shot of my mom seated in a molded plastic chair, the background dark, anonymous. I focused on the familiar gestures and intonations from my mother, strangely flattened out and stiff in front of the cameras. She was nervous. I could tell that much from the way she fidgeted before answering questions—shifting in her seat, tugging at the neck of her sweatshirt and then the too-short sleeves, which had been pushed up at the wrists.

"I had no idea what I was getting into," she said, her gaze distant as she answered the reporter. "I . . . We needed the money, and GTX was the largest employer in town. Maybe

I should have been more cautious, but I never dreamed that they were . . . doing what they were doing." She tugged her sweatshirt down in place, smoothing the front, which had been perfectly smooth to begin with.

I frowned. That was . . . weird. Not her behavior—*that* I could write off as nerves. But she had never in her life worn a school team sweatshirt like that. She'd always dressed up more than other moms. Even when my brother had been star quarterback, breaking records left and right (except for my dad's, of course), I'd never seen her in a Hawks shirt.

So for her to go on television in a school sweatshirt now, for an interview that had to be one of the biggest, most important moments in her life, that made no sense. Let alone a shirt supporting . . . I squinted at the screen. Who the hell were the Mustangs?

Of course, it could have just been a giant, convoluted "eff you" to my dad, who was no doubt watching all of this with the vein throbbing in his forehead like a separate heartbeat. Mom was calling his beloved GTX onto the carpet, very publicly.

But as I stared at those red, looping letters, I couldn't get past the feeling that the shirt looked familiar.

"I'm going to go," Ariane said. "The longer we wait . . ." Her words broke off in a pained sigh.

But I couldn't acknowledge it. Couldn't agree to her leaving, even if in such a tacit manner.

"Oh, they were very well aware of what they were doing," my mom said on-screen, her chin lifting in defiance. "Dr. Jacobs and Dr. Laughlin were creating children to experiment on them."

Even though that wasn't the whole truth, the damage from that bombshell wasn't going to go away any time soon. God, my mom might even go to jail. So much for any kind of discreet ending to all of this. Justine was going to be so pissed. . . .

Then it clicked. I knew where I'd seen that shirt before, why it looked so familiar.

"Ariane, wait," I said sharply. I turned to make sure she was listening to me.

She'd just opened the French doors and crossed out of the bedroom, but she came back. Her hair swung loose around her shoulders; I'd been the one to pull the rubber band free from her ponytail. Or, rather, I'd tried and she'd had to help me. Her hair was both heavier and softer than I'd remembered and completely wild, but I'd loved seeing her like that, her white-blond hair a corona around her head and snaking down her naked shoulders, like the last piece of her public "I'm normal" persona had vanished.

I knew, logically, that she was still the slightly strange-looking girl from my Algebra II class. Her skin was too pale, her eyes too dark, her chin too pointed, but now she was so familiar, so beautiful, it made my chest ache like someone had taken a wrecking ball to it.

"Look at what she's wearing," I said, pointing at my mom as soon as Ariane was close.

Ariane blinked at me, taken off guard by my sudden willingness to speak as well as the shift in topic. She glanced at the television. "Yeah, I saw that," she said, her voice rough. "I have no idea who the Mustangs are, but—"

"No—I mean, yeah, but that's not what I mean." I

hesitated. "I think that's Justine's shirt." I didn't know what that meant or why she would do that, but it had to mean something, didn't it? Were the two of them working together? How? Why?

She frowned. "What?"

I nodded rapidly, my certainty growing. "Justine wears stuff like that all the time. It's like part of her 'pay no attention to me' disguise or something, I don't know. But my mom never does, never did." That may have changed a little once she'd left, but I kind of thought it might be too much of a coincidence that she'd choose to wear something like that for an interview of this magnitude. "And . . . I think Justine was wearing it earlier."

Ariane tilted her head to the side, her expression distant, searching her memory. But she'd been so preoccupied during that meeting, I wasn't sure she'd remember. I did, but I'd had weeks of interactions with Justine, in which she'd dressed very similarly.

I saw it the moment the scene fell into place in her brain. She stiffened, her hands balling into fists, and bright color flooding her cheeks. "Damn it," she muttered.

"Okay, but what does it mean?" I demanded.

"Justine set us up is what it means," she said, her expression grim. "You called your mom from her phone. But after we bolted and Justine couldn't catch us, she was stuck." Her mouth curved in a bitter smile. "When she couldn't find us easily enough, she decided to drive us out instead."

"You sound almost like you admire what she did," I said, troubled.

"It's clever." She shook her head. "She used your mother to orchestrate all of this without revealing her own role in it. Which explains how Mara got the media to respond so quickly," she added more to herself than to me. "She might have already had something in the works, talking to a reporter or whatever, but a story backed by an 'anonymous' government source is going to go a lot further than just that of a disgruntled ex-employee."

"Wait, so you're saying Justine putting my mom on the news and exposing us was her way of trying to bring us in?" I asked.

Ariane nodded.

"Didn't she know what they would do?" I asked in disbelief. "That the Committee would hit the panic button?"

"Probably," Ariane said flatly, then she shrugged. "Maybe. She might not have realized how touchy they'd be, but then again, she might also have been counting on it. She wanted to force our hand."

"Even if that got us killed?" I asked incredulously.

"Nothing more effective to prove you're the better option than to take away all the others," she said. "Play her way, or die in the street. A remarkably powerful message."

"And the sweatshirt, that's her signature," I said, slowly putting the pieces together. "She wanted us to see it and know she was behind this." I stared at Ariane. "That's insane."

"No, it's manipulative, brazen, and kind of genius," she said. "She was counting on us being as good as Jacobs and the others claimed in order to stay out of harm's way."

Fat lot of good Adam's skills had done him. About the same mine would have done me. Which made sense, because the only person Justine was really interested in was Ariane. If I happened to survive as well, then, bonus. Jesus.

"If we weren't good enough to stay alive long enough to

hear her message, then we likely wouldn't have been sufficient to meet their needs." She shrugged. "Or, that's probably what she'll say in her report, anyway."

Cold, efficient, and daring—all of which matched everything I knew about Justine.

Ariane shook her head. "It doesn't change anything, though."

An idea flashed at the back of my brain. "Does that mean if we could get to her, she'd be willing to protect us?" Protect Ariane was really what I meant. And that was something Justine would have had to consider before yanking the curtains back on this particular sideshow.

After all, it wouldn't do Justine any good to have manipulated Ariane to her side if she couldn't keep her safe and, therefore, useful.

Ariane eyed me warily. "It doesn't matter. Getting out of here without being caught by whoever's hunting us—"

"But if we could," I persisted.

"Then, yeah, maybe," she said reluctantly. "But it would mean throwing ourselves on her mercy. We'd be under her thumb forever."

"But alive. *We* would be alive." I hit that word extra hard. Not just me. I wasn't looking for half measures; I wanted a solution that would get us both out.

Ariane's shoulders sagged, her face sad and etched with weariness. "You don't understand," she said. "Any leverage I might have had by being a needed resource is gone if I can't live outside their protection. I would have to do whatever they asked of me, and with that kind of absolute power, it's only a matter of time before corruption sets in."

"But eventually, Jacobs, the Committee, whoever, they'll have to stop looking," I pointed out, "and then—"

She reached out as though she would touch my cheek, but then her gaze skittered away from mine and her hand fell away. "Justine, DHS, they would own me, and I wouldn't be able to say no." She shook her head. "I can't do that again, whether it's for a few months or years. I won't."

"You'd rather die?" I demanded.

"Yes," she said, and the truth rang out in that single word. She meant it.

"That's stupid," I said, frustration getting the better of me.

"No," she said sharply. "It's a hard-learned lesson. You want me to believe that I deserve to have my own life, make my own choices. If that's true, then this existence is mine now for as long as I have it. I'm not blindly following someone else's rules, obeying their commands or even giving in to their well-meaning wishes." Her voice softened on those last words. "I have to do what I think is best."

"I'm not asking you to compromise yourself, Ariane," I said, struggling for patience and trying to make her understand. "But you have to give yourself a chance to—"

"This is a moot point," she reminded me. "I don't think we could get to . . ."

". . . live on the scene at the Manderlay Hotel." The news, which had continued as a murmur in the background of our argument, suddenly recaptured my attention as that familiar name registered.

Manderlay Hotel, that was where we'd started this little adventure this morning, which, honestly, felt like years ago.

Ariane, hearing it as well, stopped and swiveled to face the screen.

On the television, a reporter stood in front of a very familiar set of glass doors. She was in front of the west entrance to the hotel, just feet away from where I'd met Ariane this morning. Flashing red and blue lights behind her, along with an area cordoned off in yellow caution tape, showed she was as close as she was allowed.

"We don't have much information at this time, Rebecca," the reporter said to the anchor. "But there are reports of shots fired on the third floor. Also, interestingly . . ." She paused, consulting a notebook in her hand. "According to a source inside the hotel, Dr. Arthur Jacobs and Dr. David Laughlin, of GenTex, Inc. and Laughlin Integrated Enterprises, respectively, are inside, among others."

"Those would be the companies mentioned in our featured story this evening, 'Corruption in the Heartland,' " the anchorwoman prompted.

"That's correct, Rebecca." The onsite reporter seemed a mix of astonished and gleeful. The story was practically writing itself, high ratings included. "Specifically, the two individuals whom Ms. Bradshaw has referenced in her account."

I felt a sudden creeping dread. This didn't make sense. We were missing something, a key piece of information or a fact that changed everything. And when we missed something, that's when things got treacherous. Well, *more* treacherous.

"That's got to be wrong," I said. "Right?" I looked to Ariane. "You said they left."

"They should have," Ariane said with a puzzled frown.

"There is no reason for them to stay. No *good* reason," she amended.

"You think the Committee decided to take them out, too?" I asked.

"No, they'll need Jacobs and Laughlin to answer for Mara's accusations," she answered, but her voice sounded distant, distracted. She was working it through, trying to see the pattern, understand the strategy. "To be scapesheep for the government."

Now I knew she was preoccupied. "Scapegoats," I said.

She didn't acknowledge my correction. She moved past me, scooped my hoodie off the floor, and handed it to me.

"Where are we going?" I asked, turning the sweatshirt right side out before putting it on.

She frowned at me before heading toward the main room of the suite. "*You* are following our original plan: head for the nearest police station and identify yourself as Mara's missing son in need of protection."

"While you do what?" I demanded, following her.

"I will provide the distraction, as discussed," she said, but the caginess of her answer, combined with knowing her as well as I now did, told me all I needed.

I stopped. "You're going to that hotel, by yourself," I accused.

She spun around to face me. "If Jacobs and Laughlin are dead . . ." Her face lit with an unholy determination. "I need to see for myself."

"No. Hell no," I added. "I'm going with you."

Ariane shook her head, her hair falling over her face. She brushed it back impatiently, fumbling for the hair band on her wrist. "There's still a chance this is a trap, something designed to lure us back to them." She pulled her hair up into the sloppy ponytail that I remembered from the months of sitting behind her in math.

But I couldn't allow myself to get caught up in sentiment at the moment. "If Emerson St. John is inside, I need to find him. Preferably alive," I said grimly.

Ariane frowned, registering the tension in my tone or perhaps something from my thoughts. "What's wrong?"

I hesitated. She was going to be so pissed. "Emerson wasn't done with me. You know that. He had to speed up the process to save my life and to be ready for the trials. But there's a tipping point where the body either rejects or accepts the changes going on. It requires monitoring and adjustment. You can't exactly go cold turkey on this stuff." I paused, grimacing in anticipation and memory. "There was a video. Emerson made me watch it so I'd know what I was getting into. There was a rabbit he'd done some testing on. He let the virus run its course without interference. It died . . . badly."

If you could call bleeding out of pretty much every opening of your body for hours something as simple as "dying badly."

She went very, very still, her eyes dark and wide in her pale face. "Why didn't you tell me?

"Because what were you going to do? What could you have done differently?" I asked, holding up my hands in defense. "Besides, it wasn't a guaranteed outcome, so I didn't—"

"You should never have done this," she hissed at me. "You should have stayed home and safe in Wingate. None of this would have happened."

"Too late now," I pointed out. "What's done is done. The only choice now is what to do going forward." I was actually pretty proud of that last bit. It was exactly the kind of logic she would have used against me. Never let it be said that I wasn't learning anything through all of this.

Ariane closed her mouth with an audible click. Her cheeks were flushed and her eyes bright with fury and anguish.

"So, to the Manderlay?" I asked with forced brightness.

She didn't respond.

"I don't need to go with you," I reminded her quietly. "I can just go on my own later, as soon as you're done throwing yourself beneath the wheels of whatever disaster you can find. If there's a chance Emerson St. John is still alive, I need him."

She folded her arms across her chest protectively, and I hated that I'd done that to her, made her close off like that. Then she shook her head. "No, we need a distraction first. That has not changed." Her voice was thick, almost guttural in her distress.

But at least she was speaking to me again, and seemingly agreeing to take me with her.

"I need some supplies." Avoiding my gaze, she pushed past me on her way to the bedroom.

"For the record, I liked 'scapesheep' better," I called after her, trying to lighten the mood.

"Shut up."

Yep, still angry. That was okay. There was very little in this situation that wasn't infuriating, one way or another.

Sirens screamed outside, mingling with the fire alarm shrieking overhead as we exited the Ulta lobby and cleared the overhang with the other guests. When Ariane said we needed a distraction, she wasn't messing around.

A cavalcade of emergency vehicles roared into view. Fire trucks, police cars, ambulances, a little bit of everything.

With their arrival, everyone around us turned to watch them pull in, whispering among themselves, wondering what was going on.

"Come on." Ariane tugged at my hand, pulling me after her as she threaded through the crowd, moving away from the safety in its chaotic midst.

When we reached a clear patch of sidewalk, I watched in surprise as Ariane moved to the curb and lifted a hand to hail a cab, like she'd done it a thousand times.

A yellow taxi pulled up next to us within seconds.

"Trouble at the hotel, eh?" the driver said, gesturing at the Ulta as he pulled away.

"Fire alarm," Ariane said at the same time I said, "Bomb scare." Technically, it had been a little of both, thanks to Ariane's scheming and "supplies."

The driver frowned at us in the rearview mirror, and Ariane's mouth tightened with displeasure.

She straightened up in the seat. "We're switching hotels. The Manderlay, please," she said with smooth authority.

But the cab driver shook his head vehemently. "No, no, you don't want to go there today, lady. They got their own trouble at the Manderlay."

Clearly, he'd heard something over the radio or through his dispatch service.

Ariane stiffened, not expecting the refusal.

"Just get as close as you can," I said easily. "We're meeting my uncle over there."

Ariane held her breath, obviously preparing for further resistance, but the cab driver just shrugged. "Okay." He started whistling tunelessly, weaving in and out of lanes.

I leaned in next to her. "Breathe," I said. "We're fine."

"In this particular second. Maybe. I still wouldn't be shocked to hear someone landing on the roof of the cab," she murmured. "And you're still not forgiven for lying to me."

"I didn't lie," I said, avoiding her gaze.

She glared at me. "Fine, for not telling me, which is a form of lying."

"I don't think you want to use that argument, do you?" I asked, raising my eyebrows.

"You know everything about me, everything," she whispered. "Even the horrible things. Why wouldn't you tell me about the potential consequences?"

"Because I don't know for sure what's going to happen," I said, exasperated. "And . . . I knew you'd take it on." I turned away from her to stare out the side window. "You'd make my decision your problem, like you always do, and I didn't want to make things any more complicated."

"How am I not supposed to take it on when it's a decision you made because of me?" she demanded.

"It wasn't just because of you, Ariane," I said. "Not entirely. I knew the risks, and I wanted what St. John was offering. I could have stopped after the initial injections, had him try to wean me off instead of trying for stabilization, but I didn't."

"Why not?"

"Because it was a chance to be more, to finally be good enough," I said a little too loudly, losing my grip on my frustration. "So I took it, and now I'll have to live with whatever happens." My mouth twisted in a strained smile. "Or not."

She didn't like that answer. Ariane turned her head away from me, staring silently out the side window for the rest of the trip.

Ten minutes later, we pulled up near the Manderlay, finding a scene similar to what we'd just left behind. The front entrance was cordoned off with police caution tape, with uniformed officers patrolling the line. Emergency vehicles occupied the turnaround and the street out front. One news crew was already stationed as close to the tape as possible, with two others pulling equipment out of their trucks.

Some guests still lingered nearby. They were the ones with the uncertain expressions and missing shoes or random pieces of clothing. Others were obviously tourists, passing by and taking in the drama, recording it with their phones.

"This is fine," Ariane said in a clipped voice to the driver. She handed over the last of our cash. Then she got out of the cab without waiting for me, or even looking to see if I followed.

I climbed out of the cab, shutting the door behind me. Ariane was still pissed, obviously. But I suspected at least some of it might have been because she was scared, not for herself but for me. My mind-reading abilities were weak. But fear had a distinct flavor to it, for lack of a better term. It was metallic, cold, powerful. And that's what's radiating from her more than anything, even anger.

And she kind of had a point. Knowing what I knew now, I had to admit that, given the chance to do it all over again, I would probably choose differently. Adam had been pretty close to perfect as a candidate for Emerson's experiment, and even being skilled and better than the average human hadn't saved him.

Everyone had limits, blind spots, weaknesses, peculiarities. Maybe the key was just figuring out how to live with them. I loved Ariane for who she was, including the parts she didn't like and other people feared or hated.

Was it so impossible that she felt the same way about me? Maybe not.

I caught up with Ariane when she paused on the sidewalk, near a clump of people watching the spectacle.

"What do you want to do?" I asked.

Her expression had clicked over to that distant, evaluating mask that I recognized. She'd retreated within herself, letting the training she'd had and the nonhuman instincts she'd been born with rise to the surface.

"When the GTX guards brought me here, they used that garage." She tipped her head to indicate the structure looming over us. "There was a walkway to the hotel."

Which would mean fewer people watching, maybe even the possibility of no police at that particular entrance.

But a few steps toward the garage entrance revealed red and blue flashing lights and squad cars blocking the ramp to the upper levels of the garage. The officers inside the cars were on the radio, and their stiff posture screamed, "We are not kidding around."

"They are taking this really seriously," I muttered.

She nodded, her head cocked at an angle and her forehead wrinkled with concentration as she focused in on their thoughts. "Hostages. That's what they're worried about. They're not talking about it with the media yet, but that's what I'm hearing. They think someone's still alive in there." She frowned.

I felt a spark of hope. Someone still alive was good. Even

better if it was Emerson St. John and not Dr. Jacobs or Laughlin. Though, the odds of just one of them surviving weren't good. The scar on my stomach began to itch and burn again.

"But they can't get confirmation, so they don't want to go in yet. They're waiting for something . . . maybe." She shook her head in frustration. "I don't know, the adrenaline is making their minds . . . buzzy. Hard to read."

I nodded. My limited experiences with telepathy had given me more than a taste of that. It was amazing she could pick out anything from the noise, in my opinion.

"What about another entrance to the hotel?" I asked. "They have to have a door for deliveries or whatever, right?"

She nodded absently, her mind working to make all the pieces fit. "Yes, I'm sure they do. But it will likely be under guard equal to this. They're trying to make sure no one escapes."

I edged toward the hotel for another look. "Ariane. What about a window on the side? They have all the doors blocked, but if we circled the block and came through from the other direction, we might be able to get in—"

She followed me and then shook her head. "It will take too long. And that's additional exposure for us, wandering farther away from the hotel. Eventually the shooter may figure out that we came back here, if he or she hasn't already."

"What do you have in mind?" I asked. She had *that* look on her face now, that sharp, determined one that was also somehow empty of feeling. The one that said she'd ceased to see the human factor and simply viewed everyone and everything as obstacles to her ultimate goal.

It sent an instinctive shiver of dread through me. I wasn't afraid of Ariane. But occasionally, I was smart enough to be afraid of what she could do.

"I don't suppose I can talk you into staying here or going to the police on your own," she said, her eyes trained on the activity in the distance.

"No."

"I don't know what will happen," she warned. "It may end badly." She paused. "Very badly."

If Emerson St. John was already dead inside that building, "very badly" was pretty much my only option anyway, unless Justine had had someone else studying up on his research. "What's the plan?" I asked, though it may have taken a bit more effort than usual to push the words free.

"Sometimes simple and direct is the best." But that was all she'd say.

She led the way down the sidewalk toward the hotel, moving confidently.

People moved out of her way, perhaps sensing something, a potential threat, that even their conscious minds didn't register.

I tagged along in her wake as she crossed the side street and reached hotel property. Skirting the turnaround, she kept to the road, moving around the news vans and equipment on the perimeter of the police line.

Three police officers moved around inside the cordoned-off area, talking to each other on their radios and generally just looking intimidating while blocking off the main entrance.

Ducking around the last news van, Ariane headed closer to the hotel, along the short side of the caution tape line.

No hesitation, no fear. That probably should have been a clue. But honestly, I thought she had something up her sleeve, some opening or opportunity that I'd just missed. By the time I figured out what she had in mind, it was too late for second-guessing either her plan or my decision to go along with it.

I followed her lead and then watched in disbelief as she slipped smoothly underneath the caution tape.

Damn it.

I ducked beneath the caution tape after her, my heart hammering.

But the officers were preoccupied with the people outside the tape, watching to make sure the reporters weren't edging too close, and keeping the crowd at a safe distance.

None of them bothered to turn and look behind them. At least, not at first.

"Hey! They're going inside!" someone shouted.

"You, stop!" That was a new voice, one filled with authority and unused to being disobeyed. Definitely a cop.

But Ariane had already reached the revolving door, so I kept moving. She pushed through, and I scrambled in after her, sharing the same glass division to save time.

It spilled us out into the lobby, which was empty, surprisingly.

Just inside, Ariane pivoted, raised her hand, and stopped the revolving door in motion as the first officer attempted to follow us in.

"The bolts," I said quickly. "At the bottom on a couple of the sections. They lock into the ground." I pointed, and she nodded.

A second later, they snapped into place with a solid-sounding clunk that made the glass reverberate, like someone had tapped on it with a hammer.

"That's, um, not going to work for very long," I said, watching the trio of officers shouting into their radios and glaring at us.

I swallowed hard.

"It doesn't need to," Ariane said, unperturbed. "This way."

She moved away from the entrance, heading deeper into the lobby, her steps virtually silent on the black-and-white tile floor. Every thud of my shoes sounded magnificently loud by comparison.

Ariane stopped in the far corner of the lobby in front of the small alcove holding the elevator bank.

I raised my eyebrows. "The elevators? You're kidding," I said in a whisper.

"Why not?" she asked, but not like she was really interested, more just filling the silence.

But I persisted. "You're supposed to take the stairs in emergency—" I began.

"Which means that's where everyone else will be," she said.

Uh. Okay. "Sometimes they shut down the elevators—"

The quiet chime of the arriving elevator cut off the rest of my words. "Never mind," I muttered.

She slipped in as soon as the doors were open far enough, and I hurried in after her.

A burst of running footsteps hit the lobby floor, no doubt someone had taken the stairs. The doors shut, though, before anyone reached us.

Feeling vaguely dizzy from the buzz of adrenaline and fear, I leaned against the wall, closed my eyes, and tried to catch my breath. The soft music playing overhead was still on. It sounded like an instrumental version of Nirvana's "Smells Like Teen Spirit." That was wrong in so many ways.

"Do you have a plan?" I asked Ariane. "I mean, the doors are going to open and we're going to be right there in front of them." Probably at least a dozen police officers, maybe SWAT guys, firefighters and EMTs . . .

"No," she said, after a moment. "Honestly, I wasn't sure we'd get this far."

I opened my eyes to check her expression. Nope, she wasn't joking. "Maybe a little less honesty would be better," I said.

"I need to see for myself," she said quietly. "It would be too easy for someone to simply say that Jacobs and the others were dead, particularly if this is a cover-up." She shifted, tilting her head until she caught my gaze, her dark eyes so serious and sad. "I don't want to live the rest of my life, however short it is, looking over my shoulder and—"

"I know, I know," I said, reaching out and taking her hand in mine. Her fingers were so damn cold, and I realized that no matter how little she showed on the outside, she had to be scared.

"I love you," I said, moved by a sudden wave of affection and needing to say the words out loud.

Her mouth curved up in a small smile. " 'I know.' "

"Right. Because you're Han Solo in this scenario," I said, trying to tease to lighten the mood and because the thought that she was being predictive—Han Solo ends up pretty much dead moments after he says that in *Empire*—killed me.

But she didn't have time to respond, because, unlike the endless moments it had taken for the elevator doors to close, it took mere seconds for us to reach the third floor.

Before the doors opened, I could hear the squawk of radios and low, urgent voices. This must be the place.

She let go of my hand and moved to face the doors. "Stand behind me," she said, eyeing me carefully, as if expecting me to fight her on this.

And you know what? I wasn't going to argue. We all had strengths—mine, at the moment, did not happen to be stopping a hail of bullets. I wasn't stupid enough to let my ego get in the way. It wasn't bulletproof, either.

I nodded and stepped back as the doors opened.

A uniformed officer, his broad face red and sweating, greeted us with a glare as we crossed the threshold out into the small alcove housing the elevator doors.

"Brody, what the hell is this?" he said into the radio on his shoulder. "I got kids coming up in the elevator."

Brody's response came in a rush of static that was mostly indecipherable. ". . . came in the front . . . locked the damn doors somehow" was all that came through.

The big cop in front of us—his tag said Donnelly—narrowed his eyes at us.

"I don't mean anyone any harm," Ariane said, her voice mild.

And some part of me felt the insane urge to laugh. *Take me to your leader* was probably next.

"But I need to see inside the conference room," she continued. "The one called Meadowlands." As if there might be a different conference room holding their attention.

Donnelly's expression shifted from dark fury to disbelief and then confusion as he looked back and forth between me and Ariane, pausing to take in her appearance from head to toe. Uh-oh.

"Chandler, give me a status on the room," he demanded into the radio on his shoulder, his gaze glued to Ariane as if I'd ceased to exist. If he'd recognized me from the news, he might very well think she was involved in the "abduction."

"Unchanged." This voice came out much clearer and with a faint echo from down the hall, closer to the conference room.

Ariane tilted her head, listening to someone's thoughts. I wasn't sure if it was Donnelly or the more distant Chandler. Either way, she got something. "Oh," she said, after a moment, sounding surprised. "Okay."

"Okay what?" I asked warily.

"Stay close," she said. "Move quickly. And I'm sorry."

"For what, exactly?" I asked, feeling my stomach clench with dread.

But she didn't answer. "Let's go," she said, sidestepping away from Donnelly and waving for me to follow.

"No, no, you're not going anywhere," Donnelly said in a booming voice meant to intimidate. And it was working.

He reached for his service weapon, but Ariane was ready.

She lifted her hand to direct her power, pinning Donnelly to the closed elevator doors on the opposite wall, his body frozen in position, like a cartoon character who'd been slammed back and just hadn't fallen over yet, usually with a matching chunk of wall.

"Please don't struggle," she said to him. "I don't want to push too hard. You could get hurt."

His eyes bulged as if she'd waved a knife in his face, threatening him.

And to be fair, to him, that probably sounded way more like an intent to harm than the fair warning it was.

But she didn't have time to reassure him further, because the sound of running footsteps was coming toward us from the other end of the hall—Donnelly's fellow officers responding to his raised voice. He hadn't had time to radio for help. He might not have thought it was necessary. It was very easy, and stupid, to underestimate Ariane.

They stopped abruptly as we entered the hallway from the elevator alcove. There were four of them, all CPD officers, and they immediately dropped into formation, two of them on their knees, the other two standing, and four guns pointing straight at us as they shouted:

"Stop!"

"Don't move!"

"Raise your hands and get on your knees!"

Contradictory orders, and Ariane, of course, ignored them, focusing her attention on holding the men in place.

Only the change in their expressions, from harsh and commanding to alarmed, revealed that she'd succeeded.

Several strained curses followed.

"Please stay calm. I won't hurt anyone," she said, removing the weapons from their hands with a gesture, neatly and easily, without so much as a stray shot. With the guns floating in the air ahead of her, she simply stepped between the men, easing through the narrow gap between them.

Jesus. I followed—a much trickier move for someone of my size—and I could feel the force they were exerting against her hold. If sheer muscle and determination (and pissed-offness) could break them loose, they would have done it.

Unfortunately, that was no match for what Ariane had working against them. She could stop a freaking heart. Arms and legs were just no contest for her.

As soon as we were clear of them, though, three more came charging toward us with more of the same. Guns. Threats.

Ariane neatly brushed them aside, but one of them recovered faster, breaking loose as we passed them.

I was closest, so he made a grab for me first.

With a strained expression, Ariane swiped at the air in front of him, a gesture that should have sent him reeling, or at least knocked him back a step or two, but it seemed only to slow him down, and barely.

She was exerting too much of her energy holding the others in place, I realized. That telekinetic ability, however amazing it might be, was a finite resource. It could only be used to do so many things at once. Emerson had treated us to many lectures on that topic at the lab.

I focused on the officer and concentrated on where I wanted him to be, just as Adam had condescendingly instructed during our sessions in the lab.

The officer slammed into the wall, his head hitting with a disturbing thunk that sent a shudder through me. His eyes snapped closed, but his chest still rose and fell. Unconscious, or maybe just stunned. Either way, I hadn't meant to push quite that hard.

"Shit. Sorry," I muttered to him.

Ariane stared at me.

"I got it," I said tightly. Yeah, for the moment.

With a surprised arch of her eyebrows, Ariane nodded, not bothering to argue with me. Which could only be a further sign that I was right. She was tapped out or close to it.

She moved on down the hall—good God, how long was this hallway? It felt much longer when people kept trying to attack us—and I turned, pressing my back against hers to keep an eye on them.

Always cover your six. That was basic Call of Duty strategy. Just never thought I'd actually use it in real life.

I could feel a dull throb starting in the center of my brain, and blood trickled out of my nose and into my mouth at a rate that was unprecedented. Damn it. We needed to hurry up, or I was going to bleed to death before someone got a chance to shoot me.

Ariane stopped abruptly, and I glanced over my shoulder to see what the issue was.

Outside the first conference room, dubbed Sherwood Forest, according to the metal plaque on the wall, five, no, six bodies were laid out on the floor, head to toe, and three on each side of the hall. Oversized sheets, which had obviously been appropriated from a hotel supply closet somewhere, covered them.

Oh God.

Ariane inched forward and bent down to grab the corner of one sheet. I turned to watch.

A pair of EMTs leaned out from a room down the hall, and Ariane froze.

But they looked at her, at the police behind us, and then abruptly retreated, shutting the door after themselves. Smart move.

Ariane returned her attention to the sheet and the body it covered.

I held my breath, not sure if it was out of anticipation or dread at seeing a familiar face. If it was Jacobs under there, I'd celebrate as surely as Ariane. Though that would also drastically raise the odds that Emerson was beneath one of the other sheets.

But when Ariane flipped the cover back, the man was a stranger, dressed in the security team uniform. The bright red GTX logo on his sleeve identified him as one of Jacobs's men.

She dropped the sheet in place and repeated the same process for the corpse across the hall. Another GTX guard. So was the one after that.

But the next three were Laughlin's guys.

Six security guards dead, three from GTX and three from Laughlin.

Weirdly, though, only two of the sheets had blood on them, the men having been shot. The other guys were just . . . dead.

What had happened here?

Ariane frowned and left the last of the bodies to step toward the door to the Meadowlands room door.

"Get in, get in now," I said, panting. I had no idea what her endurance was, but I knew mine, what little I had, was fading fast. A quick glance back showed movement at the far end of the hall, someone working his way loose from the hold one of us had put on him.

She paused long enough to wave her hand at the guns, still floating in the air a few feet from us, directing them into a tall green can with a recycling symbol on the other side of hall. They landed inside with a cascade of echoing clangs and thumps. Then she tugged on the silver doorknob with a finger, but it didn't so much as budge. To my complete and utter shock, she then lifted her hand, made a fist and . . .

. . . knocked. "It's Ariane," she said.

"What the hell?" I spluttered.

But the door silently popped open a few inches and stayed that way, even though there was no sign of a hand.

Ariane pulled the door back just far enough to squeeze through, locking her hand around my wrist and pulling me through after her.

As if I'd want to be left behind in the hall.

But as it turned out, it wasn't me she was worried about making that decision.

The door closed behind me with a decisive snap, leaving no alternative for escape, even if I would have wanted to.

I hadn't actually considered what we might find inside the room. Some combination of Jacobs, Laughlin, and St. John, in states ranging from alive to dead and somewhere in between. I suspected the Committee would be long gone.

In that one aspect, I was right. There was no sign of the Committee. But everything else was pretty much beyond anything I could have imagined.

The table that had been Emerson's this morning was flung across the room, leaning against the one that had been Jacobs's, and broken glass and the shattered remains of laptops sprayed across the floor.

In the far right corner, I found Emerson, sitting on the floor, his knees drawn up to his chest like a kid sent to the naughty corner in kindergarten, only in this case it looked far more like a refuge than a punishment.

He saw me watching him and gave a tiny shake of his head, as if to tell me to get out or vehemently disagreeing with this version of reality.

Yeah, right there with you.

The table that had been Laughlin's, on the right side of the room, had been upended, the legs sticking up in the air now, with more of the same kind of destruction and debris around it. It looked like a small, very specific tornado had torn through the room.

Which, from one perspective, wasn't all that far from the truth.

In the center of the room, in what had been the open space between the tables and was just now empty space in general, Dr. Jacobs knelt on the floor, his hands bloodied as he applied pressure to a leg wound on one of his guards. The only living one left, actually.

The last Laughlin Integrated guard was dead at his employer's feet, merely a foot away.

But no one was paying any attention to any of this.

Because Dr. Laughlin, his face a mask of effort, his hair rumpled, and blood splattered across the front his white lab coat, held a gun trained on someone else.

There in the middle of the room, her back angled to the corner so she could see anyone approaching, stood a very familiar figure.

Her white shirt was bloodied on the left side, and that arm hung slack at her side, as though it were barely connected to her body. More like something she'd picked up by brushing too close, a dead leaf or a piece of lint.

Blood dripped down her left hand, plinking into a growing

puddle on the floor where the carpeting had already absorbed as much as it could hold. But her right hand was raised against Laughlin, clearly the reason for his preternatural stillness and the only thing keeping him from firing.

The room crackled with an electric tension between them, as if lightning might still strike.

"It took you long enough," Ford said to us through gritted teeth.

CHAPTER 19

Ariane

ASSESS THE SITUATION.

Even in the hardest, most surprising situations, that combination of training and instincts always surfaced, whispering like a ghost in the back of my mind.

You're not human. Don't react like one. That was my father, or rather a perfect reproduction of his voice in my head, lecturing me. *Don't freeze up, don't hesitate. Use what makes you different. Analyze, weigh the odds against your objective, and take action.*

The room was torn apart, tables tossed aside, broken glass, laptops shattered and spread across the ground. Power cords and wires still snapped and hissed from where they'd been torn apart.

And in the center of the room, Dr. Jacobs knelt on the ground, a GTX guard at his feet. Jacobs's hands were bloodied, pressed as they were to the guard's leg wound in an attempt at first aid, but my creator appeared otherwise unharmed.

Disappointment spiraled through me, followed immediately by a hot rush of fury. He was alive. So many others were dead because of him, even if not directly by his hand. I'd been so hoping to find him under one of those sheets in the hall. The loss of that possibility, along with the discovery of him in here pretending to be a human being with feelings as he attended to the guard, opened up a well of despair and desperate hatred so deep I could feel it coring out the center of me, obliterating some essential piece of myself.

"107," Dr. Jacobs said with relief, as if I were one to be greeted with such calmness, such lack of fear. As if I were such a knowable, controllable quantity that he didn't have to worry.

The lights overhead flashed and jumped in response to the power growing in and around me, but I clamped down on it, much to the howling rage of my human side. I couldn't afford to lose control here. We were all balanced on a line thinner than a human hair. No, a line thinner and finer than my own hair.

Because not two feet away from Dr. Jacobs was Dr. Laughlin, blood spattered across the pristine white of his lab coat. The last Laughlin Integrated guard was dead at his feet, and Laughlin was holding one of the guard's sidearms, aiming directly at Ford's head.

I wasn't surprised to find her here; I'd gotten that much from the first policeman's thoughts, the one guarding the elevator. He couldn't figure out how I'd gotten out of the conference room without anyone noticing.

But I hadn't expected to find her in this state.

Ford stood perfectly still, swaying perhaps a little but

making no move to run away or duck. Her left arm hung useless at her side, her white shirt dark with blood.

But her right hand was raised against Laughlin.

I could see the tendons in Laughlin's hand and neck standing out with his efforts to pull the trigger, but there was no movement and certainly no bullet being fired.

Ford had him tight. Which did not explain why she hadn't pulled the gun away from him already or simply stopped his heart. I could try to take the gun from him, but I didn't want to upset whatever delicate balance she had established. If we slipped up for even a microsecond, the gun would go off, and Ford was standing far too close.

The air in the room was thick with anticipation, like the moments before a big thunderstorm.

"Ford?" I asked cautiously, trying to concentrate without losing my temper or my hold on the seven full-grown angry men in the hallway outside. Otherwise they'd be barging in here within seconds, and that seemed like a very, very bad idea.

"The humans," Ford said, her voice strained. "The ones outside."

"They're still out there," I said. "I'm holding them."

"Let go of them and take the doors," she said, a fine tremor running through her whole body.

"Oh, think very carefully who you want to take direction from, 107," Laughlin said, his smile all teeth.

"She's not yours to command," Dr. Jacobs said indignantly from his position on the floor. It seemed as though he would raise a hand to gesture at Laughlin, but the abortive move of his shoulder muscles indicated that he'd thought better and decided to stay still. Or maybe he had no choice.

All the better.

A light burst overhead, raining down glass and sparks, and he hunched his shoulders against it. "I'm not yours to command either," I said, pushing hate into the words.

"Ariane?" Zane asked, his voice shaking. His skin was clammy beneath my hand on his wrist. I still had ahold of him, and a glance back revealed blood running freely from his nose and past his mouth to drip off his chin. I realized, then, he was still holding on to the one officer out in the hall, the one he'd stopped for me.

"Do it," I said to him. I let go of Zane's arm and released the men in the hallway, shifting my attention to the doors. Not just the handle, but the entire surface. I didn't want anyone getting the creative idea to remove the hinges or bash through the wood with a fire ax. Holding the doors shut and protected against any form of interference was easier than keeping all those people motionless. It was like dropping a boulder to pick up a single piece of paper; it felt like almost no effort at all.

Almost immediately, the blood flow from Ford's arm slowed, and she seemed steadier on her feet.

Because . . . Ford had been holding the doors shut, keeping Laughlin from firing (and likely holding Jacobs still as well), and stanching her wound. Holy crap.

I checked on Zane, who had leaned against the wall, his face gray with bright fever patches of pink, his arm smeared with red where he'd wiped his face.

He nodded at me.

"Where's the Committee?" I asked, mostly to Ford, but really to anyone who would answer. In the hallway, I could hear shouting and running steps. The door handle rattled, and then someone tugged, trying to open the door. But they would not get in. I could hold it all day and against all of them, if need be.

"They were gone before I arrived," she said. She let out slow breath that sounded ragged and fluid filled. Where was she wounded? I couldn't tell from behind. If she'd been shot, the most likely scenario, the bullet might have nicked a lung.

Ford and I didn't always see eye to eye, but she was . . . We were all we had left. We were the only ones. I didn't want her to die.

"They killed him, Ariane," she said, her voice flat. "They killed Carter. They sent him out as a target. I figured it out, what they'd done, and I was trying to find him. . . ." She shook her head. "I felt it when he died. He knew for a moment. He felt pain, sorrow, and aloneness because I wasn't there." Her voice rose with anguish and hatred and grief. "I. Wasn't. There! *They* did this. *They* planned this."

My eyes stung with tears, and I bit my lip hard enough to taste blood and regret. "I know, I'm sorry. I was trying to find you both, but I wasn't fast enough. . . ."

"That is true," she said. "But it is not your fault. It is theirs." That single word contained a universe of raw rage, untempered and destructive.

There wouldn't be anything left of Laughlin by the time someone outside this room reached him. He would be unrecognizable, not just as himself but anything human. She would take him apart piece by piece.

And I couldn't bring myself to feel anything but relief, and perhaps a little glee, at the prospect. Inhuman? Perhaps, but so was I.

"Ford, where is your target?" I asked. Before this went any further or devolved into chaos, I needed to know. I had no particular fondness for Rachel, but if she was dead . . .

"Ari," Zane said.

I glanced at him, and he nodded to the back left corner of the room. *A corner you should have checked,* the imitation of father's voice scolded in my head. *You left yourself vulnerable to attack.* What else was new?

Emerson St. John sat, wide-eyed, with his back against the wall. He was well out of the line of fire for the moment.

And behind him, almost hidden by his body . . . Rachel Jacobs, her fist pressed against her mouth as if she were afraid of what words might escape against her will, but seemingly unharmed.

At least there was that. One life saved. Or one more at stake in this room.

"I knew you were involved in this," Rachel hissed as soon as our eyes met, her voice shaking with anger and fear. "I was minding my own business in the lip gloss section, and *she* comes out of nowhere." She glanced at Ford and shuddered, making no move to leave the corner where she was huddled. Whether that was the effect of Ford's presence or because Rachel had just watched people get shot right in front of her, I wasn't sure.

"Are you all right?" It had to be asked.

Rachel shook her head, a jerky, uneven motion. "She dragged me through the city all the way to the park," she said, her voice thick with tears. "And then . . . and then she pushed that guy off a building." Rachel swallowed hard, pale beneath her tan.

It took me a second to put Rachel's words in context. The suicidal jumper mentioned on the news.

"The man with the gun," Ford said tightly. "The one who killed Adam before I could."

The assassin the Committee had sent after us. Ford must have arrived in the park just a little before we did. In time to see Adam get shot but not soon enough to save Carter. Then she'd tracked the shooter with Rachel in tow, as leverage most likely, and took her revenge.

That made a strange kind of sense.

"This is your fault. You just can't stand to see me happy. It's like your mission to destroy my life," Rachel said, her face a mess of tears, mascara, and sweat.

"It's not, actually." I could not understand why everyone kept assuming that this girl, the closest thing I had to an archnemesis, quite frankly, meant anything significant to me.

I'd have been more upset over the death of any number of other people, as cruel as that sounded. Using Rachel had been a risk, an unnecessary one as far as I could see, but maybe the Committee had been aiming to hurt Jacobs as well. Who knew? It didn't matter now, with more pressing matters at hand.

I turned my attention back to Ford. "What's your exit—"

Laughlin laughed suddenly, a loud sound that echoed in the almost-empty room, drowning out the sound of activity in the hallway beyond.

I looked over, startled. I didn't see anything particularly amusing about this situation.

"You don't know, do you?" he asked me. His gaze bounced from me to Rachel and then back to Ford. "None of you do."

Ford tensed.

Jacobs glared at Laughlin, his face red and the veins in his forehead an alarming shade of blue. "Don't," he said, staring down his former mentee. He sounded almost frightened.

But Laughlin ignored him. "Such a supposedly superior specimen and it's taken you this long?"

Unformed instinct told me to shy away, to duck my head and cover my ears to stop his words from reaching me. Some might describe it as seeing a wave and knowing it will pull you under and yet being unable to do anything to escape. I wouldn't. I still hadn't managed to see the ocean.

"I'd have thought you'd piece this together on your own, even subconsciously," Laughlin continued, and dread swelled in me, but I couldn't bring myself to stop him, to stop whatever was coming next.

"That girl"—he tipped his head at Rachel—"is your niece," he said, cracking my world open with his carefully enunciated words. "Or your half sister, depending on how you look at it. You are quite the twisted family."

"What?" Rachel shrieked from her corner.

I didn't move, couldn't speak. Dizziness washed over me, and a high-pitched buzzing started in my ears.

"Shut up," Zane snapped at Laughlin. "He's lying. Ariane, don't listen—"

Laughlin *tsk*ed at him. "I don't need to lie, young man. Three DNA sources are required for this kind of work. The extraterrestrial source and a *fertilized* human egg. It doesn't work any other way," Laughlin said, shaking his head with a mock sorrowful look. "And Arthur here didn't want to take any chances. He wanted to make sure he was using top-notch genetic material. What better than his own?" He laughed. "And it would have been a waste not to use the perfectly good daughter-in-law of childbearing age at his fingertips, wouldn't it? Especially one with fertility issues who was eager to have another child right away, one who was already used to medical assistance and invasive procedures."

My stomach churned. The blond woman in the photo, the one Jacobs had shown me. She'd looked familiar . . . because she looked like me? Or because she looked like Rachel? Like both of us?

"He used the harvested eggs she'd preserved as part of her previous fertility efforts in his experiment. When the most promising one split into twins, we . . . obtained the other half for implantation," Laughlin said with a lurch of his shoulders that might have been a shrug had he been capable of such mobility.

I summoned the image from the photo in my memory. Her fair complexion and hair were nothing like Rachel's, but those fine eyebrows, high cheekbones, and that smile, the way the lines broke between her mouth and cheeks, in the shape of perfect sevens, forward and backward . . . I sucked in a deep breath, struggling to get air circulating in my lungs again.

Rachel's version of that smile was tighter, pissier, but it was the same. My own resemblance was murkier, harder to see beneath the alien influences, but still possible. I'd never had cause to look for it before.

But more than any potential resemblances, what made me believe what Laughlin was saying was that I could so easily see Dr. Jacobs doing exactly just that. Using his daughter-in-law because it suited his needs. His project. His pursuit of fame. He'd done it before.

My knees wobbled underneath my weight, as if the realization carried physical mass. Ford and I were twins; that was not news to anyone who looked at us. The fact that we were actual sisters—rather than clones—was new but within reason. The connection to Rachel, to Dr. Jacobs, though . . . my brain could not seem to adjust to that idea, finding it all sharp edges and slippery sides.

"Your criticism of my work and my methods is of little interest to anyone," Jacobs snarled at Laughlin, but it was a weak, ineffective defense that everyone ignored, a papier-mâché dam against a tsunami.

"It's not true," Zane said. "It can't be. Rachel and Ariane are the same age."

"Yes, exactly!" Rachel rallied, nodding rapidly. "That."

"I doubt that's true," Laughlin said easily. "You, Jacobs girl. When is your birthday?"

Rachel glared at him but answered through clenched teeth. "December twenty-sixth."

"Ariane?" Zane asked.

I shook my head. "I don't know, they never said. Sometime in August, I think, is what my father—"

"See?" Zane demanded, triumph and relief coloring his voice. "They're not twins, and there wasn't enough time for both of them."

Laughlin laughed again.

And this time, I knew why. Staring down Dr. Jacobs—my father, oh my God—as he avoided looking in my direction, I heard his words about my "surrogate" echoing in my head. "Six months," I managed, my voice a hoarse whisper.

"What?" Zane asked.

I couldn't look at him, couldn't move, feeling rooted to the spot. "It's only six months from implantation to full term for hybrids," I said, forcing myself to speak louder. "He told me that." Even though he'd lied about everything else, including the identity of my surrogate.

So, Rachel's mother had given birth to her in December of the year before I was born. Then, evidently, either she'd volunteered, or Jacobs had talked her into another pregnancy. If she'd gotten pregnant in February, that would have been more than enough time for . . . more than enough time for me.

I lifted my gaze to meet Rachel's, and she read the truth in my expression, her face paling further.

"No," she said, shaking her head fiercely. "No. I am not . . . my mother is not . . ."

Laughlin smirked at her. "I heard Jacobs had to have her committed, eventually," he continued in a faux whisper. "She never recovered from the loss of her second child. Rumor has it, she didn't believe him about the late-term 'miscarriage' and went a little crazy. All because he thought it would be better, more natural for 107 to be carried in the womb of her genetic mother."

Rachel looked poison at me. "New Harbors in Malibu. Off and on since I was eight."

Ford turned just enough to see me. It was hard to tell, but even she looked shaken by this revelation.

My eyes burned with unshed tears. My mother. Her mother. Rachel's mother. The same woman. Alive. Locked away in a facility in California. But before that, had I passed her on the street? In the hallways at school? I had no memory of ever seeing Rachel with her mother. But she'd been there, at least for a while, within reach.

"It was completely unnecessary, of course, because as you can see, Ford turned out just fine after gestation in a surrogate," Laughlin said dismissively.

The fact that Laughlin could describe Ford as "fine" with even a reasonably straight face was yet another sign of his complete detachment from reality.

But the overwhelming punch of realization was reserved for that one big piece of news. Dr. Jacobs had used his own DNA to create me. We were related. I was even more closely related to him than Rachel was. I was his daughter.

I stared at him. Those dark, soulless eyes in his face, the ones that had shone with eagerness and scientific curiosity during my most horrible moments in the lab, they were mine.

I'd always hated looking at myself in the mirror without my tinted contacts, seeing the alien-ness in the almost-black color of my eyes and the nearly indistinguishable iris.

But maybe that wasn't it at all. Or not entirely. Was it possible I'd recognized that similarity on a level without even realizing it?

My stomach lurched, and I gagged, cold rushing over me, turning my skin damp with sweat.

"Ariane," Zane breathed behind me. But I couldn't look at him. How could I?

"107," Jacobs said with an attempt at regaining authority. "There's no need to overreact. Our early specimens were failing to thrive. I did just what was necessary to—"

"That's all you care about, isn't it?" Rachel demanded, her voice choked with tears and hatred.

I turned to see her rising to her feet unsteadily.

"What your *project* needs." The bitterness and despair behind her words curdled the air. And as much as I despised her at times, I didn't blame her one bit. He'd used his family, destroyed their lives, and left them with nothing but lies.

Rachel lurched from her corner in Dr. Jacobs's direction, her hands stretched out in claws as if she might strangle him or tear at his throat, but a look from Ford froze her in place, made her cower.

I, however, was under no such restriction. The urge to kill Dr. Jacobs thrummed beneath my skin. He wasn't just a stain on humanity. He was a stain on me. In me. Between the cells. In places I could never scrub clean.

All the emotion rioting within me bled away with a single epiphany: I would never be free of this man. Of GTX. Of what I was.

Everything I hated was part of me. No matter how far I ran or long I lived, I would never, ever escape it. I would question every decision, every act, looking for signs of that self-righteous arrogance and inhumanity in me.

I wanted to scream. To cry. To end it.

"Ariane," Ford said softly, catching my attention. Her gaze locked with mine, staring at her mirror image of my own face.

We were the same. And that, somehow, was reassuring in this mess. I wasn't alone. She didn't have the memories I had of Dr. Jacobs in the lab and what he'd done, but she understood, better than anyone, what it meant. Why the thought of it made me want to crawl out of my own skin.

"Hold the others for me?" she asked, and understanding passed between us. She couldn't do everything at once, but with me here . . . we could finish it. End everything right here and now. I'd hold Jacobs and Emerson St. John and Rachel while she killed Laughlin. Then we'd complete the work together. The deserving would be punished.

"Ariane," Zane said, sounding alarmed. "If you do this, if you kill him, you won't be able to come back from it."

But did that matter? Coming back . . . to what? What was there left for me?

I nodded slowly at Ford, my neck creaking with the effort.

"Even if you make it out of this building somehow, you can't survive without the Quorosene, Ford. You'll die tomorrow. The next day, perhaps, at the latest," Laughlin said, realizing his efforts to direct our attention to Jacobs instead had failed. His gun arm was starting to shake. Fatigue, or perhaps his first taste of genuine fear?

The thought of the latter gave me a greasy feeling of pleasure and satisfaction. I *wanted* him to be afraid. And the depth of that desire terrified me. All along I'd been attributing my darkest impulses to the alien side of myself. And instead, it could just as easily be my humanity.

I felt like a person with no country to claim, no safe space for home. I had no place to stand with the water rising and no ability to swim. I was nothing but equal parts unknown and despised. I'd never realized how much I'd counted on the human side of myself to be something not . . . awful.

"Yes," Ford said to Laughlin, lifting her right shoulder in a shrug that looked painful. "But you're overestimating our desire to survive against our eagerness to repay what was given to us."

I found myself nodding again. Not in agreement but in

understanding of the inevitability of this moment. Of course it would end this way. We were the created rising against the creators. How else but in blood, pain, and fear? It was our legacy.

But the worst part, the bit that made me feel smaller and more lost to myself than ever before, was I couldn't think of a single reason why it shouldn't end this way.

CHAPTER 20

Zane

ARIANE HAD GONE SO STILL, SHE MIGHT AS WELL HAVE been in Ford's grip like the others, except for the faint trembling over her entire body.

She was teetering on the edge. I could sense it. She wanted to listen to Ford. She wanted to give in.

If she did, it would destroy her. I understood the urge to kill Jacobs, more so now than ever. But the kind of person Ariane was, it would break something in her. She was a defender of the weak, the innocent. This girl had been so guilt-stricken over the death of a mouse, it had blocked out a portion of her mind for years. Stopping that guy's heart temporarily, just to get entry to the trials, had pushed her toward self-sacrifice at every opportunity, made her believe she wasn't worthy of breathing anymore. Murdering someone in cold blood, even a person she hated, would end her. She wouldn't be able to live without punishing herself. Ariane, the girl I loved, would disappear beneath waves of misery and self-loathing.

Running on nothing but adrenaline and panic, I straightened up, keeping ahold of the wall until I was sure I was steady, and then I reached out for Ariane.

As soon as my fingers touched hers, she pulled away, staring down at her hand as if she didn't recognize it, as if it were coated in some kind of filth that she didn't want to spread to me.

"Stop," I said, my voice hoarse and my throat dry. "It isn't too late. You haven't done anything irrevocable."

"What I am is irrevocable," she said softly. "That won't change."

I raked a hand through my hair in frustration. "You're the same person you were fifteen minutes ago, five days, a month. It doesn't matter. Please listen to me."

But she gave no sign of hearing me.

I grabbed her hand again, and this time I didn't give her the chance to pull away. "We aren't where we come from. We make our own choices, remember?" I squeezed her fingers. "That's what you told me. Unless you were lying to me," I said, pushing the words into a challenge.

Her gaze finally shifted to mine, emotion flashing briefly in the dark hollows of her eyes. "I wasn't lying."

"Then why are you any different from me and my messed-up family?" I asked, trying to sound logical even when all I wanted to do was grab her and run out of the room, assuming either of us had the strength for it.

"Yes, 107, listen to the boy," Laughlin commanded.

"Shut up," I snapped at him. Jacobs, at least, was wise enough to keep quiet, but he was watching everything with wide-eyed fear.

"Ariane, take the others," Ford instructed. "Now." I could only see her in profile, but she didn't look good. Too pale, but more than that. A chalky white that spoke of blood loss.

The police, and whoever else had joined them in the hall, chose that moment to begin hammering at the door in earnest. "We're coming in! Stand away from the doors."

Ariane flinched at the sound of a motor starting up. Was that a saw? So much noise and chaos. It only added to the feeling of events spiraling out of control, like we might reach a point of absolute anarchy where she just gave in to make it all stop.

"Ariane, please. You'll hate yourself for this. Self-defense is one thing, but murder . . ." My voice broke. I was desperate to find the right words, and those were the only ones I had, which felt so deeply inadequate for the moment.

She blinked and looked away from me. "I want Zane, Rachel, and Emerson St. John left unharmed," she said to Ford.

"Yes!" Rachel shouted.

"No!" I said at the same time, even as I wanted to cry. Ariane was always looking out for everyone else. Even now.

Ford considered a moment. "Your human and the girl can be spared. But not the other."

"But St. John took only volunteers," Ariane argued, showing more spark than I'd seen from her since we walked in this god-awful place. "He didn't experiment on anyone who—"

"One of those volunteers killed Carter," Ford said in a tone that brooked no argument.

"Zane needs him alive," Ariane said, sounding weary. "He's infected with a virus that's making changes to his DNA."

Ford raised an eyebrow, looking almost interested for a moment, then it disappeared. "Carter is dead. That's a debt that must be paid."

Ariane let out a slow breath, then she turned to me, and oh God, I knew what was coming before she opened her mouth.

"If I don't do this," she said, "I'll never be free of it, of him. And he deserves punishment for what he's done and to make sure he never does it again."

"107," Jacobs said in protest.

"She's right," Rachel said. "She should kill him."

God damn it, Rachel. "He does deserve it," I said loudly and without hesitation, as if I could drown out Rachel's words in Ariane's head. "But this isn't about him. It's about you. If you do this, Ariane, you'll never be free of it. You'll know what you did, always. It'll be in the back of your mind forever." I paused, just for a second to force the next words out, cruel as they were. "If you do this, he gets off easy, being dead. But it'll haunt you, knowing he was right about you. That you weren't meant for a real life, that you've become exactly what they said, a weapon."

Ariane sucked in a sharp breath, and the pain on her face made my eyes burn with tears for her. But I would not take it back. It was a low blow and deliberately so. She needed to hear it.

"Ariane," Ford warned. "Don't be weak."

I glared at Ford. "You are *not* like him, and he does not control you," I said to Ariane fiercely. "Make a different choice, and prove it."

"If he lives, he could start again," Ariane said, shaking her head, but I could feel her wavering.

"No," I said firmly. "He won't. He'll be stuck in lawsuits,

investigations, and public humiliation for the rest of his life. We'll make sure of it."

Ford gave a creaky laugh. "What does any of that matter? He should pay in blood. One life for all those he has taken is nothing."

It was hard to argue with that. "The future or the past, Ariane," I said finally.

She looked to me, her eyes dull.

"You have to choose. In the park, you said you missed what might have been. But you can still have that, a chance to live, to be free, to have friends and a normal life. That's the future." I swallowed hard, praying not just for words, but the right ones. "Killing Jacobs, any of them, that's choosing the past and letting it—"

"There is no normal life for us, Ariane," Ford cut in. "Not now, not ever. You know that."

"For you, maybe," I snapped. "But she has a chance, if she just takes it. You wanted her to put family first? Then what the hell are *you* doing?"

Ford cocked her head, as if I'd spoken a new language, one in which she was not fluent. And then her gaze flicked to Ariane, and I felt a shift as if something had changed in the gaps between our words.

"Is that true?" Ford asked. "Do you want this life?" She sounded tired.

"Ariane, you know I'm right," I said desperately.

But she was locked in a stare-down with Ford, neither of them registering my existence, and I held my breathing, waiting for her answer, praying that she would for the first time in her life admit that she had the right to *want* something. *Say it, Ariane. Please!*

Ariane shook her head. "I did," she said slowly. "But what difference does it make now?"

Ford straightened up, though it must have been painful. "It always makes a difference. What we want matters, even if no one else will acknowledge it."

I felt like I was eavesdropping on a conversation in code. *Something* was happening; I could feel it in the weight of the air. Everyone else could too, evidently. Even Rachel and Laughlin had gone silent, watching the exchange.

"If these men do not start the program again, another will," Ford said in a warning tone.

Ariane nodded with a confused frown. "I know. But at least we can stop these from—"

"Then you know what needs to be done," Ford said, as if this were the end of a long discussion.

Then she looked straight at me with that flat but somehow still defiant expression. "Family first," she said, her normally uninflected voice carrying a tremor of emotion.

Ariane's eyes widened then, a spark of alarm within them. "Ford, no."

But before she could say anything more, Ford stepped out of the way, leaving Laughlin and his gun aimed at us. Her intent was clear: she was going to let him go and he would fire on us. He wouldn't be able to stop, even if he wanted to. His finger was already pulling on the trigger.

"Ariane," I shouted, dropping to the ground and covering my head out of instinct and the very near and real memory of being shot. Rachel shrieked and hit the floor, following my lead.

The pressure change in the air when Ford released her

hold on Laughlin and the others was palpable. And immediately after, the sound of multiple shots echoed loudly in the enclosed space, making it impossible to tell where they were going.

With my head down, I didn't have a clear view of everything, but peering through a gap between my arm and the carpet, I could see enough.

Ariane didn't run or duck. Instead, she lifted her hand in a wide-sweeping arc that was almost a blur.

Bullets hit the wall behind Laughlin with a quick *rat-a-tat* sound, knocking bits of drywall to the floor.

Then it went quiet. Even the police outside had stopped trying to get in. Or maybe I couldn't hear them anymore over the ringing in my ears.

I scrambled to my feet. "Are you all right?" I asked Ariane, searching her for wounds and finding no obvious ones.

"I am." But she didn't sound like it.

Ford swayed on her feet, turning toward us as she did, and I saw the new hole in her ribs, just below her heart. She'd caught one of the bullets Ariane had deflected.

Oh, shit.

Ford sank to her knees.

"No," Ariane whispered, moving to her side.

I stayed back, giving them some room.

"We could have found another way," Ariane said, her eyes bright and overflowing with tears.

Ford shook her head, her face a mask of pain, blood trickling from her mouth. "Your human is right. There is no other way for me. And I couldn't let him go."

I didn't know who she meant by "him" at first, until

I realized that Laughlin was no longer standing. A quick glance at where he'd been showed him on the ground, gun still clutched in his hand. Ragged red circles now decorated his forehead and his cheek.

I grimaced and looked away.

Ford had done it deliberately, knowing Ariane would protect us the only way she could. It was a testament to Ford's character that I wasn't sure if she'd used Ariane or protected her from the guilt of doing what needed to be done.

"You will make sure that it *never* happens again," Ford said, her gaze seeking Ariane's for confirmation. "If we are all one, all of us who suffered and died and hang in display cases for the humans' pleasure and advancement, then someone must stand for us."

Ariane shook her head with a bitter smile, tears leaving bright tracks down her face. "It should never have happened at all."

"And yet we are here. . . . Here you are." Ford coughed, spraying blood in a fine mist.

I swallowed hard. Ford had made our lives more difficult, unquestionably, but that didn't mean I wanted to see her die.

Slowly, Ford sat on the floor and then lay down, curling up on her uninjured side, like she was preparing to go to sleep.

"Ford." Ariane reached for her hand, taking it into her own, the same slim, long fingers entwined. "I can't . . . I don't know if . . ."

But Ford's eyes were now fixed at some point beyond Ariane, beyond this room, perhaps. "I wish I could have seen the mountains," she said, the words barely understandable over the liquidy sounds of her breathing.

I had no idea what that meant. Maybe nothing, a product of whatever dying vision she was seeing. But Ariane's shoulders bowed in grief, as if she understood.

And when Ariane rose to her feet a few moments later, I knew Ford was gone.

"Are you all right?" Emerson asked from his corner of the room. I looked over to see him standing up cautiously.

I nodded, resisting the temptation to pat my arms and legs to confirm their bullet-free status.

Rachel pushed herself up to her hands and knees, and then curled in a ball with a half sob.

"Are you all right?" I asked.

She glared at me wordlessly.

Guess that meant she wasn't hurt. Or not shot, at least. "Do you think—" I started to ask Ariane, only to realize she'd moved away.

She stood over Dr. Jacobs, who was now lying on the floor, next to the injured and unconscious guard.

Uh-oh.

She stared down at him.

"Help me, please." Blood coated the side of his face and ran down his neck. He'd been shot somewhere. From where I stood, it was hard to tell the exact location and severity of his injury; there was so much blood. "107."

I felt the faintest return of panic, watching her watching him. It would be so easy for her to finish off what Ford had started. And to destroy the gift Ford had given her.

But before I said anything, she turned away from him, leaving him to his fate, whatever it would be.

She headed straight to me, and as soon as she was close enough, I grabbed her in a hug, lifting her off her feet for a moment and squeezing her tighter than I probably should have. "You're okay," I whispered, as much for her as for me, because in that moment it was true and I was still having trouble believing it.

She wrapped her arms around my neck and let out a long shuddering breath that I could feel.

"Rachel?" Jacobs tried, his breath rattling in his throat.

But Rachel ignored him, the pallor of her face and tightening of her mouth the only signs that she'd even heard him. She stood slowly, her balance wobbly, and then moved past us toward the doors. "Can you open these now?" she asked Ariane. "I want out. I want to go home." She was trembling, but her gaze was focused on us as she steadfastly ignored her grandfather on the floor. She was very clearly done with him, and when Rachel made up her mind, there was no changing. Stubbornness was a family trait, it seemed.

"Rachel is right. We can't stay in here forever," Ariane said against my shoulder and over the sound of the police shouting to be let in. "I have to open the doors, and I don't know what's going to happen when I do."

"It's all right," I said. "We'll figure it out." My voice was muffled by Ariane's hair, and I didn't want to let her go, not even long enough for her to let them in. Technically, she could do it just as easily without me putting her down.

But she pushed against me gently, and I released her, setting her on her feet.

"No matter what happens, it was worth it," she said. Then she pushed me out of the way, and the doors opened slowly out into the hall.

And that should have been my first clue that even if she

wasn't sure what was going to happen next, she had a better idea than I did.

The floor shook with the boot steps of black-uniformed men in tinted face shields and unmarked body armor as they poured through the doors. Not the police anymore.

One of them pulled Rachel out into the hall, "rescuing" her presumably. "Get down, get down, get down!" Their shouts overlapped one another, making it hard to understand the individual words, but the gist was clear.

Ariane knelt on the ground, her hands raised above her head, offering no resistance. She looked so small and vulnerable. And they didn't seem to care, surrounding her and blocking my view of her until I caught just flashes of her pale hair in the gaps between them.

"It's not her. You're looking for that one," I shouted at them, pointing at Ford's body.

But that caused only more angry shouting and more guns pointing at me until I sank to my knees as well.

"That boy is my patient. He's in my care. Do not harm him," Emerson shouted from his position near the wall.

"I've got three dead and two injured," one of the men in the center of the room said into his radio. "Hostiles are contained."

Did he mean Ariane and me? I guess, considering we were the only ones currently being threatened with weapons, three guys on me and about six on her.

"She's not hostile," I snapped. I couldn't say the same for myself; I was feeling a little angry and misunderstood at the moment.

The lights sputtered overhead.

"Zane. Don't." Ariane's voice came through loud and clear.

"Are you all right?" I asked.

"I'm fine. Don't—"

But I didn't get to hear what she was forbidding me to do because as quickly as the strike team had flowed in, the six surrounding Ariane had her up on her feet and moving out of the room.

"Hey!" I protested. "Where are you taking her?" I tried to stand, but the business end of a rifle suddenly two inches from the end of my nose convinced me otherwise.

A familiar figure came through the doors then. Justine, looking much thinner in a dark suit, her dark-red hair sleek and smooth in a knot at her neck. It took me an extra second to recognize her without her "hassled average mom" disguise.

"Justine." I sank back on my heels in relief at the sight of a familiar and theoretically friendly face. "Where are they taking Ariane?"

She ignored me, listening to the man reporting in to her and surveying the room and the damage.

"Justine!" I bellowed.

And this time, she glanced in my direction, her forehead wrinkling with annoyance, as though I were the neighbor's puppy left unattended and barking on the porch all night long.

"Where are they taking her?" I demanded.

She stared at me, as if she'd never seen me before. "Taking who?" she asked.

Cold seeped into my skin. She'd set this up. She'd gone to my mom to orchestrate that news story, to push us out of hiding and to make the Committee/DOD run. She probably wasn't even "here," officially. And if this wasn't official, then that would make it even easier for Ariane to disappear. Forever. "You know who!" I shouted.

She returned her attention to the man on her team, as if I didn't exist.

No. Just no. Not after all of this. "Justine! You have to tell me. You can't lock her up. You can't just take her away! She has rights!" Except . . . did she? Did any of us these days, let alone someone who wasn't entirely human?

"If I may?" Emerson approached the guys guarding me, who were getting a little twitchy with my shouting. Not that I was going to stop. They wouldn't, most likely, shoot me just for being loud. The paperwork would be a bitch. "I'm his physician," he added.

Justine gave a nod, and they let him approach, though they didn't withdraw. None of them even asked why I would have a doctor here, which should have struck at least one of them as odd.

"Not now." I glared at him. "They took Ariane!" As if he hadn't witnessed it himself. But I certainly hadn't heard him protesting.

"Zane." Emerson squeezed my shoulder and then handed me a wad of tissue from his pocket. "Wipe your nose, calm down, and listen."

I hadn't even realized my nose was bleeding again. Damn it. I snatched the tissues from him and cleaned up my face.

"You're not going to be able to help her if you're dead or tucked away in a cell that they're doing their best to forget exists," he said quietly.

He smiled placidly at the armed men surrounding us.

"These gentlemen are just doing their job," he said in a louder voice. Then he muttered, "So just shut up for now and wait for your moment."

He was, unfortunately, right. And I had to figure he knew what he was talking about, as he was the only one who'd successfully struck a deal with Justine. And he'd survived.

With an effort I gritted my teeth and swallowed my protests, even when Justine, after a final look around the room, walked out, followed by the men guarding me.

Before I could get to my feet, though, EMTs were rushing in to tend to Dr. Jacobs and the injured GTX guard, and there were lots of angry Chicago police officers with them.

Better to stay down, then. I wouldn't be going anywhere anytime soon.

So, I waited, impatience burning in me, for the right moment, the one that would be mine.

Six hours later—after I was mysteriously released from police custody to my mom—I realized that Emerson St. John's seemingly sound advice made a rather large and risky assumption: that there would ever *be* a more advantageous moment.

And there were no such guarantees. Ever.

CHAPTER 21

Zane

"ZANE! COME ON, MAN, YOU'RE GOING TO MAKE ME late for class!" Quinn pounded on my bedroom door impatiently.

"In a minute," I said, not bothering to look up from my laptop. I had time for one more e-mail. The best thing was that once you figured out the Homeland Security address formula—firstname.lastname@dhs.gov—you could e-mail any DHS employee whose full name you knew.

Last month, after I got back from my treatment and recovery at Emerson's lab, I'd started out looking for a reference to Justine, any Justine. When I couldn't find her, I'd begun e-mailing every valid address I could find at that domain with a condensed version of the story, then asking if the recipient knew anything about Justine or Ariane.

Most of the e-mails went unanswered. Some of them came back with very carefully worded threats. I'd even gotten several "anonymous" phone calls, warning me to stop.

Right. I'd taken those as signs that I was getting closer than they wanted me to be. That, or I was just annoying them. Which was fine. If I had to be the irritating mosquito and risk getting swatted to get their attention, so be it.

It was December now, and I'd last seen Ariane over two months ago. With every day that passed, it felt more and more like I'd never see her again. Life had returned to almost normal, and sometimes it seemed like I'd made her up. I didn't even have a picture of her.

"Now, asshole!" Quinn said with an extra thump on the door for emphasis. "Let's go, or you can find your own way."

The funny thing was, even with the irritation in his voice, I could tell he wasn't really angry.

Since Quinn had come back to live in Wingate after the incident with GTX and Dr. Jacobs, he'd mellowed considerably. We'd talked a little about what had happened, but mostly he seemed to be trying to forget it and move on. He was taking classes at New Century Community College and working at Dick's Sporting Goods in his spare time. His arm had healed, but his scholarship to Madison was long gone. And he actually seemed much happier. It had occurred to me that as hard as my dad had ridden me as a "failure," Quinn probably hadn't had it much easier as "the success." No room for mistakes. No room to breathe. No wonder he'd flunked out. The pressure alone must have sucked.

So we were getting along a lot better. That, however, did not mean I wanted to push him too far. It was a long walk to school, and Trey was on Rachel duty this week. She needed someone to drive her since the bank had repossessed her car.

"Okay, okay," I shouted.

I hit SEND on the last e-mail, grabbed my backpack where it hung behind me on the desk chair, and then headed for the door before doubling back for my coat.

It was supposed to snow today. Again. And one of the lasting side effects of Emerson's viral experiment was that I still had trouble regulating my temperature. When it was cold, I was freezing.

Quinn was waiting at the table in the kitchen when I got there, his foot jiggling with impatience.

After opening the pantry cabinet I grabbed the last foil-wrapped package of Pop-Tarts from where I'd hidden it behind the oatmeal my mom had purchased and sent home with me. I stuffed them, wrapper and all, into my mouth, while I shrugged into my coat.

My dad watched from his perch at the island, coffee mug in hand. "Did your mother buy that for you?" my dad asked, his mouth tight with disgust. "You look like you're about to go shovel manure."

I hoisted my backpack onto my shoulders. "Well, it's called a barn coat, I think," I said, after taking the Pop-Tart package out of my mouth. And yes, it had been a gift from my mom, who was doing her best to make up for lost time and the fact that her place, an apartment on the other side of Wingate, was too small for me or Quinn to join her right now. But as soon as her role as a witness in Dr. Jacobs's trial was over and she could find another job (maybe), that would change, she hoped. I thought that was a little overly optimistic, but she was trying, so whatever. I wasn't going to crap all over her dream.

"Because you wear it in one or because you smell like one?"

Quinn asked, pretending to consider the question seriously.

"One more crack about my coat, and I'll leave it in your car so that girl in your Poli Sci class thinks it's yours," I said around a mouthful of strawberry Pop-Tart.

Quinn immediately held his hands up in surrender, his key ring looped around his finger. "Not cool." Then he got up and led the way out the door.

"Bye, Dad," I said, more out of habit than anything else.

He grunted in response but made no further attempt at communication, critical or otherwise.

Ever since GTX had faltered in the public eye, he'd seemed smaller somehow and almost bewildered, a man in a changed world without any idea how to adjust. He'd lost his guiding star. And he blamed me for it, unquestionably. But he had at least tried to help me, cooperating with the news report about my "abduction."

That being said, it didn't make up for the fact that he'd pretty much left me for dead in a parking lot, and we both knew it. So there really wasn't much he could do or say in retaliation.

And frankly, it was better that way.

But if home had gotten a little better since I'd come back, school was worse.

How had I accumulated so many memories of Ariane in such a short amount of time? I saw her *everywhere*, my heart picking up an extra beat every time I caught a flash of pale hair or heard a laugh that sort of sounded like hers.

It was never her.

On my first day back at school, I'd used the last of my waning abilities to pop open her locker. Ariane's official story was, I guess, that she and her father had moved away unexpectedly. The school hadn't needed her locker and there was no one to claim her stuff, so the office just left everything there.

Her locker was, as far as I could tell, exactly how she'd left it. No personal items at all, unsurprisingly. Just textbooks in a neat line, with matching folders and notebooks, and maybe a hint of dust and lemons.

I'd stolen one of her notebooks, which was filled with a careful precise script that I recognized from sitting behind her in class, and the one note she'd written me all those months ago.

I just had so little of her.

According to Linwood Academy High School, when I'd called them pretending to be the parent of a concerned friend, Ford, Nixon, and Carter had transferred to a private school in some small European country. Never to be heard from again, of course. That was the official story for their fate.

I was swimming in official stories these days. Or just plain gaps in information. No one had ever reported the discovery of Carter's body or Adam's.

Based on what I'd heard last from Emerson, Adam's family was still searching for him, and I hated that. But I didn't know what either of us could do without pulling the entire house of cover-ups down around our ears. Emerson agreed.

So I just kept doing what I could—going to school, sending e-mails, waiting for my freaking moment, whenever or whatever that was.

Quinn dropped me off at school with just minutes before the first bell, which was how I preferred it these days. I didn't want to be hanging around the parking lot, trying to pretend everything was okay.

My morning classes were, as usual, endless. I lived for the moments between when I could check my e-mail on my phone, even though I knew that odds were against my ever hearing anything useful. I had to keep trying.

Reaching lunch every day felt like an accomplishment. But I wasn't the only one suffering.

Rachel was sitting alone at the table today. Pretty much every day now.

"Hey," I said, setting my tray down next to hers.

"Missing your little girlfriend? Looking for an easy substitute?" she asked as I sat down.

I just waited, staring at her. She still snapped at people, but it was more like an automatic defense mechanism. She had no ground to stand on, and she knew it.

"Sorry," she muttered, dropping her fork in her wilted salad.

If my dad was sort of lost without GTX, Rachel was even worse off. She'd have rather pretended that the last few months hadn't happened, but that wasn't an option.

The company still existed, but her grandfather was no longer in charge. Bedridden and partially paralyzed from the bullet that had damaged his spine, he would never be in charge again. Prosecutors were still trying to decide if he was even fit to stand trial on the ethics charges being brought against him, thanks to my mom's very public allegations.

So, yeah, the shine was definitely off GTX and the entire Jacobs family.

Rachel hunched her shoulders a little tighter. Her sweater,

in her characteristic red, looked too thin for the weather. Her tan had faded. No one to take her on expensive vacations to warm places anymore.

"How's everything going?" I asked.

"I wish everyone would stop asking me that," she said, but the heat was missing from her tone. "It's going crappy. How else should it be going? My grandfather"—she said the word like it tasted gross—"is a sicko perv criminal, my father is useless, and my . . ." She trailed off and shook her head.

For a second, I thought she was going to mention Ariane. Her sister. Or her sisters, if you counted Ford. That, too, had to do a number on her head.

But instead, she said, "My mom is coming home next week."

I looked up from my pizza, startled. "Really?"

"My grandfather is the one who pulled strings to put her away in the first place, and without him around to keep pulling . . ." She shrugged. "Besides, my dad has no clue what to do without someone telling him. I think he's hoping she'll be able to boss him around."

I imagined Rachel in that huge, empty house without anyone checking on her now. Her grandfather had been the only relative to visit her fairly regularly. Now that her dad was laid off, another casualty of the fallout from this scandal, he should have been there more often, but somehow I doubted it. They still had the house only because Dr. Jacobs had bought it through an LLC separate from his other enterprises—the one saving grace he'd provided his granddaughter.

"I'm sorry," I said.

"Don't." Rachel waved her hand, and the bangle bracelets on her arm gave off halfhearted chimes, as if they couldn't be bothered anymore, either.

She retrieved her fork from her salad and stabbed the lettuce with more force than was necessary.

Guess that conversation was over. It had lasted longer than most of the ones I had with her, or anyone else, these days.

I pulled my phone from my pocket surreptitiously to check e-mail.

"You know that's never going to work. She's gone," Rachel said, gesturing at my phone with her fork.

I ignored her.

"I'm serious, Zane." She touched my arm, a quick, fleeting brush almost as if she was afraid I'd shove her away.

I looked up to find her frowning at me. Genuine concern looked strange on her face, like she was sitting on something uncomfortable.

"How long are you going to keep that up?" she asked. She knew, if only in general, about what I was doing because I'd been forced to ask if she'd heard anything while I'd been away.

"I'm fine," I said.

"Uh-huh. That's why you're glued to your phone twenty-four-seven and you barely leave your house anymore."

"I'm recovering from severe trauma and memory loss, remember?" I asked tightly. That was my official story. Yeah, I got one, too. I'd been "found" in the conference room along with the injured and the dead, which only lent credence to my mother's claims of kidnapping. Jacobs denied it, of course, but Laughlin was too dead to do the same, so most of the blame for my abduction and the mass shooting landed on him.

My weeks of mental and emotional "recovery," as well as my continuing memory loss, had been officially documented at a facility I'd never seen. Emerson had handed me the paperwork on my way out of his lab. But no one had even bothered to ask for it yet. More of DHS's influence, I was sure.

Rachel snorted. "Yeah, okay. You're crazy if you think anyone believes that."

"Whatever," I muttered.

"Look, I may not like her, but she did what she had to do. And I'm just . . ." She made an exasperated noise and rolled her eyes to the ceiling, as if she couldn't believe the words she was about to say. "I'm just asking, do you think this is what she would have—"

"If you say, 'Do you think this is what Ariane would have wanted you to do,' I'm going to walk out and never speak to you again," I said.

Her mouth fell open before she snapped it closed with a loud click. "Fine. God. Whatever. I'm . . . trying to be a friend."

"Well, stop," I said.

She gathered up her tray and stood. "Fuck you, Zane." And she sounded shockingly close to tears.

I sighed. "Rachel . . ." But she was gone before I could apologize. Or explain.

The truth was, I knew Rachel was right. This was absolutely *not* what Ariane would have wanted for me. In fact, she probably would have been pissed that I was wasting all these opportunities at "normal" experiences.

But I didn't know how to let go. I didn't want to. It was like the world had been opened up to this whole other level—aliens, government conspiracies, a hybrid girl who loved french fries and kicked ass—and now I was trying to cram myself back into this one tiny corner of it and pretend that was okay.

I dragged myself through my afternoon classes—playing the role of a still dazed and recovering victim to the hilt, though I had no idea how I was going to manage next semester—and stared out the windows at the snow that had started to fall.

After the last bell, thank God, I was at my locker, slowly gathering my stuff, when my phone buzzed.

My heart immediately jumped, thinking it might be an e-mail. But it was just a text. Quinn. He was going to be later than usual picking me up because of the roads.

Which sucked because everyone else I knew with a car had already bolted, trying to get home before the weather got any worse. So now I'd have to wait.

I put my coat on, hitched my backpack on my shoulders, and slammed my locker shut before heading for the main doors to wait for Quinn.

The entryway was quiet except for the roar of the heaters and the thoughts—just mine, but that was enough—circling loudly in my brain. As much as I'd hated Rachel asking those questions, now I couldn't seem to shake them from my mind.

How long was I going to wait? There were only so many e-mails I could send. And then what?

How many months? How many years?

As long as it takes, I promised myself.

But at a certain point, I'd have to give up, wouldn't I? I'd have to admit that she was gone or . . . dead. That seemed inevitable suddenly.

My breath caught in my chest, and I felt like I couldn't get enough air, the dry heat pumping too hard from the vents on either side of the entryway.

I pushed through the outer doors, the snow immediately seeping into my shoes and turning my feet to ice. The fresh air burned my lungs, a distraction I welcomed.

I started trudging in the direction Quinn would have to come to get me. Movement was an improvement over standing still. Action helped focus my attention elsewhere. A temporary fix, I knew, but better than nothing.

I hadn't gotten more than halfway into the parking lot when a clump of snow hit the back of my neck, dripping down under the collar of my coat.

Damn it. I was not in the mood for whatever dumb-ass had decided to pick a fight with me right now.

I turned sharply, furious words on the tip of my tongue, and froze.

Ariane, or a very vivid hallucination of her, stood in the middle of the snow-filled parking lot. She wore a puffy blue coat, shades lighter than anything I'd ever seen her in before, as if she didn't mind if someone noticed it or her. Her hair was pulled back, snow dusting the top of her head, and her cheeks and ears were pink. She wasn't wearing her contacts, her dark eyes a stark contrast to her skin.

"Sorry. I always wondered what that would feel like." She made a face at me and held up her bare hand. Her fingers were red with cold and dripping with melted snow. "It's cold, messy, and provides too much opportunity for retaliation and escalation." She paused with a contemplative tilt of her head. "An arms race, I suppose."

And that was what sold me. This was not a hallucination. Only the real Ariane would say something ridiculous and weird and perfect, just like that.

I stumbled and clomped toward her in the snow, hurrying as fast as I could, which wasn't very, while she did the same.

"This looks a lot easier in the movies," she observed with a frown at her feet.

"Yeah, they're not usually slogging through six inches of snow," I said breathlessly when I finally reached her. "Are you okay? How did you get here?" I didn't wait for her to answer before grabbing her in a tight hug, bending down to bury my face against her neck. Her puffy coat released a burst of warm air scented like lemons, like Ariane. The familiarity of it, and the reminder that, until this moment, I'd thought I might never experience it again, made me eyes burn with more than the cold.

She pulled back to smile at me and touched my face. Her fingers were like ice, but I didn't care. "I'm all right." But the tightness around her eyes and her mouth told me that maybe that hadn't always been the case. "You look better than the last time I saw you."

"Four weeks at St. John's lab in Rochester, letting him try to undo everything he'd done," I said, making a face.

She raised her eyebrows. "Really?"

It had not been an easy decision. But the vision of Adam lying on the ground, shot and dead despite all of his acquired skills, had stuck with me. Not to mention the bloodbath in the conference room at the hotel.

There were no guarantees in life. What NuStasis had

given back to me—the chance to live—could just as easily be taken away again, perhaps even by NuStasis itself.

"My body still wasn't adjusting well, not stabilizing," I admitted. "More nosebleeds, headaches, dizziness, passing out." I shook my head. I could have kept fighting, trying to hold on to those abilities, but at what cost? I'd seen firsthand how pricey that kind of shortsightedness could be. And I hadn't liked who I was becoming. Confidence was one thing; perpetually spoiling for a fight was another.

Plus, if NuStasis killed me—or kept me in a lab under permanent observation—I wouldn't have been able to search for her.

"And?" Ariane searched my face anxiously, as if the answers were written there, and they sort of were, in that I didn't look permanently ill anymore. I hadn't realized how bad it had gotten until I looked in the mirror one day and was startled *not* to see dark circles embedded under my eyes.

"Most everything is back to normal," I said. "It was mostly keeping my immune system from overreacting and killing me, I guess. Lots of IVs, and antibiotics I'd never even heard of. Sometimes my ears ring still, and I pick up a word or two out of nowhere. And if I really concentrate, I can make the TV remote kind of wobble a little. Unless that's just Quinn messing with me, which is definitely possible." But I didn't want to talk about any of that.

"Did they let you go?" I asked. "Did Justine . . ." I paused and glanced over my shoulder instinctively, half expecting to see a black van barreling toward us. "Does Justine know you're here?"

"Justine knows I'm here. She'll know wherever I am." Ariane pulled out a slim phone from her pocket, almost as thin as a credit card. "I have to keep it on me at all times. A compromise for no embedded tracking device. I made them remove the one under my skin from before."

I nodded but had to wonder what would have stopped them from inserting another at the same time.

She smiled tightly, obviously following my train of thought or just plain hearing it. "Because I wouldn't let them use any anesthesia or numbing agents, and they had to show me the removed chip afterward."

Jesus. Yes, confirmed once more: Ariane Tucker was a badass.

I shook my head in wonder, my thoughts trying to catch up with everything she was telling me. "Do you want to go inside? I don't have a car, and it's freezing out here." I clamped down to keep my teeth from chattering.

She shook her head. "I can't stay long. I just wanted to see if I could catch you here before you went home."

"Oh." The word escaped before I could stop it, more like exhaling than actually speaking. So that was what it felt like to have your heart crushed. It wasn't just a sinking feeling, the way everyone described it. It was more like someone had reached in my chest and removed said heart with a clenched fist.

But it made sense. Of course she wouldn't be staying. How could she? Why would she even want to, assuming they'd let her?

Ariane regarded me with a faint wrinkle of confusion in her forehead. Then her expression cleared, and she raised herself up on her toes, pressing her cold lips against mine.

Hell if *that* was going to be our last kiss. I bent down and looped my arms around her waist, lifting her up.

Her mouth was as impatient as mine, and her fingers curled into my coat collar, pulling me closer. And suddenly I forgot about the cold, the snow, everything except her body pressed against mine.

After a long moment, Ariane pulled back, her rapid breath appearing between us in little white puffs, and I set her down reluctantly.

But she kept her hand on my chest. "I'm going to the apartment they set up for me," she said to me slowly, as if she was afraid I would misunderstand. "Here in town, in that new complex."

"Over on Forest and Lombardi?" I asked, confused, my brains kind of scrambled from the kiss.

She nodded.

"But . . . that's where my mom's new place is." Which meant Ariane would be close to where I already spent a lot of time.

Ariane just smiled.

It clicked. "You knew that already."

She grinned. "I might have heard something to that effect. But we're in Building B, across the courtyard from her apartment." She pulled gloves—knitted in bright pink and purple stripes—from her pockets and put them on.

"We?" I asked.

She wrinkled her nose. "The agent assigned to me. Not sure who it's going to be yet. I was hoping maybe . . ."

I didn't have to have my former (limited) mind-reading thoughts to know she'd been hoping Mark Tucker would reappear. I considered mentioning what Rachel had told me about her/their mother, but decided it could wait.

Ariane shook her head, dismissing Mark as a possibility

even though neither of us had said his name. "It's okay. I think it's going to be Marta, one of the DHS agents assigned to me when I was with them. And she's fine. Kind of dry, not much of a sense of humor, and she doesn't believe in watching movies—"

"Obviously she's an alien," I said.

"Clearly," Ariane said, her eyes bright with amusement.

I stared at her in disbelief. "How did you manage all of this?"

"I can be very persuasive," she said.

"I'm aware," I said dryly. "But they're just letting you go?"

"Not exactly. They need me." She shrugged. "And when you're the only one on the entire planet who can make all their recovered alien tech light up and send out incomprehensible streams of data that will take them years to decode, they're pretty motivated to keep you . . . cooperative."

"Dr. Jacobs needed you," I pointed out, stomping my feet in place to keep warm. Ariane, in her boots and brightly colored cold weather gear, didn't seem bothered.

"No," she said. "Dr. Jacobs wanted to control me. There's a difference. He was willing to break me, wanted to, even. Justine . . . she knows better." Her voice took on an ominous tone, and I wondered what, exactly, Ariane had had to do to convince her of that point. "I'm no good to them if they push too hard." Her mouth curved in a tight bitter smile. "Not to mention all the tales I could tell if someone does show up here from another planet, wanting to know if you all are worth keeping around."

Leverage. That's what she'd been talking about when we'd first met with Justine. And now, with Ford and the others dead, I guess she had it, though I was betting she would have rather it not happen quite in this way. "So you could have gone anywhere," I said. "You didn't have to come back here for . . . I mean, I'm not . . ."

"I didn't come back just for you," she said. "Dr. Jacobs is . . . currently out of commission. But he's not the only one who knew what was going on at GTX." Her expression darkened. "He's not the only one who could start it up again. I want to make sure that doesn't happen. Here or anywhere else. I promised Ford." Her gaze dropped to the ground.

I nodded, even as my brain chewed on the fact that she'd said that she hadn't come back "just" for me. Which meant that she had considered my presence in Wingate and it had been a factor in her decision. And that made a ridiculous grin spread across my face.

The sound of tires crunching on snow came from behind me. I turned and saw our battered SUV slowly making its way into the parking lot. Quinn braked as soon as he saw me, unwilling to go farther into the unplowed parking lot, and honked the horn in a short, impatient burst.

I waved at him so he'd know I saw him. "That's Quinn. He's living here now and hogging the car. I have to go," I said to Ariane. "Come with me," I added on impulse.

"Considering the last time Quinn saw me," she said after a moment, "I think it's probably better if we work up to me being in an enclosed space with any member of your family."

I thought about the nightmares that Quinn had occasionally, after all that he'd been through while being held by Dr. Jacobs as a bargaining chip. He sometimes woke up screaming loud enough to wake everyone. Once, even Mrs.

Kripke next door had called to make sure everything was okay. Proof perhaps that Quinn's "pretend it never happened" method wasn't working as well as he might prefer.

Ariane had done nothing to Quinn, but she'd been at the parking lot during the exchange that had gone horribly wrong. And while Quinn didn't know her, he had to know that she was the reason he'd been taken. He'd never mentioned it, but seeing her marched out in handcuffs and surrounded by guards had to be a pretty big clue.

I wasn't sure how Quinn would react to her now, being in our car or at our house.

My dad would probably foam at the mouth.

"You might be right," I admitted. "But I don't want to just leave you here." Or ever.

She smiled at me. "I really do need to go to the apartment," she said. "It's not far. I'll be fine."

Quinn hit the horn again, harder this time, but I stayed put.

"But you're going to be here tomorrow, right?" I asked, hating that I felt the need to be reassured. But I knew all too well how quickly the world could shift, your entire understanding of the universe changed in less than a day.

"As long as the world as we know it doesn't end," Ariane said. "I'm on call for that."

"Okay," I said with a laugh. "I can work with that." But I found myself walking backward, keeping her in my view. I was still reluctant to leave, afraid she'd disappear again.

"Zane," she called after me.

I stopped immediately. "Yeah?"

"Can you come over tomorrow? After school, assuming they let me back to classes," she asked, not quite meeting my eyes.

I ignored Quinn waiting, my heart picking up an extra beat in alarm. "What's wrong? Do you think Marta might not be on your side or—"

"No, no. Nothing like that." She paused, biting her lip. "Just maybe bring a DVD or something? I'll have my laptop set up by then. And I'll get popcorn."

"You want to watch something?" I asked, baffled by the contrast between what she was asking and her reaction to doing so.

She nodded, her face brighter red than I'd ever seen it, as though she were asking me for some huge favor or extreme task.

And then I got it. This was a big deal. She'd never invited *anyone* over to her house before. Of all the amazing things she'd done and could do, this simple, everyday part of life was new and *huge* for her.

"Unless . . ." She hesitated. "I mean, if that's not something you'd want to—"

"Yes, I want to," I said quickly and firmly. "Definitely. If the snow clears up, we could even go out to the movies. In public."

She blinked, as if she hadn't even considered that possibility in her newfound freedom.

I grinned at her. "Maybe we'll even sneak some French fries in and skip the popcorn."

"That's against the rules, isn't it?" she asked.

"Thought you were all about that," I said.

Her face lit up with one of her rare, uncompromised smiles. "I guess I am," she said. "I'll see you tomorrow."

That sounded like a promise to me.

CHAPTER 22

Ariane

THE PALE WINTER SUNLIGHT, REFLECTING OFF THE NEW snow, was so bright it hurt my eyes. And when I took a deep breath, the cold air made my lungs ache.

But it was worth it. To be outside. To be unmonitored. Well, mostly. But the cell phone in my pocket was as little encumbrance as could be imagined, particularly compared to before.

My promised new life at the ocean had never materialized, and that was fine. I'd get there one day, now that I had the freedom to make my own choices. Instead, I'd spent the last eight weeks indoors, surrounded by Justine and her people. Moving from one safe house to another, and then to conference rooms that were all very similar, and finally to a secure facility outside Phoenix where scattered metal pieces and fragments of a ship—some with strange characters on them, some without—had been carefully cataloged and organized.

The engine, that was what they were mostly interested in.

Well, after I'd told them there weren't any weapons systems. Which was, and was not, true. I didn't actually know for sure. The main AI, what was left of it anyway, had reacted to my presence, just as I'd told Zane. I'd gleaned some information from it, though it had been mostly through the exchange of images rather than actual words. It was heavily damaged, and I was part human, so our communication had been limited at best. Still, I'd seen some very interesting things, including mapping a few constellations that I recognized. Yet it was in my best interests not to reveal everything at once.

I was valuable to Justine and her crew, but I wasn't stupid enough to count on that alone. Always have a backup plan. One of my father's earliest lessons.

Thinking of him, my feet followed a familiar route automatically, leading me to my old house before I realized what I was doing.

A FOR SALE sign leaned crookedly in the yard, accumulating snow on the sign post, and there were tire tracks in the driveway. A few more steps down the sidewalk revealed a dark blue SUV full of boxes, the cargo door open for unloading.

Of course. GTX wouldn't, or couldn't, hold on to the house now. They'd sell it if only to provide more distance between anything that could connect me to them.

A man in a baseball cap and a heavy denim jacket walked out on the front porch and moved stiffly down the steps to the vehicle.

My breath caught in my throat. He looked like my father. But he'd just been on my mind, so perhaps it was simply wishful thinking. I'd asked Justine to find him, to ask him to serve as my guardian, but she'd told me they had no luck. I hadn't been surprised to hear that, but definitely disappointed. I'd learned a lot from him, and not all of it had come from a training manual. He was my father, for better or for worse, the only one I would ever have. I refused to consider any other possibility.

The man at my former home must have sensed someone watching. He stopped on the edge of the driveway and turned to face me. "You going to just stand there, or are you going to help me load this stuff?" he demanded. The brim of his hat shadowed his features, but his voice left absolutely no doubt.

It *was* my father.

Stunned, I hurried forward, my feet kicking up small whirlwinds of snow. "What are you doing here?" I asked, wrestling one end of a box out of the cargo area.

"No," he said. "The other way. We're moving out."

I let go of the box and stared at him. "What?"

"The apartment is a fresh start. I agreed with them on that. It's important, but I don't see any reason why we should abandon everything," he said. He dug into the open top of the closest cardboard box and produced our silver toaster. "I, for example, have no emotional attachment to this toaster. I can't see a reason to spend twenty bucks on a new one."

"Good point," I said, even though I still had no idea what he was talking about overall. I hesitated. "But does this mean . . . Are you working for Justine?" I steeled myself to hear the answer. I didn't mind if he was being paid to keep an eye on me again, but I wanted to *know* this time.

"No," he said sharply. Then he took a breath and let it out

in a sigh. "No," he said again, in a softer voice. "That was a mistake I'm not making again. I'm retired. I'm not working for anyone anymore."

"But then I don't understand. . . ."

"They found me after that mess in Chicago. Well," he amended, "I found them. A few weeks ago."

I nodded. That made more sense to me. He could have disappeared forever. I had no doubt of that.

"That woman, Justine, told me the deal you'd negotiated." His voice held gruff admiration. "You really held their feet to the fire."

I shrugged, as if I didn't care, but the unexpected warmth of the compliment filled me. "I learned from the best."

He rolled his eyes. "Save it for someone who's buying, kid."

I grinned, the familiarity of his words providing that sense of home I'd been missing. But I still had questions. "So, if you're not working for them, then who is?" Someone had to be. There was no way Justine would let me have that much unsupervised freedom, not until she got more of what she wanted from me.

"They'll still have an agent on site," my father said. "Marta something or other. She'll have her own apartment next to ours, I guess. I'm not quite sure of the setup. They're playing it pretty close to the vest. They didn't even tell me you were showing up today." He frowned. "You know they probably have trackers in some or all of your new clothes." He nodded at my coat.

"I'm sure," I agreed with a shrug. "But I didn't see any reason to cause panic by removing them before I needed to."

"True. But it would be a shame if some of them met their

end through an accidental scrubbing or a rough trip at the dry cleaners. Just to keep Justine and Marta"—he made a face, which made me think he'd met the painfully humorless DHS agent already—"on their toes."

I grinned. "It would."

"You know not all of this is going to fit," I said, looking at the house and considering the floor plans I'd seen of the two-bedroom apartment.

"We'll take the important stuff," he said.

"All of it," I added, hoping he knew I meant the photos and items from his former life with his wife and daughter. He'd hidden his past in the basement for too long.

He nodded wordlessly, his bright blue eyes a little damp.

Then he said, "And if we run out of space, I think I know a place where I can get a good deal on a storage unit."

I laughed. "I bet you do."

He wrapped an arm around my shoulders cautiously. "I missed you, kiddo," he said into the top of my hair.

Acting on impulse, I ducked under his arm to give him a real hug, surprising both of us.

"Good," I said. I felt like I'd been waiting my whole life to hear exactly that. And it was so worth it.

EPILOGUE

Ariane

My name is Ariane Tucker. I share that name with a girl who died a long time ago, but that's all. This is *my* life. And my rules:

1. Be in by ten on weeknights, midnight on weekends (with exceptions made for special occasions, which do not, apparently, include marathon viewings of the entire original Star Wars trilogy alone with Zane in his mom's apartment while she's out).
2. Keep quiet on the whole being genetically-engineered-from-human-and-alien-DNA thing.
3. Check in weekly with my DHS handler, Justine, and make a quarterly trip to the secret warehouse in Phoenix.
4. Figure out what I want to do with the rest of my life, now that it appears I will have one.
5. Be on call in case of first contact with extraterrestrials

(of any kind, but especially those with whom I share a genetic connection).

Oh, and most important . . .

6. Don't sneak across the apartment courtyard to spend illicit time with my boyfriend. Rather, don't get caught.

No problem. I was made for this.

I owe a great deal to my local Starbucks. When I'm writing a first draft, I'm there for hours, and everyone is so patient and supportive. So, a huge thank you to Megan, Caroline, Stacey, Sharon, Sean, Dawn, John, Kayla, Michelle, Jacob, Kiley, Shane, Sarah M., Brianna, Sarah P., Jessica, Heather, and Roberto.

And when I'm not at Starbucks, I'm at my local Barnes & Noble in the café, scribbling madly away. Thank you to all the booksellers and staff, especially Alma, Ann, Jay, and Roger.

A big thanks to the following blogs that went above and beyond to help promote *The Hunt: Jacque's Book Nook*, *Lili Lost in a Book*, *Just a Booklover*, and *Bows & Bullets Reviews*.

Okay, I feel like this is one of those Emmy speeches that just keeps going . . . but I'm not done yet! Don't cue up the orchestra!

Thank you to Becky Douthitt, who has been reading my stuff since we were eighteen. And we're still friends, which speaks to a lot of patience on her part. Love you!

Thank you to Age and Dana Tabion who remind me to take a breath, have fun, and eat some mashed potatoes every once in a while. To Ed and Debbie Brown, who keep inviting me to dinner and refuse to give up on me, even though I often have to say no more than yes. I'm so grateful that you keep asking!

To my parents, Steve and Judy Barnes, and my siblings, Michael and Susan. Thanks for always listening.

And finally to my very patient husband, Greg, who is supportive even when the people in my head are getting most of my attention. Love you, and thanks for the chocolate.

Acknowledgments

THANK YOU TO EVERYONE AT HYPERION FOR EVERYTHING you've done to support this series and G&G before it. You are amazing, and I'm so grateful.

As a writer, I'm always looking for ways to improve. Tracey Keevan, you taught me so much about making a story (and my writing) tighter. You can bounce a quarter off this book. (I mean, you totally can because it's a book, but the story is tight, too.) Thank you!

To Christian Trimmer, thank you for believing in me and Ariane and Zane. (And Alona and Will, for that matter!)

Tyler Nevins, I love the new covers—thank you. I think this last one is my favorite. Ariane looks so badass!

Linnea Sinclair, thank you for always being the calm voice of reason in my ear and the shove in the right direction when I need it. I couldn't have done this without you.

Librarians are the most awesome people in the world. A big thanks to two of my favorites, Amy and Kim, whom I'm lucky to also call friends. Houlihan's doesn't know how to close without us!